The Spinster

Chloe Laube

Andrew Benzie Books
Martinez, California

Published by Andrew Benzie Books
www.andrewbenziebooks.com

Printed in the United States of America
First Edition: October 2021

10 9 8 7 6 5 4 3 2 1

Laube, Chloe
The Spinster

ISBN: 978-1-950562-31-2

Cover and book design by Andrew Benzie
www.andrewbenziebooks.com

To those who are tucked in my heart.

CONTENTS

CHAPTER ONE

The silver-framed scroll sat on top of my dresser, a grand proclamation that I, Amy Archer, had survived four years of academic stress to graduate from college—cum laude, a modest accolade. I didn't qualify for the more extensive honors of magna or summa because I wasn't that smart.

Nor was I brave enough to escape my mother's stifling household or her tenacious grasp. And despite my academic feat, I still lacked the one piece of parchment that mattered in 1960—a marriage license.

Four frilly bridesmaid dresses drooped in the back of my closet, annoying reminders that the four girlfriends I preceded down the aisle had become euphoric brides while I remained miserably unattached. I couldn't bear to look at the offending fluffs and slammed the closet door shut.

A foolish move that invited the inevitable invasion.

Knock. Knock-knock. Knock-knock-knock.

"What's going on in there?"

Mom, at it again, patrolling with the intensity of a hound on the hunt. Now she positioned herself outside my room, most likely with her ear pressed against the door—or was she peering into the keyhole?

I collapsed on my bed, a narrow twin-size that personified

my chaste existence. Snatching a pillow to stifle the howl of protest I dared not let out, I wallowed in dark thoughts.

No matrimonial prospects had survived Mom's onslaught—*none*. Possibly marketable at twenty-two, I dreamed of a garden wedding under a lush bower of sweet fragrant wisteria. But by age twenty-three? I'd be a shriveled old maid. Parked on a parlor settee sniffing a lavender-scented hanky. Crocheting a doily.

A prime example? Aunt Jane, my mother's older sister. She didn't crochet, but jigsaw puzzles occupied much of her time. When I was a little kid, I thought she looked like a movie star. She swirled in stylish skirts, flipped her wavy, shoulder-length hair, and, to my fascination, glued on long sultry eyelashes.

But for whatever reasons, the matrimonial boat had sailed on by her, and now my aunt epitomized the plight of an unwed woman.

"I'm doomed to the outskirts of existence," she lamented, achingly aware of her solo status. "Don't let this happen to you, Amy. Find a fellow while you're in bloom, because the flower withers fast."

Aunt Jane spouts poetic metaphors the more she sips from the flask in her purse.

The absence of a husband has molded her life. In the insular couples-culture of the early 60s, men ruled, women fawned over and fastened themselves to one, and those who missed out languished. My aunt's rants, angry and poignant, haunted me.

"I pound in anonymity on that damnable Underwood typewriter for $35 a week, transcribing the pompous words of male mucky-mucks who don't give a damn about me or any of the other women trapped in their ghastly steno pool.

"No breaks anywhere. I sacrificed my precious lunch hour to hurry over to the bank because I wanted a credit card. The snotty teller told me the bank would issue me a duplicate using my husband's account—if he okayed it. 'But I'm single,' I reminded him. 'Sorry. No cards for unmarried women.' Like hell he was sorry."

Aunt Jane became further incensed when she inquired about a mortgage.

"I harbored the foolish hope of buying the flat where I live. When I asked the finance officer if I qualified for a loan, the arrogant ass laughed at me. 'In your dreams. Maybe you've got a father or a brother who can cosign, but don't count on it. You won't qualify because you don't have any credit.'

"How do I get credit if you won't give me a damn card?" I asked. I felt steam coming out of my ears.

"'No need for rancor or uncivil language, ma'am.' The pompous jerk sat back in his chair and tore up my application.

"And the social scene is just as unfair. God forbid that I should mingle with the married. What if I stole someone's husband? The highlight of my existence is lunch with the girls. Take heed, Amy."

Well, even without my aunt's admonitions, I was all too aware of the need to acquire a husband. Every young woman growing up in the 50s knew the simple truth—find a man or forfeit a colossal chunk of life.

So far, prospects were lousy. When I plunged into the college scene as an eager freshman, I hoped—no, *expected*—

to discover the magical man who'd fill my yearning heart and open the door to a wider world.

I thought I was attractive enough—five-feet-four inches tall and a petite size six maintained by compulsive calorie counting. Flecks of green and a touch of blue liven up my bland brown eyes. The sun has streaked my long, copper-brown hair. I smile a lot.

But two thousand other coeds on campus shared that expectation, and the stampede to land a guy turned brutal. I'd limped into the fray and, on the upside, tweaked the interest of a fair number of admirers who flitted my way. A lost cause.

Almighty Mom swatted away the fellows like flies invading her kitchen to desecrate her chicken potpie. Squashed under her crushing thumb, I longed to escape my wretched situation, but my chances dimmed with each passing day.

A cruel twist of fate had walloped me early in life, and Mom's steamrolling personality finished the job. I had been crafted into a timid, submissive, jellyfish.

*　　　　*　　　　*

The catastrophe struck a few days after my fifth birthday. Mom was giving me a fierce scolding because I had decorated all ten of my fingers with pitted olives left over from my birthday party.

"Missy, those olives were hard to come by with war-time rationing. Last year was bad and now 1943 is worse. You've spoiled the olives, so now you're going to eat every last one." Hands on her hips, elbows jutting out, she meant business.

This was the best punishment ever because I loved olives, but all of a sudden, I felt bad—real bad.

"I can't eat, Mom. I feel sick—and hot."

She put her hand on my forehead before plucking the olives from my fingers and boosting me up to wash my hands in the kitchen sink.

"Most likely a cold coming on," she said, but I didn't sniffle or sneeze.

"I'm tired, Mom. Can I go back to bed?" I asked.

Mom frowned her face. Her forehead wrinkled and her eyes looked worried as she led me to my room and tucked me under the covers. Then the doctor came carrying a big brown satchel. He talked to Mom out in the hall, and after he left, she phoned my dad.

Dad came home from work early and rolled the wringer washing machine from the porch into my bedroom. He shoved the big white machine up right next to my bed and filled it with hot water. Then Dad, Mom, and Aunt Jane took turns wrapping me in hot, moist towels from the wringer all day and night.

I couldn't move or pay attention, and I don't remember much except I kept hearing them whisper the same word—*polio*.

*   *   *

Nobody knew where it came from. The grownups talked about flies and water and mosquitoes and how the awful disease popped out all over the world to destroy kids.

Everyone was afraid of catching it, so Mom said I had to

be quarantined, which meant I had to stay inside the house. No playing with anyone for a long time.

That made me sad, but worse yet, I wasn't able to walk. My right leg wouldn't work anymore. I couldn't make it move. Lonely, scared, and weak, I didn't even try to get out of bed.

Sometimes the air-raid sirens screeched out in the night. I felt spooky and afraid because then the radio crackled, and the newsman whispered that Japanese soldiers might be sneaking into California. They might catch me because I couldn't run. Somebody turned off all the lights in the whole city. Mom would hurry through the house, pulling down the thick window shades, and Dad lighted his block-warden lantern so we could see.

So many scary things to worry about. What if the war came into our house? I was glad to be a girl, so I didn't have to shoot people. What if I got sick again? The rest of me might stop working the way my leg had. And what about the dark picture hanging above my junior-size bed? A gloomy little girl with a big bow in her hair stared down at me. I worried why she looked unhappy.

"Who is she—what's her name, and why isn't she smiling?" I asked Mom.

"Her name was Alice, and she was your father's sister. People didn't smile for photographs in those days."

"How come I don't know her?"

"She got sick and died when she was only five. Caught the flu or something. Nobody knew why back then."

Five, just like me.

Would I die next? More terror. I shivered in my bed under Alice's mournful gaze and wondered if she could see me.

Three goldfish kept me company, but one day my mom took away their bowl to change the water. When she brought the bowl back a few days later, three goldfish were swimming in circles, but I *knew*. They weren't my fish.

Then I overheard Mom talking to Aunt Jane.

"I had to run out to the pet shop because I accidentally turned on the hot water instead of the cold and boiled those silly fish." Mom chuckled.

Goldie, Swishy, and Bubbles—my only pals.

Scalded. Dead like Alice and gone forever.

Hiding under the covers, I longed to rise in defiance like Wonder Woman, my favorite comic book heroine. Her amazing bracelets protected her from many evils, including wicked Vulcan's lightning-bolt daggers.

But were they strong enough to fend off Mom? I doubted it, and things have been dicey between us ever since she wiped out my fish.

CHAPTER TWO

Aunt Jane is brave. Everyone's afraid of my mother, but not her.

My aunt lived not too far away and visited me a lot when I was six or seven. She sipped medicine from a flat silver bottle she kept in her purse. The medicine made her extra talky, and she was still mad because Mom stole my dad from her.

"Your mom pushed the limits even as a kid," Aunt Jane told me. "Wanted everything her way. A bossy brat. On Friday nights, everyone gussied up to go to the big dance at the Veteran's Hall. Your dad was a hazel-eyed, good-looking country-boy who'd just moved to town. I spotted him first thing, and my heart fluttered like a butterfly when he asked me to dance. Then your mother had the *nerve* to cut in. Ladies don't do that."

"Why not?"

"Terrible manners. A proper woman waits for a fellow to invite her to dance. But my selfish baby sister Harriet bulldozed in. She'd set her sights on handsome Henry Archer, and when she found out that he could do the Charleston, the poor man didn't stand a chance. Neither did I." She took a drink from her bottle. I liked the big bird etched on the side of it.

"What's a Charleston?" I asked.

"A real fast dance where people flap their arms and legs and kick up their heels."

"Did she dance it good?" I had a hard time imagining Mom dancing a fast dance. She wasn't very tall, and she was chunky around her middle. Mom was pretty enough with her big brown eyes and fluffed brown hair, but she didn't look at all like my ballerina doll.

"I thought your mother resembled a chicken running amuck, but your father thought otherwise." Aunt Jane shook her head. Her hair was red today.

She and Mom looked a lot alike, except my mom had round cheeks, like apples. Aunt Jane was taller and thinner and did herself up more fancy. She wore bright red lipstick and drew on dark eyebrows and colored her hair. One time, I drew on my eyebrows with a black crayon and Mom gave me a talking-to.

Aunt Jane drank more medicine before she went on with her story.

"Your dad was twenty-one and your mother was only seventeen when she conned him into running off to Reno to tie the knot."

"What knot? Like on a shoelace?" Her stories were complicated.

"No, that means they got married. And then your mom began obsessing about having a baby. She rushed out and bought a fancy bassinet. But after four years, still no kid. I was tired of her bitching, so I told her to stand on her head after the deed. Bingo. The seed was planted, your mother swelled up like a watermelon, and here you are, kiddo."

I didn't understand what Aunt Jane was talking about, but to be on the safe side, I wouldn't eat watermelon for a long time.

After a while, I got stronger, and one morning when I woke up my knee worked again. I was able to bend it and straighten it out.

"Hey, Mom. Come and see," I called out, surprised and excited. I tossed the covers off and jumped out of bed to stand up. But I still couldn't walk. My right foot dropped down. It just hung there. I wasn't able to raise it or wiggle my toes.

Mom was disappointed too. She phoned the doctor, and he said he was sorry, but the rest of my leg wasn't going to get any better. "Bring her in to be fitted for crutches," he told her.

*   *   *

The crutches were made of wood and hurt under my arms. I hated them, but to go anywhere, I needed to hop on one leg, struggle with the crutches, or scoot on my bottom. I mostly liked to stay at home because if I went anywhere, grown-ups stared at me with pity all over their faces.

"Too bad. What a shame," they'd say.

Please don't look at me that way, I silently cried and wished I had Vulcan's awesome powers to zap the offenders.

CHAPTER THREE

I figured something was up when Mom woke me up early on a Monday. She laid out my yellow-daisy dress for me to put on instead of my pull-on overalls.

"You're going to school today, and a special bus is coming to pick you up." She fussed with my hair. I *hated* the braids she made me wear.

"*Real* school like other kids? How come you didn't tell me?" I felt confused, scared and happy all at the same time. I'd already learned the alphabet and numbers, but Mom worried because I was almost seven years old and other kids my age were way ahead of me in schoolwork.

"Because we signed you up to go to this school almost a year ago, but there was a long waiting list. The attendance office called this morning and told me they finally had an opening."

"Are you coming with me?" She had on a house-dress and not her going-out clothes.

"No. The principal thought you'd do better by yourself— to get acquainted with the other kids on your own. Hurry up and eat your Rice Krispies. We can't make the bus late. I made you a peanut butter and jelly sandwich for lunch, and it's going to be hot today, so you don't need a sweater."

My favorite kind of sandwich and *real* school. I was so surprised and excited that I didn't want to have breakfast.

When a loud horn honked outside, I pushed away the cereal bowl.

"That's the bus," Mom said. She handed me a small brown paper bag and my crutches, and I hobbled as fast as I could to follow her to the front door.

An orange bus was outside, parked at the curb. The bus driver was a big lady, bigger than Dad. When she saw me, she climbed out of the bus, picked me up off the sidewalk along with my crutches, carried me inside the bus, and sat me down next to a boy who kept twitching.

Kids in wheelchairs were shoved together at the back of the bus. Other kids had crutches and sat on hard double seats. Some cried or yelled, and a few even hit one another. Others didn't make any noise at all. They sat frozen, like me. I was terrified and too afraid to cry.

The doors closed, and the bus rattled as we drove. When it stopped in front of a crumbly old building, a few of the kids got off on their own. I couldn't move or talk. The bus driver finally picked me up and stood me on the sidewalk with my crutches. I just stayed there like a statue, trying to balance on my good leg.

Another lady came over and talked at me, but I didn't understand her words. When I didn't move, she stopped talking, ducked behind a hedge, and rolled out an empty wheelchair. She sat me in it and pushed me to an office where a gray-haired lady was busy on the phone.

"Flo, you'd better call this one's mother. She's not going to make it," the wheelchair lady said. I heard her words, but what did she mean? That's how people talked in stories when someone was going to die.

I didn't move an inch until Mom charged through the

office door about an hour later. Then I started to cry. I cried all the way home in the taxi and couldn't stop, not even when Dad came home from work.

When I finally was able to speak, all I kept saying was, "I don't belong in that place," in between sobs and hiccups.

I stopped crying when Mom and Dad promised I never had to get on that bus or go back to that school again.

Mom gave me a peanut butter and jelly sandwich for dinner because I had lost my favorite lunch, and then she put me to bed and shut the bedroom door. My bedroom was next to the kitchen, so lots of times I listened to stuff when the grownups forgot I could hear everything, even with the door closed.

Dad had been reading the evening newspaper at the kitchen table. I heard Mom pull out a chair. She started to cry.

"I should never have put her on that terrible bus," Mom kept saying. "Never. It's *disgraceful* to treat children that way. Sticking kids on a dilapidated vehicle with no adults to help them. Someone's going to answer for this."

"Harriet, you meant well so don't beat yourself up. We'll figure something else out," Dad said.

It didn't take long. Two days later, Aunt Jane came over to stay with me because Mom needed to go to a meeting at the board of education. Mom had on the same outfit she always wore if she went out on errands or to the doctor or dentist. Her gray-colored Victory suit had a skirt shaped like an A, and the jacket had fat shoulder pads that stuck out. I wondered if that's why Aunt Jane said Mom had a chip on her shoulder.

Mom's shoes were black with little heels. She called them

sensible pumps, and they matched her purse and hat. She ratted up her dark brown hair high and used gel stuff to make it stay in place, so the hat sat on top of her hair. A single red rose on a long stem looked like it was growing out of the front of the hat, and whenever she started talking, the rose bobbled up and down. When Mom had a hissy-fit, that rose bounced like a Yoyo.

"What's a board of education?" I asked Aunt Jane as soon as Mom banged out the door. I thought it might be a Monopoly board with tiny schoolhouses to move around on it.

"No, Amy, this kind of board means a group of people deciding things such as who goes to what schools. Now let's get rolling before your mother comes back."

She reached into her big purse and pulled out her medicine bottle and a deck of cards. Aunt Jane always surprised me with what we were going to play. We used to play War, but after she taught me numbers, it was too easy. For a while, we played Go Fish or Old Maid, but then Aunt Jane said she didn't like that game.

"Why don't you like to play Old Maid?" I was disappointed because I thought it was fun.

"I don't like the game because I am one, and it's your mother's fault. When you grow up, Amy, you need a husband if you want any kind of life. Now I'm going to shuffle and then we'll practice our new game, Rummy. After that we'll move on to Gin Rummy to help you with your numbers even more. You're a fast learner, and your mom will be quite surprised when you trounce her at the card table someday."

When we heard Mom at the front door, Aunt Jane

scooped up the cards and hid them and her bottle in her purse. The cards were our secret, and the best part of the game was fooling Mom.

Mom barged in, and the rose on her hat was leaping like a jumping jack. She plopped down on a kitchen chair, bursting to tell Aunt Jane what happened at the board of education.

"I marched into that meeting and gave those two-bit bureaucrats a piece of my mind. Special education program, my eye, I said. You endangered those helpless kids by parking them on a relic of a bus with inadequate adult supervision.

"The chairman was all schmooze. 'Well, there should have been a monitor on the bus that day. Thank you for calling the issue to our attention, Mrs. Archer,' Mr. Big-wig says.

"And how is my daughter going to receive an education?" I asked.

"'The board will need to confer on a solution, and we'll notify you of our decision.' He stood up and stuck out his hand like I was supposed to shake it and leave.

"I sat back in my seat. 'Take your time, buster. I have all day. My attorney thinks it would be easy enough for you to send a home teacher for Amy and a lot simpler than a lawsuit.'"

Aunt Jane interrupted. "Did you really call him buster?"

Mom's lazy cousin Buster pretended to be sick because he didn't want to go fight in the war. Mom thought he was a no-good draft dodger, and if she didn't like someone, she'd call him buster. Dad signed up to be a soldier, but the Army excused him because he couldn't see good enough to shoot a gun. That made him okay with my mom.

Mom kept talking.

"Don't interrupt me, Jane. Yes, I called him buster. I was fuming, and that's the worst disparagement that came to mind. One of the other men on the board sensed trouble and took charge. 'Will you excuse us for a moment, Mrs. Archer?' he asked.

"Go right ahead, I said, but I didn't budge. So, all six men got up to go out into the hall for their moment. Only big-wig Buster came back.

"'Good news, Mrs. Archer,' he says with his phony smile. 'Your daughter is eligible for home tutors twice a week.'"

Aunt Jane jumped up and hugged Mom, something she never did. "Harriet, a great job. But where did you come up with an attorney?"

"Oh, I use that one all the time. It helps people to see my point of view."

*   *   *

The next night, Dad came home a little early from his job at the telephone company. I wanted to see him climb up and down the telephone poles, but he said he worked in a big office doing hard numbers.

Mom made a meatloaf with baked potatoes. My war-time job was to pop the orange ball in the package of white lard and mush the stuff around until it turned yellow to look like butter. It tasted good on the potatoes.

When dinner was over, we stayed sitting at the kitchen table while Mom finished giving me another talking-to for drinking the juice left over in the olive bowl. I pretended I was sorry.

Dad interrupted.

"Harriet, you did a bang-up job handling the school business. I'm treating you and Amy to a special day."

He leaned over to me to explain.

"Now I want you to listen to the story I'm going to tell you. That's so you'll understand where we're going and why." Dad looked serious. "Amy, the President of the United States caught the same bug you did, so don't ever think that you can't accomplish great things."

"I hated FDR." Mom frowned and snapped a dishtowel.

"Harriet, the man worked wonders for the country before he died last month."

"That's *your* opinion. I never liked Eleanor either."

"This isn't about politics. Please let me finish."

Dad sighed and turned back to talk to me.

"Amy, the President liked to go to a place in Georgia called Warm Springs to swim in special warm mineral water. There's a town not too far from here called Calistoga that has hot springs and a mineral pool. We're going to check it out."

"But I don't know how to swim, Dad. And why did the President die—did he drown?"

"No, he died because he got old. The good news is, I'm going to teach you to swim. I seem to remember your mother bought you a swimsuit and some water-wings just before you got sick."

"The suit won't fit her now, and this place is probably a filthy hole-in-the-wall. Henry, you ought to have consulted me." Mom glared at Dad and flicked the towel again. She liked to be the boss.

"Well, Harriet, buy her another swimsuit because we're

going next Thursday." Wow. Dad hardly ever sassed her, but I could tell he meant business—and Mom knew it, too.

"Why are we going on a Thursday instead of a Saturday? Now you have to waste a vacation day." When Mom didn't get her way, her bottom lip stuck out, all pouty.

"It's not a waste, it's an opportunity for Amy." Dad scowled. "Thursday is their least busy day. I phoned and checked with the manager. Knock it off, Harriet."

*   *   *

Mom took the trolley downtown to Woolworths and bought me a new swimsuit, a pretty pink one to match the water-wings still in the box from a long time ago. She also bought a new summer outfit for herself. Instead of separate slacks and a blouse, this was all one piece with a zipper up the back. The light blue material was shiny—polished cotton, Mom called it.

"Well, la-de-da. Aren't we the fashion-plate sporting the newest rage in overalls?" Aunt Jane looked miffed when Mom showed it to her. "Did you get yourself a new bathing suit too?"

"No, I didn't, Jane. I tried on a couple, but they were too lumpy. Besides, I really don't like to swim."

"It's not the suits that were lumpy," Aunt Jane said. Then there was a ruckus.

CHAPTER FOUR

A trip—to someplace *new*.

"Will there be ocean and mountains?" I asked, wondering because I never got to go anywhere. Mom said no, but I was still super-excited. She was making a picnic lunch, and best of all, I would be going swimming with Dad.

We left at 10:00 Thursday morning, on the dot. That made Dad happy. Mom looked pretty in her new outfit and her summer wedgie shoes. She'd made cheese and baloney sandwiches, potato salad with sweet pickles, and she filled the empty pickle jar with black olives. Plus, she baked my favorite treat next to olives—Toll House cookies.

Dad settled me in the back seat of his Ford and placed a small ice-chest on the floor under my seat. Mom must have read my mind, because she kept the cookies in a separate bag up front.

As Dad pulled the car out of the driveway and onto the road, I asked why we needed the ice-chest.

Mom explained that the food had to be kept on ice because the mayonnaise on the sandwiches and in the salad might go bad and give us terrible ptomaine poisoning.

Because of the road-noise, I didn't hear all the conversation. I thought Mom said toe-mangle poison and worried how mayonnaise could wreck your toes.

I kneeled on the seat and looked out the window. When

we drove away from the city and into the country, the sky turned bluer. Green hills stretched out as far as I could see.

"Look at all the yellow flowers—like a carpet on top of the grass. And purple and orange flowers are popped up everywhere."

"The yellow ones are mustard greens, Amy," Mom said. "The purple and orange ones are wildflowers. Lupus and poppies—the state flower." She knew all about flowers.

"Harriet, you're mistaken. The purple ones are lupin. Lupus is a disease."

"I do not make mistakes, especially when it comes to flora and fauna, Henry."

"I'm not going to argue with you, but you're wrong." When Dad got mad, his voice stayed quiet, but his face turned red. I couldn't see his face, but the back of his neck and ears looked pink.

"We'll just see about that, Mr. Know-it-All." Now she was mad. Mom liked to know it all.

Dad's neck turned pinker, but he just kept driving.

Then we came to fenced ranches that had hundreds of cows—the cutest, prettiest cows ever. Most were white with big black spots, but some were black with white spots.

"Those are dairy cows. That's where our milk comes from," Dad explained.

"I thought cows were brown," I told him.

"The brown cows are the ones we eat," Mom said. Then she started fussing about when we were going to have lunch.

"Henry, we need to stop for lunch an hour before we get to Calistoga."

"Why's that, Mom?" I asked.

"Because you're going swimming, and if you eat and

don't wait an hour before getting in the water, you'll get awful stomach cramps and sink to the bottom of the pool."

Now the back of Dad's neck and ears looked like they were on fire.

"For God's sake, Harriet, you've terrorized her with poisoned mayonnaise, agonizing cramps and possible drowning. If you say one word about the beef industry, you can walk home."

"Henry, she needs to understand these things for her own protection," Mom snapped.

I wasn't sure what he said back, but Mom stopped talking, and Dad pulled over to the side of the road for us to have lunch. Mom couldn't figure out why all I wanted to eat were the olives and cookies. I told her it was because I didn't want my toes messed up, but she didn't understand.

After Dad drove some more, we came to a dusty old town. I saw a few horses in a field, but I liked the black and white cows better.

Dad stopped at a rickety grocery store with what looked like a cowboys' saloon attached on one side, and he went inside. When he came back to the car, he had a purple stamp on his hand and smelled the way Aunt Jane does when she drinks from her medicine bottle.

"We're good to go to the pool," Dad said, lots cheerier. He drove around to the back of the building and parked in a dirt lot. Mom sniffed her nose and put on her thunder-face.

A green meadow sprawled out in front of us with a pool in the middle. Funny little closet-like shacks were lined up on each side of the pool. A picture of a lady was painted on a sign on one side, and the other side had a drawing of a man.

The grass was too uneven for me to use my crutches, so

Mom carried me to one of the ladies' shacks and helped me get into my pink swimsuit. Something smelled bad—like when Mom didn't cook eggs right.

Dad had changed to his swimming suit, and he carried me to the shallow end of the pool. We sat on the edge while he took a big breath and puffed to blow up my water-wings.

"The water smells yucky." I held my nose.

"That's because there's sulfur and other minerals in it that make it special. Put your feet in, Amy," he said.

I expected to be struck by a terrible tummy ache and sucked to the bottom of the smelly pool. But I carefully dipped in the toe of my good foot, and the water felt warm. Not hot, just right—like the perfect bath. The water-wings hooked on to a harness and Dad fastened it, so the wings fit under my arms and puffed out in back.

Dad took my hand, and I hopped beside him as we waded into deeper water. When he got waist-deep, he said, "The wings will hold you up, Amy. See?"

He let go of my hand, and sure enough, I floated on top of the water. "Now kick your legs. Or pretend you're riding your tricycle the way you used to before you got sick."

I thought I'd burst from being so happy. I pretended to run and jump and hop and dance like regular kids do. My floppy foot didn't matter at all. I forgot all about the smell.

Mom kicked off her wedgies and rolled up the legs on her fancy new overalls. She sat down on the edge of the pool in the shallow end to put her feet in the water.

"Harriet, Amy's going to be a top-notch swimmer," Dad called out to her. "This mineral water is so buoyant I think she'll be fine without the water-wings."

Mom smiled. I thought she waved at us, but then I saw a

bee buzzing around her head. She flapped her hands to shoo it away.

Dad unhooked my water-wings, and without them it was easy to float on my back. Next, he showed me how to turn over and paddle my arms the way dogs do in water. Before I knew it, I was swimming—all by myself.

I didn't think the day would get more wonderful, but it did. Dad and I kept practicing how to dog-paddle, and all of a sudden Mom stood up in the pool, shaking her head like crazy. The bee was in her hair.

She didn't know that the special water made the bottom of the pool extra slippery. Both of Mom's feet slid out from underneath her, and there was a giant splash. Mom landed in the pool, sitting waist-deep in the water, and the only way for her to get rid of the bee was to dunk her head.

I laughed so hard I got the hiccups and almost tinkled in the pool (I did a little but never told). Dad tried to dive before Mom saw him laughing, but he was too slow.

Mom wore a beach towel home and told off Dad for laughing because the vicious hornet might have stung her, causing a life-threatening toxic reaction. Dad said it was only a little bee, and it wouldn't have gone after her if she hadn't put so much goo in her hair.

Now I had to worry about mayonnaise poison, mutilated toes, stomach cramps, eating nice brown cows, and bee stings—but I wasn't afraid of drowning. I knew how to *swim*.

A short-lived comfort, because of Mom's new project— repairing me.

CHAPTER FIVE

What a *commotion*. Car horns honking, yelling, and when Mom pulled aside the ruffled yellow curtains to look out the kitchen window, she saw people running into the street. I was too short to see anything from my chair.

"Must have been an accident. I'd better check." Mom put down her dish towel and started to go to the front door, but the phone rang. It was Dad, calling from work. They talked a minute, and when Mom hung up, she flew into a tizzy, dancing what I think was a Charleston. She wiggled her knees and bounced up and down so hard that even her hair moved. Then she raced to turn on the radio.

"Amy, you're only seven years old, but you need to remember this day. May 8, 1945. The war is almost over."

Our neighbors opened their doors and windows, shouting and waving to one another above the noise of the car horns and the voices of newscasters coming from their radios.

"It's over in Europe," the grownups kept yelling. "Damned Germans surrendered." Except they called the Germans a lot of bad names I wasn't allowed to say.

The radios blared patriotic music real loud, and I listened to Kate Smith sing *God Bless America* so many times that I knew the words by heart before bedtime.

All the kids ran out into the street and made a parade,

banging on pots and pans since no one had any drums.

I watched from the picture window in the living room because marching and crutches didn't go together. Mom gave me a little flag on a stick to wave when the kids paraded by, but it wasn't the same.

Even winning a Kewpie doll when Dad took us to the big parade downtown wouldn't make my sadness go away. I didn't want to be different and stared at by grownups who shook their heads and looked sorrowful before they turned the other way.

Not long after the parade, Mom surprised me. She'd hurried off to a last-minute appointment, and Aunt Jane pretended to be sick to stay with me instead of going to work.

When Mom came roaring back home, the rose on her hat was whipping up and down like a seesaw.

"Amy, I've found a new doctor who's going to fix your foot."

"You mean he'll make it work again, so I can run, and skip, and play jump-rope?" I wanted more than anything to be like regular kids.

"He's a top-notch specialist, and that's what he told me." She sounded so sure. And Aunt Jane hugged Mom and shared her medicine with her to celebrate.

*   *   *

My Wonder Woman magic bracelets were only plastic, so they didn't have enough power to save me from that scary doctor. Mom called him an orthopedist. I called him bad names in my head.

"How is the girl today?" he'd ask my mom, as if I wasn't sitting on his exam table right in front of him. I can still hear his white coat crackling with starch as he moved. He never smiled or talked to me or acted like I was a real person.

"Doctor has ordered orthopedic shoes for you so he can make you a brace," Mom told me after a few visits. She didn't call him Dr. Whitecoat. Just "Doctor" like some grownups say Jesus or God.

I was excited. I didn't know what orthopedic meant, so I imagined the shoes would be pretty white Mary Janes.

When Mom washed the breakfast dishes, I liked to sit at the kitchen table and play with my Paper Dolls Cut and Color book while she tidied up. Today, I decided to color one of the dresses green, to match the house-dress Mom had on. It was tricky because of the white polka-dots.

When the mailman rang the doorbell, Mom hurried to the door, even though she still had fat curlers in her hair.

"The shoes are here," she said, coming back to the kitchen. She put the package down on the table. I could hardly wait for her to open it. She tore off the stiff brown wrapping paper, lifted the lid of the box, and took out the shoes.

I burst into tears when I saw them.

"Mom, they're *ugly*. The ugliest shoes ever. Brown and square. And look at the laces up the middle. Like boys' shoes." I had to snuffle my nose because I cried so hard.

"Doctor says you need to wear them to fit in the brace he's making for you. So that's that. We'll try them on."

I was sure Mom would do whatever "Doctor" said. I gulped down some tears, and then I had an idea. Maybe half-ugly wouldn't be so awful.

"Can I wear a Mary Jane on my good foot?" I asked.

"Of course not," she snapped. "Don't be silly. Shoes have to match."

"Why?" I asked.

"Because," she said. "Don't sass."

When she turned back to the table to pick up the scraps of wrapping paper, I wiped my nose on the hem of her dress.

*   *   *

The shoes fit. I curled the toes on my good foot so it wouldn't go in the shoe, but Mom figured it out. Then we had to take them to Doctor Whitecoat.

The heavy metal brace he'd made fit around the shoe. It had steel spokes that climbed up my leg and clamped to an iron band just below my knee. A cage for my leg. The brace was cold and hard, and weighed almost as much as I did. I struggled to drag it around.

Pity, pity. The adults stared. I hated it when they looked sad and felt sorry for me. I wanted to neutralize them with Vulcan's dagger—*zap*.

The creepy doctor thought of more torture. After a few months, he told my mom that if he operated on my leg, I wouldn't have to wear the brace anymore.

"Amy, Doctor is going to move some muscles around so your foot won't drop down. Won't you be glad to not wear that brace?" Mom asked. Her question wasn't a real one.

"I guess so," I said. It didn't matter what I thought or felt because Mom was the boss of me, and the doctor seemed to be the boss of Mom.

So I had to go to the hospital, which scared me so bad I don't remember much except when I woke up from the surgery, a white plaster cast covered my whole leg.

And after I came home, the doctor started changing the casts, slapping on slimy wet rolls of plaster, one after another. Each time he sawed off the old one, he used a real saw, like the little one Dad kept in the garage. More panic—what if his hands slipped?

The last cast stopped below my knee and had a stub under the heel for walking.

"Have the girl put as much weight on it as she can," he told Mom. "It will be easier for her when the cast comes off.

"Is this the last cast?" I asked Mom.

"That's what Doctor said," she answered.

It turned out to be the last cast and the final straw. While he sliced through that itchy plaster, I was too excited to be afraid, but then I looked at my bare leg.

Fix my foot?

Big, rotten fibbers—both Mom and Dr. Whitecoat. That skinny, shriveled-up white stick wasn't my leg. I tried to point my foot down, but it didn't move. He'd *wrecked* my ankle and it wouldn't go up or down. My step was flat—no way to rise on my toes or rock back on my heel.

"You *cemented* my ankle. How am I supposed to play hopscotch on this?" I yelled at him, so angry that I didn't care if my mother punished me for sassing—which she did. No dessert for two days.

*   *   *

I needed to use my crutches for a while because it hurt a lot to step on my foot. But I hoped if I toughed through the pain the way Wonder Woman would, I might be able to snatch olives from the refrigerator—and to escape from the house.

Dad helped me practice every night, and when I could walk without the crutches, Mom let me go out to play in the neighborhood as long as she was able to see me. Our second-story back porch stuck out over our backyard, where Mom had planted her victory vegetable garden. She stood out on the porch to keep tabs on everyone else's backyard and could easily check on my whereabouts.

On nice summery days a little pack of kids got together to play dodgeball, ride bikes and chew on blades of delicious sour grass that grew wild. Jimmie Olson had two wiggly dogs that always came along. No one seemed to mind if Fido or Spot lifted a leg to sprinkle the grass.

At first, I was afraid the kids would make fun of the ugly orthopedic shoes I still had to wear and the funny way I had to walk, but the gang was okay with me and my foot so long as I kept up and didn't spoil any games. Jimmy was the oldest, but he acted younger. His big brother had smacked him in the head while teaching him how to swing a baseball bat and ever since, he made clacking noises with his tongue.

Penny Tanner had red curly hair and turned out to be my first best friend. We were both eight years old and loved our story-book dolls—and most any game we thought of. It didn't bother me that every now-and-then she needed to run behind a Juniper bush and throw up.

Mom was at her lookout station when she saw Penny upchucking.

"Something's wrong with that child. I'll have a talk with

her mother," she said. Jimmie's noises were not a worry for her because she knew about his accident.

I sat on the squeaky wood steps of our front porch and watched Mom march two houses down on our side of the street to grill Mrs. Tanner. My mother was about five feet tall—and a little chubby. Not fat, but plump with a pudgy waist. Somehow, her bundled-up bossiness and puffed-up hair, glued with hair gel, made her seem much bigger.

Mom knocked on the door, Penny's mom opened it, and they disappeared inside.

Please, please don't spoil everything and make Penny's mom mad.

After a long time, the Tanner's door flew open and Mom charged out. She didn't notice me because I'd moved to sit in the glider on the porch behind her big ceramic pot full of red geraniums.

As she bustled up the street toward home, Mom paused to look down at the sidewalk where Penny and I had drawn white chalk outlines for hopscotch.

Now we're in trouble for messing up the sidewalk.

Then Mom glanced around, and when she didn't see anyone watching, she started hopping. Double jumps, splits, up on her right foot, down on her left. She flapped her arms, I guess for balance, and she never landed on a single chalk line.

I couldn't believe it. I'd never seen my mom play at anything, except for Canasta, which didn't count because she always ended up in a fight with Aunt Jane. For that brief few minutes, I saw Mom having fun, and it made me happy.

When Mom climbed up the stairs to our front porch, I pretended I hadn't seen her because I thought it would spoil it for her.

"Well, Penny doesn't have anything you can catch, so it's okay if you play with her." She huffed, a little out of breath.

Mom sat down beside me on the glider and started plucking dead leaves off her geraniums. She kept talking, almost like we were friends. I wished she would be that way more often.

"Mrs. Tanner told me her family was living in Honolulu in 1941 when the Japanese bombed Pearl Harbor. She said hundreds of planes swarmed overhead out of nowhere, dropping bombs relentlessly. Penny doesn't remember the attack or the horrible explosions, but the sound of the planes stuck in her head."

Mom pinched off a dried-up flower.

"A shame," she continued. "Penny doesn't understand why, but if a plane flies close, she runs around retching. Her pediatrician says she'll get over it someday. I wanted to know why that family was in Honolulu in the first place, what with the war. Those Japs and Krauts have spies everywhere."

Mom hissed when she said those names, just like she did when she talked about black people.

"I needn't have worried, though," she added. "Penny's father is an engineer, and he managed a government factory on the island that made generators for our brave armed forces. He's a genuine patriot."

After Mom okayed the Tanners, Penny and I moved from outdoors to their big indoor playroom so she wouldn't hear any airplanes. Doll houses, paper dolls, jacks, Pick Up Sticks—we reveled in a summer of fun.

Until Mom decided that since Dr. Whitecoat had fixed my foot—*ha*—it was time to deal with my neglected religious education.

CHAPTER SIX

"I refuse to engage in this holy war, Harriet." Dad was not going to discuss religion, and he meant business.

Religious talk always led to a ruckus. Dad's family were mostly Mormons, and Mom thought they were too churchy and had too many kids. Mom claimed her kin were Presbyterian, but Dad called them red-necked Bible-thumpers.

Both sides argued all the time and agreed on only one thing. Black people were no good. Dad's folks said that was because it was written in the Bible that God had cursed them, and Mom's kin said it was just because.

Mrs. Tanner came up with a solution. A non-denominational church three blocks away was offering a summer Sunday school program. She planned to enroll Penny, and because the two of us were now inseparable, she asked my mother if she'd consider sending me, too.

At first, Mom said no, but I howled and cried, which I never did because I needed to be tough and strong like Wonder Woman. That's when Dad stepped in. He couldn't handle any confrontation, but when he saw how upset I was, he risked Mom's wrath and put his foot down.

"Harriet, this tribal squabbling is ridiculous. Amy will go to Sunday school with Penny. Period."

*　　　　　　*　　　　　　*

Mrs. Tanner walked Penny and me to the church that first Sunday. We met up with Jimmy and his mother along the way. His dogs stayed home. When we arrived, a church-lady, Mrs. Holly, greeted us. She offered to show us kids to our class and to take us home afterward since she lived on the same street. Sounded good to everyone.

Penny and I held hands and followed Mrs. Holly to a classroom. Jimmy had to walk behind us. We wouldn't hold his hand because he was a boy.

When we walked into the classroom, about ten kids had already settled into little desk-chairs. A lady stood handing out brightly colored picture-books, and Mrs. Holly led us over to her.

"Children, this is your teacher, Miss Simmons," she said.

Miss Simmons closed the book she was holding and looked at Penny.

"Penny—a lovely name, dear. Have you heard the story of Penelope, a famous lady in the history of ancient Greece?" Miss Simmons asked her.

"No." Penny whispered, blushing.

"Well, I promise to tell you about her."

Then she turned to me. She smiled and said, "I'm happy you're in my class, Amy. Two darling girls with pretty names."

I was entranced. Too often, adults looked at me and said, "Poor child. She would have been so cute," as if I were ugly, invisible and unable to hear them. *Zap.*

I knew I was broken, but Miss Simmons never let on, and

I began to think I might not be so freaky. She read stories from the Bible and taught us songs. Her voice was beautiful. So was her skin—a soft chocolate color, like a Hershey's candy bar.

During the first hymn, I figured out that Miss Simmons was one of those people Mom called bad names, even though she was a lovely brown, not black. Grownups had their colors confused, calling folks black when they were brown or white when they were beige. I never understood why color mattered.

It sure mattered to my mother. If she found out about Miss Simmons, she'd never let me go to Sunday school again.

For the next seven Sundays, Mrs. Holly—Jimmy called her "holy Holly" and Penny tattled to his mother—collected us to walk to and from the church. I hobbled to adjust to an ankle that wouldn't bend, Jimmy clacked, and, depending on happenings in the skies, Penny upchucked in the nearest bush. Nobody paid us any attention because all the people in the neighborhood knew everybody else's business.

I learned a lot at Sunday school. *Do not tell Mom anything about Sunday school and don't believe her or anyone else when they say bad things about black people.* I'd already figured out not to trust what doctors said.

Sunday school classes ended in August with tearful hugs and goodbyes to Miss Simmons, but big excitement lay ahead for Penny and me. Real school began in September, and we'd be in fourth grade.

Except for Sunday school, I'd only been schooled by the ladies who came to the house with study-plans and books. The home-teachers taught me to read, and I loved my books.

They had been my friends. But I still remembered the awful ride in the orange bus, and it terrified me to think of being in big classes, mixing in with a lot of other kids.

"Don't worry," Penny assured me and promised to show me the ropes.

That's when Mom *ruined* my life.

CHAPTER SEVEN

"You won't be going to the same school as Penny because we're moving," Mom announced in the school-supplies aisle in Woolworth's.

Did I hear her right?

"What did you say?" I asked.

"You and Penny will be going to different schools because we're moving to a better neighborhood."

Sheer panic washed over me. I put back the pink pencil box I had selected. I didn't want it anymore.

"But why?" My hands started shaking. Mom had treated me to an Eskimo Pie, and I thought I was going to throw it up.

"Too many of the *wrong* kinds are filtering in around here," she said, jerking her head left to right as if an evil beast was creeping up to pounce on us. Her hair didn't move. She'd ditched her old hair gel to layer on the new Aqua-Net aerosol hair spray.

Mom was as inflexible as her helmet of hair, and the buckets of tears I cried meant nothing.

*   *   *

One month later, on September 1st, 1947, the Mayflower movers came and packed up everything. We climbed into

Dad's Ford, drove away from our house in Oakland's flatlands, and followed the big van to our new house on a cul-de-sac in the hills.

I eyed the neighborhood from the back seat of the car.

"These houses are too far apart," I protested. "How will we get to know anyone—and where are the sidewalks to play on?"

"You'll adjust," Mom said.

I wanted to cry, but I didn't. Tears were useless and never changed anything.

*   *   *

The new house had a large, sloping front yard with a potting shed to one side. Mom was excited because for years she had wanted to have a big flower garden instead of her victory vegetables.

The inside of the house was laid out so that the kitchen was next to the entry hall, and the large kitchen window faced the street. This made her almost as happy as the potting shed because she could keep tabs on everyone in the neighborhood, just as she had from the second story back porch at the old house.

Heartbroken and frightened, I mourned the loss of Penny. And now we lived too far away from Aunt Jane for her to drop by all the time. I retreated into a self-imposed shell, shutting myself in the midnight blackness of the closet in my new bedroom. I spent hours seeking solace from my Lone Ranger Atomic Bomb Ring that glowed in the dark with genuine radioactive isotopes.

Why would anyone want to be friends with me? Penny

was to be my buffer as we began fourth grade, and now I was all alone and on my own.

People stared at me—far too many to zap, and my limp became an all-consuming curse. *Please don't notice me*, I cried to myself in self-conscious agony.

To compound my misery, my mother insisted that I wear white blouses with ruffled collars, yucky pleated skirts, and the boxcar orthopedic shoes prescribed by Dr. Whitecoat. She also made me wear braids like the dowdy ladies from the old country that I saw in news reels. Mom called them pigtails, which made me feel even uglier.

When I dared to complain about my hair, Mom handled the situation with a kitchen-scissors haircut and a Toni Home Permanent. The perm fried my whole head, making me look worse than ever. Back to the closet to hide—and to hope for a magical rescue.

I imagined Wonder Woman, who was still my idol, flying in her invisible plane to hover overhead. She'd reach down with her indestructible bracelets flashing, grasp my outstretched hands, pull me on board, and swoosh off to the lush island where the Amazons lived.

There, the super-women could teach me to be strong and how to fight for right and justice. Superwoman would use her Golden Lasso to rope up villains and make them tell the truth because lying and deception were bad. And I would become fierce enough to divert a lightning bolt from Vulcan to wipe out Dr. Whitecoat—and to send a zing to Mom.

*   *   *

"Missy, your father's due home any minute. It's time to set the table for dinner," Mom called out from the kitchen. How did she always know when I was about to singe her with an electric jolt? My old job was to squish orange dye in the package of lard to make it look like butter, but now stores sold margarine that was already colored, so setting the table was my new job. I liked lining up the silverware—nice and neat.

I followed my nose to the kitchen, and one sniff told me something bad was happening. Mom always changed from her gardening clothes to a spiffy dress and slicked on lipstick just before my dad came home from work. Today, she was wearing her Kitty Foyle dress—the maroon one with a white collar, almost like Ginger Rogers's in the movie.

Mom stood at the stove, staring out the big window over the sink. She'd hung white ruffled crisscross curtains on the other kitchen window, but this one just had a little ruffle on top so she could look out on the garden she was planting. Plus, she needed to keep an eye on the neighbors.

I *knew* it—Mom' soup-pot was filled with corned beef and cabbage. Yuck. Nobody liked the stringy meat, and the cabbage smelled worse than Brussel sprouts.

"Why are we having this? I asked.

"Because it's tradition, missy. Don't sass. Tomorrow is St. Patrick's Day, and children are starving in China. So that's that."

Bucking Mom was hopeless. I finished the table and sat down to watch while she stirred the pot.

Then I heard Dad's keys rattling in the front door. He opened it, stopped to hang his suit jacket in the hall closet, and came straight to the kitchen, all excited. People said he looked like that movie actor, Ronald Reagan, especially when he smiled.

The grin on his face was bigger than ever as he plunked down in a kitchen chair next to me.

"Harriet, it's our lucky day," he said, pulling an envelope out of his shirt pocket. He waved it at Mom.

"I bought two court-side tickets to the Harlem Globetrotters exhibition match in San Francisco. I've wanted to see them play for years. A guy at work turned me on to a scalper, but he only had two tickets left to sell."

Mom turned around from the stove, scowling so hard her eyebrows touched each other.

"*Our* lucky day? Henry, you've wasted good money to watch seven-foot-tall darkies run up and down a stadium bouncing a ball like adolescent fools. Worse yet, the spectators will be *black*." Mom spit out the word black.

Dad's voice stayed calm, but his face flushed from red to purple.

"The Harlem Globetrotters are world-famous athletes, Harriet. I thought you might appreciate the opportunity to see them play. And the people attending are fans. Who cares if they're black or white?"

"*I* care if they're *black*, and I'm not going. Why do you fritter away your time on such nonsense?"

"Harriet, I will not let your outlandish, unjust prejudices contaminate Amy or influence me. I'll fritter as I please."

Wow. A show-down. I sat real still, hoping not to be noticed, but then Dad turned to me.

"Amy, it's wrong to judge people by their color."

"I already know that, Dad."

"Good. Would you like to come to the game with me?"

"Yes, please."

Thrilled, I didn't even flinch when Mom banged down the lid on her pot. Her eyes were slits.

"Henry, if you have so much money to burn, I want something for myself."

"What?" His face color had faded from purple back to cherry-red.

"I want my potting shed wired for electricity." Her hands were on her hips, her elbows jutted out, and so did her chin. This meant war.

Dad's eyes jerked as though he'd received a zap from Vulcan. He sat for a few minutes, thinking hard.

A stand-off. I dared not move.

"Harriet," he finally said, "My apologies for being so thoughtless. Of course you shouldn't be in the cold or dark. I'll call an electrician tomorrow."

Mom's eyes widened and her jaw dropped. She'd primed herself for a knock-down, drag-out and now there was nothing for her to fight about. She thought she won but somehow knew she'd lost.

That's why we had to eat corned beef for the next three days.

*   *   *

Not only did Dad and I see the Trotters, as he called them, but he began taking me to other games as each sport came into season. Mom hated sports as much as she hated blacks, so she was content to stay home and pot because the shed now had an overhead light, wall-plugs, and a space heater from Montgomery Ward.

Basketball, baseball, football—even hockey. Dad and I ate hot dogs and peanuts, and it was okay to drop the peanut shells on the ground. He taught me the rules for each of the sports and talked lots about sportsmanship and fair play.

I felt special going with Dad—extra-special because other fathers brought their sons, not their daughters. And nobody looked at me or my limp too much because they were more interested in the game.

*   *   *

But school was torture. I hid in the back rows of class-rooms and stayed at the end of any line. Burrowing my frizzed head in books, I was a phantom through grades four and five, praying no one would notice me.

My classmates weren't mean, but a corkscrew-haired, limping, oddly dressed bookworm was too weird, so they ignored and looked right through me. Once again, I didn't exist.

Fate intervened. One Tuesday morning, Miss Tucker, my new sixth-grade teacher, told us to line up single file along the blackboard-wall to march to Assembly. I dutifully lined up where I thought I would be last, but three boys, including Jerry, the hot-shot class president, got in line behind me.

The three boys began giving one another friendly punch-es, and their horseplay escalated into shoving.

I faced toward the front of the line, too shy and intimi-dated to turn and look back at the boys.

All of a sudden—*bam*. Hands slammed into my back. My arms shot forward reflexively to maintain my balance and smacked wimpy Gilbert, the class genius, in his back, which caused him to lurch and shove. The line of kids tumbled down like a row of dominoes.

Unfortunately, Miss Tucker didn't see Jerry and his buddies initiate the action. She only saw me and the resulting avalanche.

"Amy Archer, I'm shocked and ashamed of your behavior. Go to the principal's office. *Now*," she shouted.

Mortified, I hesitated and wondered if I should defend myself.

No. I may have a limp, hideous hair, awful clothes, and no friends, but I am not a snitch.

Principal Boswell delayed the Assembly for fifteen minutes while he interrogated me in his grim, creepy office. He stared at me through his round-rimmed glasses.

"Amy, what possessed you? Why did you lash out in such a destructive manner?"

I squirmed but never squealed.

"I don't know why," I blurted.

"Totally unacceptable conduct. I'm sending you home with a note to your mother, and I expect both of you back here tomorrow.

Mom was furious that I had caused such a disturbance. She had to go to school with me the next day and listen while Principal Boswell gave her a talking-to about the responsibilities of a parent in molding acceptable behavior.

"You may return to class, Amy, but you'd better not cause any more trouble," he warned at the end of his lecture. I bolted out of his office before Mom could have another go at me.

I hurried down the hall, and when I opened the door to my classroom, the kids all gasped. Miss Tucker's icy stare followed me as I skulked toward my chair. I tried to be invisible, but she would have none of it.

"Amy Archer, come to the head of the class and apologize to your fellow students."

I wanted to die, but no such luck—I didn't. Stumbling to the front of the room and facing all those staring eyes, I found enough voice to whisper, "I'm very sorry."

"Louder." Miss Tucker barked, prolonging my agony until she was satisfied that my humiliation was complete. Gilbert shot me the evil eye from the second row.

Finally, Miss Tucker allowed me to slip behind my scarred wooden desk with the dried-up inkwell. I bit my cheeks and tongue so I wouldn't cry.

The bell rang for recess, and I slumped in my seat, too miserable to join the other kids as they raced for the play-yard.

Then the most amazing thing happened. Big-shot Jerry tapped me on the shoulder.

"Thanks for not ratting us out, Amy. Boswell would have kicked me out as class president. You're okay."

CHAPTER EIGHT

A game-changer.

The *class president* had found me acceptable, and I was no longer a pariah. Not on the in—but I wasn't shut out.

My hair grew back—straight, shiny, and long enough for the requisite ponytail. A big smile and cheerful diffidence helped me connect with a few girls with whom I happily shared secrets and giggles.

When we graduated from middle school and entered ninth grade at a four-year high school, I was desperate to keep my new friends. More afraid of losing them than I was of Mom's ire, I challenged my mother's fashion choices.

"Mom, I need poodle skirts and white buck shoes so I can dress the way the other girls do."

"Nonsense. Your clothes are perfectly serviceable, and your foot needs proper support."

"My foot's as good as it's ever going to be, and I hate how I look except for my hair."

I flicked my ponytail.

That sassy little flip really set her off, and the friction escalated until Aunt Jane stepped in. She pretended that we were going to the library but instead whisked me off to Capwells Department Store.

My aunt's extravagance was fueled by her lasting resentment toward my mom for hijacking Dad. And her purse strings really loosened up after multiple medicinal swigs from her flask.

White buck Spaldings, two poodle skirts, two angora sweaters, a crinoline petticoat, and a three-inch-wide waist-cincher. I was ecstatic with my new wardrobe.

The best part of the shopping expedition? The shoe salesman placed my orthopedic monsters in a bag because I wanted to wear the new shoes. When we left the store, Aunt Jane said, "My *dear* sister Harriet can't make you wear what you don't have," and tossed the bag into the Salvation Army bin on the sidewalk.

*   *   *

Outraged, Mom refused to speak to Aunt Jane from September until Christmas. Her retaliation against me was more immediate. The models in chic magazines like Mademoiselle appeared to be cavorting in Paris, so all the ninth-grade girls planned to enroll in French as a language elective.

Mom the Enforcer roared.

"Young lady, you are *not* going to be studying French. Foreigners are eroding our country right and left. You will enroll in Latin and learn the history of the Roman Empire— essential subjects for you to become an educated person."

"What makes you think so?" I sputtered in rare defiance.

"Because I read an article in *Readers' Digest*. You're going to study Latin, and there'll be no *buts* about it, missy. And you'd better keep those white buck shoes spotless."

Mom refused to budge, so I landed in a class dominated by socially challenged super-geniuses. Gilbert was building a rocket in his parent's garage and taking advanced calculus at prestigious U. C. Berkeley. He never forgave me for that sixth-grade shove and took care to keep a physical distance.

Thornton was Gilbert's best friend and already fluent in four languages. He amused himself by adding Cantonese to his repertoire.

Snidely assessing my brainpower, the two of them concluded that I was studying Latin because I was Catholic and wanted to become a nun.

Far from it. Adolescent hormones had kicked in, and romantic dreams invaded my serious study. Not dreams of Gilbert and Thornton. My classmates were brilliant but not the least bit hot—nor was I, but that was beside the point.

My tiny clique of newfound girlfriends swooned over Elvis and mooned over Tab Hunter. I pretended to be equally possessed to maintain my delicate network of blossoming friendships. But my true passion?

Julius Caesar. My crush, which I needed to camouflage at all costs, was obsessive.

Sculptors of the time depicted Caesar as masterful, oozing power and masculinity—encased in armor covering short tunics with hard, muscular legs and feet displayed in sexy strappy sandals.

Oh, how my heart fluttered. I fancied myself in a gossamer toga, swirling into an elegant atrium to join Caesar reclining on a divan in the manner of the Romans. Julius and I sipped wine from plundered gold goblets and looked deeply into each other's eyes. His were the blank orbs of marble sculptures, so I imagined them to be a glorious blue, matching the color of the Aegean sea.

But then Cleopatra barged down the Nile and ruined my fantasy. Compared to her, or most anyone, I was inferior and certainly not eligible to be an emperor's consort. I demoted myself to a devoted maidservant and hovered in the background while that conniving seductress made off with the man of my dreams.

*   *   *

At their first opportunity, the girls taking Latin switched to French, and the cool guys, dazzled by Gina Lollobrigida, transferred into Italian.

By eleventh grade, only fourteen students returned for another semester of Mrs. Dickson's Latin class and her exacting academic and ethical standards.

She always insisted that we embrace the highest principles of conduct and morality, so her opening declaration surprised none of us this semester. We'd heard it daily for two years.

"The honor of a Latin student must be above reproach," she stated, about to launch a discussion of the behaviors and politics of the ancient Romans.

Mrs. Dickson paused when the door to the classroom opened.

A new girl entered, clutching a familiar-looking, yellow admissions slip from the attendance office. Her unruly reddish-brown hair was tamed into a ponytail secured by a rubber band, her white bucks were scuffed, and her nose was sprinkled with freckles.

"I'm sorry to interrupt, ma'am, but I had to complete paperwork in the attendance office. I'm Lynn Westin." Then she turned and introduced herself to the entire class. Her confidence blew me away. If I had been in her place, I would have cowered in the first dark corner I could find.

Lots of desks were vacant, but Mrs. Dickson assigned Lynn to the one directly behind me, sensing that I could use some support.

Mrs. Dickson needed support for herself because as soon as she began a review of Cicero's extraordinary gifts as interpreter, orator, and philosopher, Thornton rudely interrupted. He delivered his own pompous speech debunking Cicero's linguistic accomplishments compared to his own.

Lynn leaned over her desk to whisper in my ear.

"What's with that guy?" she asked.

Not wanting to risk Mrs. Dickson's ire by swiveling around, I scribbled a note, folded it, and passed it over my shoulder to Lynn when Mrs. Dickson turned to face the blackboard.

"Impossible nerd," I had written. "Most of the guys with normal IQs bailed after tenth grade, so the only ones left are brilliant. If you're not on their level, you're toast."

I heard Lynn open the note. She leaned over her desk toward me and again whispered.

"I hate uppity smart-asses."

CHAPTER NINE

"You were expelled?

We sat together in the cafeteria picking at cardboard sandwiches filled with what might have been baloney. When Lynn told me why she had left her old school, I choked.

I stared at her in disbelief, but she was not the least bit ruffled by the disclosure.

"Yep. Kicked out of Carlton's Academy. What a crock. Ridiculous place—a private prep school for snooty rich girls. All white. Everyone was white—students, teachers, admin staff.

"I finally called out the so-called headmistress. 'The Supreme Court already ruled that schools can't be segregated, so what's the deal here?' I asked. The biddy told me to knock off the attitude because prosperous parents don't want their offspring contaminated by liberal concepts. I knew what she was really saying and told the bigot where to go."

Wow. Lynn was as bold as I was timid. I would never have dared such defiance.

"What did your parents say?" I asked.

"Dad's a financial tycoon," she explained. "Whatever I do is okay as long as he doesn't need to get involved. My mother is a true Berkeley freethinker. She congratulated me for standing on principle. I asked her why she enroll me there in the first place, and she said it was because the school was highly rated academically, and I needed to come to my own conclusions about the rest."

I was dumbfounded.

"Lynn, you are so lucky to have an open-minded mother." Hopefully, my envy wasn't too apparent.

"Yours isn't?"

I could only shake my head no. *If you only knew.*

"So why are you stuck in that sappy Latin class of know-it-alls? When I transferred in, I'd already taken two years of Latin because the teacher was a hunk. I tried to sign up for French here, but no luck—too late and no vacancies. But you're already enrolled in this school. Couldn't you have snagged a spot in French?"

"My mother insists that I take Latin. Most of these guys have photographic memories and strut around letting everyone know how smart they are. It's hard for me to keep up with them."

"Well, I'm no brain either. Want to study together?"

I couldn't say *yes* fast enough. We were in perfect sync, and my reserve balanced her impulsivity. At last, I had a new best friend.

*　　　*　　　*

I was frantic to minimize Lynn's exposure to Mom, so we began hanging out after school at her house—except it wasn't like any house I'd ever seen except in magazines or movies.

On the first afternoon I took the bus home with her, we

trudged two blocks through a Berkeley neighborhood of huge, stately old homes, buffered by trimmed lawns and shaded by sprawling trees.

Lynn stopped in front of a shingled, three-story mansion. She opened the wrought-iron gate, and I followed her up the cobblestone path to the oak double front door.

"Welcome to this monument to capitalism," Lynn said, unlocking and flinging open one of the heavy doors.

We walked into an entryway paved with black-and-white tiles, an awesome backdrop for the sweeping staircase leading to the second story—the kind of stairs that Ginger Rogers and Fred Astaire tapped up and down in their classic movies.

A living room with a massive stone fireplace was to the left of the stairs, and to the right was another enormous room with a gleaming black baby grand piano. Coffee-colored leather sofas and fancy velvet-covered chairs in muted colors filled both spaces.

"A drawing room and a music room." Lynn snickered as she conducted a tour. What I found entrancing, she scorned as pretentious. A butler's pantry separated the dining room from the kitchen. The maid's quarters were off the kitchen. Rolling ladders were attached to the shelving in the library. And I gasped in wonder when I peeked into the grand ballroom.

Wow. Like a swanky movie set, I thought, but this was real.

We carried our books up the imposing staircase and walked down a hall to Lynn's bedroom with an adjoining sitting room, a walk-in closet and a private bathroom.

I was speechless, but Lynne shrugged it all off.

"Like I told you, my dad's a fanatic businessman who

works non-stop to make gobs of money. A chieftain in this lopsided society of haves and have-nots. My mom loves to entertain and to play socialite with her clubs and charities, so this house is okay for them. I think it's an example of bourgeois extravagance."

Not wanting to appear the country bumpkin, I refused to acknowledge that I'd never heard that word and spent two months figuring out how to spell it before I was able to look it up.

*   *   *

Mrs. Westin was occasionally home when Lynn and I studied together. She was the polar opposite of my mother. Tall, thin, sleekly dressed in fashionable suits, dashing here and there to important civic events.

"Girls, I hope you're taking full advantage of the cultural opportunities available in this university environment," she admonished, charging out to one of many board meetings. "You must broaden your thinking and grow into independent women."

Lucky Lynn. Her mom thought it was cool that we were learning about Karl Marx and his revolutionary views. My mom deemed Joseph McCarthy a staunch patriot and cheered on his ruthless, destructive anti-communist purge.

Mrs. Westin's reference to cultural opportunities propelled us to Telegraph Avenue to hang out in musty bookstores. There, scruffy street vendors bombarded us with pamphlets decrying multiple social injustices.

Lynn had me thinking hard about my insulated white world. Sometimes we would walk under the arch of Sather

Gate to stand in the frenetic plaza and listen to student orators, dazzling in their ethnic diversity as well as in their strident messages. We hoped to be taken for university students, but our white bucks blew our cover.

"Our time will come," Lynn insisted as we endured the last two years of the high school pecking order. She and I watched from the sidelines as the A list twelfth grade girls swished their cheerleader pom-poms, flashed their spangled behinds, and flirted with hunky guys. But mostly we kept our noses buried in the books that guaranteed us admission to U.C. Berkeley.

"There are real *men* on that campus whose lives extend beyond their grade-point averages. We'll have a blast and find our guys," she insisted.

But what if we didn't find that special someone?

Neither of us wanted to dwell on that grim possibility. Graduating from college without a commitment meant our chances of finding a mate would plummet exponentially. We would tumble into the abyss of dismal spinsterhood. A fatal nosedive, as Lynn put it.

Graduating with honors, and with Mrs. Dickson's parting reminder to take the high road throughout life, the two of us proudly began our freshman year at Berkeley, thrilled to be accepted into that elite academic community.

What Lynn and I hadn't considered was the crushing workload required to compete in that environment.

"My God, this campus is swarming with the likes of Gilbert and Thornton. How the hell will we survive?" Lynn fretted.

Study groups saved us academically. Small groups of less-than-brilliant students clustered and nurtured one another through the tortures of the Pleistocene era and the mysteries of standard deviations.

Over time, I became a steady study-mate, convenient best friend and perennial bridesmaid, mostly because other girls at Berkeley didn't perceive me as a rival. I was sure this was because of my limp.

How I envied the four lucky brides I had preceded as they walked down flower-bedecked aisles to their dreams.

Lynn missed out too. She was too bold and busy with her megaphone on the steps of Sproul Hall, agitating milling students to rally to the cause of the day. Few guys wanted to date the young woman who's brash personality didn't fit the demure, doting little-wife scenario that was the prototype of the late 50s and early 60s.

To my amazement, I did attract a number of guys not put off by my ankle, my limp, or my self-effacing manner. But my trip down an aisle? A fading hope.

CHAPTER TEN

What blocked *me* on the road to a wedding chapel?

My mother, the pothole of my life.

Impassable and unyielding, she cinched in the ties on her Betty Crocker half-apron, secured her hair with an extra squirt of Aqua-Net, and came out swinging at every guy I brought home.

She chased away my admirers with interrogations worthy of the CIA. A smart fellow bolted as soon as he realized he'd be stuck with a mother-in-law who'd risen from hell's deepest bowels.

This didn't take long, because Mom always began her introductory assault with a jaw-dropping belligerent question.

"Just *what* do you intend to make of your life, young man?" she'd ask, her piercing brown eyes firing laser darts. And if he really rubbed her the wrong way, she addressed her quivering victim as "Buster."

An inquisition ranging from family origins, financial means—including who was footing the bill for college—religion, and political inclinations followed.

Bye-bye guy.

God, my embarrassment was excruciating.

Why does she do this? I asked myself over and over. To control? Well, yes. No matter how she tried to disguise herself in dainty shirtwaist dresses, she could not suppress the fact that she was born to rule.

Controlling, commanding—these were the essentials of her personality. And I wondered if there was a distorted element of protection involved, a belated attempt to shield me, her once perfect kid, from further harm.

Or did she believe that my disability reflected poorly on her parenting? Or did she have second-thoughts about her blind adherence to Dr. Whitecoat's cruel agenda?

A muddle of motives probably drove her, but it didn't matter. For as long as I could remember, my mom monitored all aspects of my life in full combat mode. Invasive, relentless, and oblivious to personal boundaries.

A phone call for me? Click—she was listening on the extension. A rare piece of mail arrived addressed to me—I'd find it torn open on the hall table. Friends? *Ha*—never good enough, especially the boys.

Lynn? Also, on the hit list.

"I don't like her." Mom stated this with absolute finality.

"Why not?" I displayed exemplary control considering how angry I was that she begrudged me my best friend.

"That girl is a Berkeley beatnik."

*　　　*　　　*

Meddle, meddle, meddle.

"You're going to become a teacher, Missy."

Mom's mantra. She had it in her head that the noble profession of teaching would give her bragging rights with anyone who inquired about her dutiful daughter.

No matter that I wasn't suited for that role. I could never

prod or discipline struggling kids without worrying. What if a child were hungry—or had been awake all night in a chaotic home?

"Ditch that teaching major," Lynn urged with her do-gooder zeal. "Look at what's happening around us. JFK's call to serve the nation. The Peace Corps gearing up. The drive for civil rights sweeping the South. It's time for action."

She was right. The altruism of the times was inspirational. Since Mom had no notion how academics worked, I surreptitiously switched majors from Education to Social Sciences and plunged down a path of liberal enlightenment with a light heart. A universe of social awareness and responsibility opened—a perfect fit for idealistic me.

Sitting in a vast campus chamber at U.C.'s Wheeler Hall, I listened to an impassioned professor denounce the systematic suppression of the underclasses. Halfway through his lecture, the lightning-bolt struck, and I realized that I'd found my calling.

I would become a social worker.

*   *   *

The reckoning for that decision came during fall mid-terms in my junior year. I'd survived two brutal exams, one in cultural anthropology and the other in early childhood development, on the same blustery November day.

Exhausted, I hurried home from campus and rushed straight to the kitchen, desperate for a Coke to wash down an aspirin. Mom was sitting at the kitchen table. Her thunder-face matched the menace in her voice.

"Missy, what do you think you're doing?" She stood up,

puffed up, and waved a ripped-apart envelope in my face.

What had set her off? I plopped my load of books down on the table.

"I don't know what you're talking about, Mom. And that envelope you're holding is addressed to me."

"So?"

"It's illegal to open other people's mail."

"This is not other people's mail. It's just yours. The letter is some gibberish about changes in required subjects for a degree in something called Social Sciences. Nonsense. I told you, you're going to become a teacher."

The jig was up.

"That won't work for me." Two aspirin might get me through this conversation, along with a sip or three from Dad's bourbon bottle.

"And why not?" She was livid.

"Because I want to make a difference in people's lives. I'm going to be a social worker, Mom."

Her eyes narrowed.

"That no-good Berkeley beatnik Lynn put you up to this."

"Lynn didn't put me up to anything. It's my choice."

"Social work is simply wasting your life on worthless ne'er-do-wells. What will I tell everyone when they ask what you're doing?"

"You might say that I'm helping disadvantaged people."

Mom slapped her hands on the table. "No one can know that you've chosen to wallow with scum."

*   *   *

Three aspirin were required to ease the migraine called

Mom. I often wondered if the compassion I felt for others and their causes stemmed from my own suppressed pain and feelings of helplessness. Or was I brain-washed by all those Wonder Woman comic books I devoured early on? Diana, Princess of the Amazons, and her heroic fight for right had been etched into my tender young psyche.

Whatever the reasons, doormat me, too submissive to stand up for myself, became fierce with the prospect of fighting for the underdog and rescuing the vulnerable.

I wasn't going to cave in to Mom on this one.

It was easy for me to slip into someone else's tattered shoes, to see and feel life from another's perspective. But not so for Mom, whom the empathy gene had skipped.

She still reeked of bigotry, worshipped political conservatives, and tilted so far right I expected her to fall off the planet. Every stereotypical prejudice imaginable remained riveted into her brain.

Her rants were *terrible*. Niggers, kikes, wops, chinks, japs, krauts, poor white trash—she used the most denigrating terms possible when attacking race and ethnicity. Commies and Democrats fared just as badly. My soul shriveled when she carried on.

Anyone not related by blood became suspect. I speculated that her rigid mind-set stemmed from her Southern-born parents who had instilled in her a blind reverence for kin and a distrust of anybody else. Good thing Mom didn't know about gays.

As a daughter, I loved my mother with primal feelings, but I was appalled by her attitude. In one of my favorite spite-fueled fantasies, Mom was whisked to Selma, where she landed in a tattered seat on a bus, wedged in between Martin

Luther King, Jr. and Medgar Evers.

"What if you had been born poor and black in Alabama?" I once asked her.

"Nonsense. A ridiculous question," she replied, incapable of comprehending anything other than her own immediate circumstance. "Just as foolish as the mistake you're making. *Social worker.*" She shook her lacquered head and sneered her disdain.

*　　　　*　　　　*

Poor Dad fretted, caught in the controversy. He still looked sharp despite his browbeaten existence, although I found it hard to think of him ever cutting loose with a Charleston.

Mom harped at him through most dinner hours, ignoring my presence at the table.

"Henry, she's making a stupid mistake. Teaching is acceptable work for a young lady. Associating with trash is not. Tell her so."

"I think Amy's made a fine, selfless choice." His response sentenced himself to this same dialogue that continued through commencement and after I had begun an internship as a social worker.

The ultimate irony. By fulfilling my dream, I had an income that rivaled that of a field-hand, leaving me financially dependent and beholden for the roof over my head.

Striking out on my own was beyond my capabilities. I'd defied Mom once, but I was still intimidated by her power and incapable of escaping her smothering grasp.

Let go. Let me be who I am, I soundlessly screamed into my pillow every night as I tried to fall asleep.

Mild and tolerant, Dad supported my career choice and shared my liberal leanings. But he needed to hide those tendencies because he, too, was afraid of Mom. Jim Beam had become his good friend and source of solace.

Neither of us had the courage to confront Mom, who roared and ruled with an iron skillet, so Dad hid behind the *Oakland Tribune* in an 80-proof haze.

And I, sober, single, and stuck, envisioned a dismal, empty future. Until Mom decided to alter it—her way.

Help.

CHAPTER ELEVEN

"**I** found him."

Mom waved her pruning shears in triumph from the door of her potting shed.

Now what? I trudged down the brick stairs and through her garden. I'd just dragged myself home from work after an awful day spent trying to save a family from being thrown out on the street.

"Found who?" I asked, still numbed by the callous indifference of a greedy, heartless slumlord.

"The perfect young man for you. His name is Bob, and he's adorable."

Augh. Mom was on the lookout for a choirboy, and I had forsaken fickle Julius for smoldering bad-boy Marlon Brando. I sat down on the garden bench and listened as she relayed the specifics.

"I was in the kitchen this afternoon chopping onions. A strange-sounding car drove up, so I poked my head out the window. I've always suspected that widower next door was up to hanky-panky, but I was wrong this time. He's rented a room to a student—Bob.

"The minute I spotted him I knew. He's the one meant for you."

Why does she have to run my life?

I suspended my anguish for the soon-to-be-homeless

family and pondered my own predicament. The likelihood of finding a qualified suitor to aid in my escape was dwindling. Most of my girlfriends, now giddy newlyweds, had exhausted their supply of eligible guys to refer.

A new boyfriend inevitably led to that obligatory and torturous Archer family dinner, dished up by Mom. Pot roast, simmered in her suspicions and peppered with her agonizing, intrusive questions.

The workplace? A dead-end. Just a few oddball male colleagues, and professional standards ruled out the clientele I served.

Mom never failed to disparage the latter as unworthy lowlifes.

"Felons, mooching off their women's welfare until they botch another hold-up or car-jacking. Good-for-nothing bums. If you were a teacher, you could meet a nice, respectable principal."

Who was she kidding? Horace Mann himself, architect of public education, would not have made the grade unless she personally had exhumed him.

No, I was not to leave Harriet Archer's household except on the arm of a husband chosen by her.

My heart was on hold, an empty void—waiting, longing for my magical man. A secret little part of me hoped, against all odds, that Mom had found him.

Ha.

*   *   *

Before the week was over, Bob moved in next door but spent most of his time enthroned in Mom's kitchen, kibitzing over chocolate cake and coffee.

She grilled him like a rack of ribs and established that he was single, a grad student and teaching assistant at U.C. Berkeley and—of course—met her ethnicity standards.

An excellent candidate, but she questioned why he chose not to live with his mother, aunt, or grandmother, each of whom lived less than a mile away.

"Wouldn't it be cheaper to stay with someone in your family while you finish your studies?" she asked him.

"Not worth it. They're fruitcakes and make me crazy," he replied.

"That dear young man needs my guidance and support," she mused, absently adding sugar, rather than salt, to the spaghetti sauce she was stirring.

*　　　*　　　*

So Bob became a kitchen fixture, with Frigidaire embossed on his forehead. He hopped over the fence the minute he got home from classes, eager to share his familial trials with Mom. And she pushed me on him like I was a big, mocha-frosted brownie.

Movie-star handsome, with long black lashes framing his violet eyes, a mop of thick, tousled black hair, slender and buff—he was heart-thumping hot.

Maybe she's done it, I thought, intrigued by a delectable first glimpse. But that initial spark flickered out fast. What a bunch of downers bundled up in one weird guy.

First problem—personality. Bob saw his can of Dr. Pepper as half empty and spewed negativity.

Second issue—his chosen field, entomology, the study of bugs. *Ick.*

Last bummer—besotted by his studies, he skittered away from me and basked in the presence of doting Mom.

Bob continued to view me with suspicion until the day he brought over one of his meticulous labeled cigar boxes full of embalmed beetles—each impaled on a pin stuck in layered Styrofoam and identified by a precise tiny label.

Mom hated bugs more than she loved Bob and bolted, remembering she had laundry in the dryer downstairs.

Staring at the carnage in the box, I repressed my impulse to throw up.

Was he my last chance? Might be, and Marlon, to my dismay, had just married a sexy actress named Movita, He also was becoming known for indiscrete, bunny-like propagation.

Make a play. Worst case, you'll end up holding a cardboard coffin filled with deceased creepy-crawlies.

I plastered a facade of dewy-eyed admiration on my face, looked up into his violet eyes and said, "Wow, what a magnificent collection."

Bob puffed with pride and described every critter, plus its dramatic capture, in stupefying detail.

I never wavered, and a tenuous connection began, punctuated with occasional dates for coffee (I hated coffee but went anyway) or a slice of pizza (Dutch treat).

His wall of reserve was always up, so he surprised me by inviting me to an afternoon barbeque at his grandmother Vi's house to celebrate her birthday.

Mom vacillated. She viewed the invitation as marking progression in a courtship, but Bob had filled her head with horror stories recounting his relatives' shortcomings.

"Well, go for Bob's sake, but don't get too friendly with those trashy people." She scowled.

"What trash?" I asked. Bob so far had never told me anything about his family, except to mention that his cousin Teddy was studying interior design at the College of Arts and Crafts in Oakland.

"You'll find out," she sniffed. "Poor boy. He's suffered so much."

CHAPTER TWELVE

This is trashy?

Grandma Vi's sprawling hacienda-style house nestled in a ritzy part of the Oakland hills.

Purple Bougainvillea climbed the rounded archways, a bubbling fountain graced the front lawn, and a shiny Cadillac sat in the driveway.

"What a lovely setting," I exclaimed when we drove up.

"Yeah, whatever." Bob mumbled in his usual monotone. *Such a charmer.*

He'd insisted on leaving the top down on his stupid, third-hand convertible. The wind had sexily rumpled his hair and had blown mine into a tangled, irreparable cobweb.

I wore my light blue capri pants and a white button-down blouse because Bob told me the party would be casual and outdoors. Seemed like appropriate attire to me.

Bob led me on a path around the house to the backyard. Did he offer a hand or an arm to assist along the way? No. That would have entailed *touching.*

Gingerly picked my way over the flagstones in my ballerina flats, I tried not to lurch on the uneven surface and call attention to my inflexible ankle—although at the moment, my disastrous hair was equally vexing.

I hoped my party conversation—current events, books,

sports, movies—would sparkle and make a refined impression.

The path opened onto a backyard patio rimmed by thick, white-blossomed oleander bushes and blooming red roses. A long picnic table ran its length, and a handful of people were scattered around it. They stared at one another in stony silence.

A heavy (let's face it—very fat) woman sat at the head of the table, dressed in a hibiscus-flowered muumuu and flip-flops. A gardenia was tucked in her frizzy bleached hair, and she had a big smile.

"Hey, sonny, you made it, and you brung along a pretty girl," she called out to Bob. "I was startin' to think you was one a them fu-fu boys." Bob's face turned redder than the roses. He acknowledged her with a grunt and gave a sullen nod to the grim-faced assemblage.

Hoisting herself out of her white plastic chair, she waddled over and hugged me.

"Hi, I'm Vi," she said. "What's your name, kid? I know I'm gonna like you."

"Amy," I replied. I sensed I would like her, too, although the "fu-fu" comment gave me pause.

"Kid, I'll introduce you." She took my hand to lead me around the table.

Two exquisite women sat opposite each other. Even their pained expressions did not diminish their extraordinary beauty.

I felt completely intimidated—like an unkempt, out-of-place frump. *What would it be like to go through life looking so utterly perfect?* I couldn't imagine.

"These here are my daughters, Lana,"—whose back was partially to us—"and Rita. Twins they was."

Lana swiveled her chair around and nodded. She wore a halter and short shorts with the panache of an 18-year-old. I wondered how often she was mistaken for Elizabeth Taylor. Cascading, wavy black hair, perfect heart-shaped face, enormous violet eyes framed by thick dark lashes—exactly like Bob's.

"Lana is Bob's mom and that guy next to her is Bob's stepfather, Dan. Bob's *real* father amounted to somethin'," Vi said.

The guy looked pinched and wary. His reply was chilly. "My name is Don—not Dan."

"Mister, your name's Mud in my book." Vi snapped back, glaring at both Don and Lana.

All eyes rolled.

Lana took a huffy puff on her cigarette and made a petulant tap with her stiletto-sandaled foot, calling more attention to her amazing legs.

Vi moved to the other side of the table and introduced her other daughter.

"This here is Rita, and she got it right."

Rita was equally stunning—straight black hair, green eyes, and sultry. I instantly thought of Rita Hayworth in *Gilda*. Her off-the-shoulder sundress displayed eye-popping double-D attributes.

Vi hugged the tense fellow sitting beside Rita.

"This sweetie is Hank, Rita's husband. He's a big-bucks orthodontist, and she made a hell of a catch with him."

Vi beamed at Hank, who was balding and had a slight paunch. He adjusted his eyeglasses, nodded, and squirmed.

"He's got bad hemorrhoids," Vi confided in a stage whisper.

"Now, next to Hank is Rita's son, Teddy. Rita screwed up. Had the kid before she met Hank, but Hank's a real gent and adopted the little bastard when he was a baby. Next one over is Teddy's roommate, but I never remember his name."

"His name is James." Teddy, the legitimized bastard, spoke up. His voice was tight, and his cheeks flushed.

The door to the kitchen flew open, and an older bald man stumbled out, leaning backwards like a marching drum corps leader to counterbalance his enormous belly. He juggled a platter piled high with turkey legs.

"Grub's ready," he hollered. "Teddy, Bob—hustle your butts in the kitchen and hall out the rest a the fixin's."

"That there is Roy," Vi said. "Me and him got hitched and damn, for the life of me I can't remember why. Another dud, like that boob Don. Let's eat, kid."

Mostly, everyone drank a potent mix of beer and bourbon—called a boilermaker—and no one gave a hoot whether my conversation sparkled.

Bob finally roused himself from his funk and said to me, "We gotta split before it gets ugly. I can't stand these people."

*   *   *

On the way home, I visualized a family tree:

Vi, matriarch and star, topped the tree and consigned each person within her dynasty to the branch she designated.

Daughters Lana (legs) and Rita (boobs) dangled beneath her like shimmering precious ornaments.

Grandsons Bob (prickly bug freak) and Teddy (fuming former bastard), occupied non-descript middle branches.

Sons-in-law Don (loser) and Hank (meal ticket) drooped on the lower branches, although Hank's position was clearly more elevated than Don's.

And dud Roy landed on the bottom, dominated and squashed under Vi's flip-flop like one of Bob's bugs.

Quite a lineup, and Mom thought she could pull off a marriage between Bob and me and make them go away. *Really?*

CHAPTER THIRTEEN

"Come on over, kid. Bob's moochin' another meal here, so's the four of us can have some dinner and play cards."

Vi had become my new best friend. We clicked—a connection as unlikely as Mom and Bob's—and after her birthday party, Vi took me under her wing.

"Can't believe Bob showin' up with a classy gal like you," she marveled. And I basked in the unfamiliar glow of her compliments.

I'd hurry over to her house after work, and if I arrived before freeloader Bob, Vi would shoo husband Roy out of the kitchen, pour us each a glass of wine and settle in to discuss her daughters.

"I raised my girls to marry rich, and they done good as they could. Bob's Auntie Rita hooked Hank, even after she had the kid."

Vi built up steam. She liked to tell this story.

"'Oops, Ma, I had too many martinis,' Rita says to me when her belly bulges. Could wrung her neck. But after Teddy's born, she found good ol' Hank. Sure, he's not a looker, but there's big bucks fixin' crooked teeth."

She picked up the chunky bottle of Lancers Rose, reached over to top off our glasses with the sweet pink wine, and rattled on.

"Gotta keep my eye on that girl, though. 'God, what a *bore* Hank is—braces, bands, retainers,' Rita says, but I tell her never no mind. Hank makes good money, lets you spend it, and treats you and Teddy right. Even gives you a new car every Christmas. Quit bitchin' and don't mess up, I say.

"Now Bob's mom Lana's another story. She starts out okay and marries a go-getter undertaker. Big buddies with the priest at Saint Anthony's and the dough rolls in with the caskets. Bob got born a couple months after Teddy. Had the colic from day one.

"Then Lana meets this boob Don who's sellin' nickel and dime insurance, and she throws over a sure thing. 'But Ma, I love Donny,' she says when she dumps Bob's dad. *Hooey*, I say. It riled me—taught my girls better, but Lana wouldn't listen. At least Rita got some sense."

*   *   *

One evening, Vi invited me for dinner, and I left work a little early, so I arrived at her house way before Bob.

I rang the bell, and she opened the door as chimes played *Lara's Theme* from *Dr. Zhivago*.

"Psst, kid," she whispered. "Come on upstairs to my boudoir. I got neat stuff to show you, but I can't when Bob's here because he's such a tight-ass."

Vi always calls it right.

We climbed the staircase and entered her bedroom. Red-flocked walls, a skirted vanity framed with stage lights, an enormous circular bed draped in crimson satin, mirrors overhead under the bed's canopy—*whoa*. Heart attack time for righteous prude Mom if she ever saw this.

Immense, old-fashioned trunks filled the closets. Vi threw back two or three brass-hinged lids and rummaged. Dozens of costumes tumbled out. Slinky silk gowns, feathers and furs, glittery thongs. Tawdry, fanciful, seductive—I was fascinated.

A brief whimsy flashed and faded. I imagined myself, Amy Archer, costumed and aglow as the dazzling star of a lavish Broadway production. *No, never me.* An understudy? No. Possibly a wardrobe assistant skulking backstage. Never good enough to be a lead, even in make-believe.

"Try this on." Vi handed me a gold lame bikini bottom, jolting me from the bleak scenario.

"Where's the top?" I asked.

"I'm lookin' for the rest." She dug some more.

I couldn't resist and dodged behind a mirrored dressing screen. As I slipped out of my Agency approved, mud brown, hemmed-at-the-knee shift dress, Vi began talking about her early life and her little boy, Billy.

"My folks was poor, and the depression hit 'em hard. We was livin' in a shack with dirt floors. Didn't have nothin.' The day I turned twelve, my grandpa and me hoofed it to town to the barbershop.

"The barber was a stinky old goat, but he liked me, so I got married off by a preacher guy. Most likely not legal, but I didn't know no better. He never did nothin' mean, plus me gettin' to live in a real house was a big deal. Little Billy come along before the year was out. You comin' out from there?" she asked,

"I need the top to this thing," I said, shivering as I stepped into the skimpy bikini bottom.

"I forgot. Here, that's what these is for." Vi passed some big white feathered fans over the top of the screen.

"Anyway, Billy was always playin' in the shop, and one day—he just turned two—his dumb-ass dad left the old iron cash register open. Billy reached up and pulled on the drawer, and it fell over on top of my baby. Kilt him dead."

I gasped, shocked, and struggled to find a response. *Hardship, tragedy—and way too young.*

"Vi, what a terrible loss. How awful for you. And you were only what—fifteen? Still a child yourself. I'm so sorry."

"Worse thing that ever happened in my life, kid. I loved that little guy. Still don't like talkin' about it. Buried him right though. Soon as the funeral was over, I packed up a valise and walked over to the bus station. Last time I seen Bakersfield or the damn barber.

"I bought a ticket to Modesto, but I conned the driver into takin' a detour to Frisco. When we hit the city, I dumped that chump and checked out Sally Rand's joint. Lots of action was goin' on—hi-rollers who liked gamblin' and good-lookin' show girls.

"I was pretty and a real smooth singer, so soon as I learnt them dances, I was on my way. Look-it what I found!"

I crept out around the screen, clutching white feathers to breast and behind, but Vi didn't notice my debut. She had unearthed a stack of faded photos and posters.

"Vi, you're gorgeous!" I gawked at her stunning face and voluptuous body.

She fluffed her frizzy blonde hair.

"I made out okay. Guys loved me in them fancy get-ups, and I listened up when they talked business. Learnt about the stock market and real estate, and makin' big bucks. When

World War II ended, I tossed them sequins and fans and rhinestones in the trunks. Had real diamonds and furs galore.

"The stocks and property put me on easy street. Kid, listen up. Make 'em happy, keep the money, invest in blue chips, and be sure you got your name on the deed."

Vi shared her wiles as well as her wisdom.

"Me and the dud are goin' to Vegas for the weekend." She winked. "The key's under the mat, the trunks are open, and I put on the satin sheets."

But to no avail. Bob was busy. Mounting a monarch, he said.

*   *   *

The *jerk*. I was disgusted.

Skinflint Bob was as tight with his emotions as he was with his money. This whole thing was a fantasy manufactured by Mom and going nowhere.

I fumed as I watched the two of them huddled in the kitchen, bonded as tight as an Oreo cookie. Bob never tired of whining about his horrible lot in life, while Mom, the ultimate voyeur, lapped up every bit of smut about his family, clucking with maternal consternation and sympathy.

*   *   *

My girlfriend Lynn detested Bob and couldn't understand why I didn't ditch him. She had, to my envy, scored a job at social services one month after our June graduation from Berkeley. Confident and assertive, Lynn was snapped up fast by the Agency. After I'd finally squeaked through the vetting process and had been hired that fall, we tried to coordinate our field days.

Taking a break from making home visits, we'd meet around twelve o'clock in Mosswood Park to eat our sandwiches sitting on a splintered wooden bench under a giant eucalyptus tree.

Motionless, alcohol-saturated bodies lay scattered on the lawn, and squirrels scampered over them to beg for pieces of crust from us. The comatose drunks were harmless, and the park was a convenient and safe place—the dangerous druggies hung out in Jefferson Park, and at the office a demonic manager terrorized us.

Lynn pulled no punches assessing my current situation.

"How can you stand that negative tight-wad? He only chose that stupid major so he could grub around in the yard and not have to buy any supplies. Dead bugs stuck on pins and pickled spiders. Even an engineer would be better."

Well, she might be right, but no engineer or any other male clamored for my attention.

Would a romance with Bob ever match the passion of my fantasies? Not likely, considering his restrained and stingy nature.

But I tried to convince myself that this was a mature compromise, and a future with him would be secure.

Get real. All he liked to talk about were spiders and searching for automobile parts to keep his junkie convertible running. Which was worse, I asked myself—pistons, spark plugs, and sow bugs, or strangling in the noose of Mom's apron strings for the rest of my life?

Mom sensed my dwindling interest in Bob and realized the only way for her to pull off this union was to groom him to be my groom, whether he liked it or not.

One day he brought me a Whitman's Sampler from Walgreen's, a bargain at half-price because it was a Halloween leftover and Christmas merchandise now filled the shelves.

I knew this largesse resulted from Mom's frantic coaching, but Bob's inherent frugality kept mucking up her instructions.

"How thoughtful," Mom said. She munched through a graying chocolate pumpkin. "See, he cares."

"Cheap is Bob's middle name, Mom. Watch out—worms breed in rancid chocolate."

I was miffed because when Bob made a big deal out of treating me to dinner on a Saturday night, he took me to Mel's Drive-in Diner. He was thrilled because he had found a coupon in the newspaper for half-off the second burger.

"Young lady, don't be snippy," Mom said. "I happen to know Bob has planned a very special surprise for you at Christmas."

"Like what? A free coffee mug from the gas station?"

"No, smarty. I saw him coming out of Give Me Gold jewelers yesterday. He was carrying a fancy little box all wrapped up, just about the size to hold a ring. And I'm sure that's why he's been a bit tight with his money."

Whoa. I envisioned Bob, whose eyes were suddenly more violet, and his soft, wavy hair invited my fingers to muss it.

"You two make a perfect couple," Mom declared, whipping the batter for a batch of Bob's favorite snicker doodles.

"But I thought you didn't like his family."

"I don't, but I have no intention of ever mingling with

such scum. That trollop of a grandmother probably was a craps dealer at a sleazy casino. Don't get too friendly with her because I will not invite her to the wedding."

"What wedding?"

"Yours and Bob's."

Was she delusional? Maybe not. A fancy little box?

Uh-oh. What if he *does* come up with a ring?

Could I go through with it?

CHAPTER FOURTEEN

"**K**id, get on over here for dinner. Pronto. Big news." Vi spoke in a secretive whisper before hanging up her phone.

Intrigued, I realized something other than food was cooking at Vi's and drove over to her house straight from work.

I parked in front of the house because the driveway to the side of the three-level hacienda was blocked by Roy's new Cadillac sedan. The kitchen window was directly above where Roy parked, but the awning over the top of the window was too small to protect his car, shining under the layers of turtle-wax he lavished on it.

Vi refused to move her car to one side in the two-car garage.

"I park in the middle so's I don't get no dents in *my* Caddy," she said. And Roy, the fourth husband to follow the barber as near as I could figure, was aware of his dispensable status and dared not protest.

When I rang the doorbell, the subsequent serenade of chimes once again reminded me of Omar Sharif's Russian passion in *Dr. Zhivago,* and Bob's lack thereof.

Vi greeted me with a big hug and took my coat. I could tell she was excited.

"Bob come over early." She whispered in the hushed

voice of a conspirator. "We got no time to play in my trunks. I sent him out for Chinese so's I could tell you quick. He's cookin' up somethin' special for you at Christmas."

Could Mom have been right?

"Get this," she continued. "Bob told Auntie Rita he was goin' over to Give Me Gold to pick up a ring. Rita calls me up and spills the beans, but I'm not supposed to know nothin'.

"He's cheap, but Bob knows the women in this family like their diamonds big. I'm bustin' for a gander. Oops, here he comes. Don't say a word."

Bob walked in carrying two takeout bags from the Silver Dragon and plunked them on top of the dining room table.

He tossed a perfunctory "Hi" toward me and then whined at Vi.

"Why didn't you order chicken chow-mien? You know I hate the pork. Greasy gunk." Complaints were Bob's favored form of communication.

"Because I'm buyin' and that's what I like. Where's my change?" she asked. "I gave you twenty bucks, and the guy on the phone said the bill was gonna be $17.65."

"I used my gas and my time." His eyes narrowed in defiance.

"Fork it over sonny, or you won't see none of it comin' back in no inheritance."

Bob fumbled through his pockets and Roy appeared, preceded by his momentous stomach. He plopped himself on a chair at the table, tucked a paper napkin into his size 50 waistband, and plowed through at least three cartons of food by himself. Then he pushed aside his empty plate.

"Why don't you do these here dishes before we start playin'?" he asked Vi, bellowing a hearty belch in her direction. She shot him a withering glance, then quickly replaced it with a bland look.

I sensed she was still smoldering inside and recalled a previous piece of her advice.

"Remember, kid, don't take no guff from no man, and you're not no goddamn maid."

Bob interjected himself into the conversation. "So, my thesis advisor said straight out, 'If you want to fast-track that Ph.D., scrap the sow bugs and go with the bees.'" He was deep in his own weird world.

"I'll help you, Vi," I volunteered.

"Keep your seat, kid. This won't take but a minute," she insisted. Her smile was pleasant as she brushed aside my offer.

With the skill of an experienced waitress, Vi stacked plates up her arms and picked up the glassware and cutlery.

Swish, swish. Her muumuu swirled as she cheerfully backed through the swinging door to the kitchen. It closed, and next I heard the creak and a groan of a window opening, followed by a cacophony of breaking glass and smashing crockery.

The sound-effects told the story. Vi had thrown all the dishes, glassware and utensils out the window and the entire mess landed on the roof of Roy's beloved Cadillac.

She swaggered back in with the same smile in place and sat down in her chair.

"Who shuffled?" she asked.

Roy's bald head pulsed with throbbing veins, a hot pink and purple gyrating road map leading the way to a massive stroke, but the game proceeded without comment.

Even Bob was sufficiently flummoxed to end his drone on drones.

*　　　　　*　　　　　*

"Kid, Bob's poppin' with that ring, so I'm throwin' a big shindig on Christmas Eve. Love a party. Your folks is invited too," Vi announced when I left to go home.

I carefully sidestepped chunks of broken Fiesta Ware and stray packets of soy sauce that had careened off the roof of Brian's car.

"Vi, that's super-nice of you, but are you sure he bought a ring?"

"I'm quotin' Rita direct. 'Ma, Bob told me he picked up a ring at Give Me Gold, plus I helped him choose a special stocking stuffer for Amy, one I wouldn't mind having myself.'

"Kid, you seen the rocks Hank's draped on Rita, so I figure the ring's a done deal. She wouldn't tell me what the other thing is 'cause I got a big mouth," she added with a wink.

Vi convinced me. That sparkling symbol of commitment was in the bag, a portent of escape from Harriet Archer's barbed wire cage.

*　　　　　*　　　　　*

When I relayed Vi's invitation, Mom's reaction was predictable.

"You must be joking. I would never demean myself to mingle with those low-lives." She snorted, with her jaw set as tight as her artichoke-shaped hair.

Embarrassed to relay the rude rejection, I called Vi the

next day and told her that the 24th was a busy holiday Saturday, and my mom and dad had already made other plans.

"And I might be late. The office will be open to handle weekend emergencies because Monday is a federal holiday. I'm the newest employee at the Agency, so I have to work and stay to close up the office."

"A damn shame your folks is busy, kid, but you come on over any time after five. It's a buffet, so you won't hold nothin' up. Now wear somethin' with oomph, not none of that nun stuff. How about stilettos?"

"Can't, Vi. My ankle."

"Well then, go for the cleavage."

Cleavage? I glanced at my chest. As impossible as the stilettos, considering my limited assets.

*   *   *

When I met Lynn in the park at noon the next day, she wouldn't buy into the story.

"I wouldn't trust that penny-pincher to come up with five bucks for lunch, much less a ring. You can do better." She stepped around a passed-out body to get to our bench.

"Well, I don't see many other prospects at the moment." I gazed at the lawn strewn with sad lost souls. But she had planted a distressing seed.

What if there was no ring?

A ridiculous thought. I didn't expect one literally to be in my stocking. Bob might slip a slender gold band on my finger. No, change that to a fat flashing diamond and a passionate kiss.

Or to a clever surprise. A lovely bauble would tumble from a maze of deceptive wrappings, or twinkle from the depths of a champagne flute.

So many scenarios flitted through my foolish head.

*   *   *

I took a chance and wore a red dress to work Christmas Eve, even though the Agency forbade employees to wear bright colors.

The day I was hired, I was handed a green booklet titled *Mandatory Dress Code* which laid out the grim rules: no pantsuits or trousers, no hemlines above the knee, hosiery at all times, modest necklines, and muted colors.

"Why is that?" I had asked my supervisor, puzzled as I looked over the archaic, misogynistic commands.

"Because Major Rampart wrote the rules, and he's the head of the Human Resources Department," she told me. "The guy's one uptight dude—says he wants to avoid inciting lust in derelicts or deranged cliental. Sack dresses are okay as long as they aren't minis."

Well, most of the staff had the day off, and nobody paid attention to me, anyway. My red wool A-line was perfect for the photos of my Christmas Eve engagement. Who would notice?

My surly co-worker, Webber, with whom I'd gotten off to a rocky start when he asked me if I had a pebble in my shoe, immediately called me out.

"Sister, you might as well have worn an American flag. If a supervisor sees that, you'll be history."

Surprised at his concern, I said, "I didn't know you'd care

if I got in trouble."

"I don't give a shit, but if you get sent home, then I'll have to stay and close up." He glowered.

So, I sweltered in my all-purpose gray trench-coat the rest of the day so no one else would see the red dress. Visions of carats danced in my head.

Lester, the security guard on the first floor, phoned the hot-line ten minutes before five o'clock.

"Miss Archer here." I answered his call in my most professional tone.

"They left you in charge? You don't know shit from Shinola," Lester declared. "A nut-job is in an interview booth, and she won't leave because she wants five bucks. You better come down here."

I took the elevator from the third floor, found the wild-eyed woman in a small cubicle, and introduced myself, but my interviewing skills were minimal, and I buckled at confrontation.

After half an hour of her tears, threats, and shouted demands, I broke another rule.

We were never to give money to a client. I had food vouchers that she could easily have bartered on the street for cash, but dare I suggest it?

No. Instead, I made a round trip—back up to the third floor to find my wallet and back down to hand the woman a five-dollar bill. She snatched it from my hand and darted out of the building toward the closest liquor store.

"Boy, you got a lot to learn." Lester grumbled as he chained the doors.

I bolted for Vi's, wallowing in self-doubt and the humiliation of not standing up to a manipulative drunk.

CHAPTER FIFETEEN

Vi's musical chimes rang out *Lara's Theme*, and my finger was still on the doorbell button when the door swung open.

Rita's husband Hank, the orthodontist, was propped up against the doorframe. He waved an open bottle of Courvoisier in greeting.

Usually well dressed, this evening he wore conservative slacks, but his sport jacket lay crumpled on the floor, his shirt-collar was unbuttoned, and his tie was half undone.

He was plastered.

"Merry Christmas, Hank," I said, burying for the moment my dismay over my appalling lack of assertiveness.

Why had I let that woman intimidate me?

"The bitch and her litter are downstairs, Amy. Go right on down." Hank tossed his head back to take a slug from the bottle.

"Is something wrong?" His agitated state alarmed me.

"*Wrong?* Three months ago, my dear wife Rita sashayed over to the Buick dealership to order her new car. Last week, she picked up a white LeSabre convertible with a custom hot-pink interior, and she also brought home the salesman.

"I said no go, and she called me a prig. I told her to screw it, so she did. They spent this afternoon between the sheets at the Jack London Inn, and then she had the balls to bring Mr. Sam Super-stud here."

Dumbfounded, I mumbled, "Sorry, Hank." Not knowing what to do, I turned to maneuver down the spiral staircase. Going down was tricky with my ankle. I cringed inside—*would anyone be watching my awkward descent?*

Vi had converted the basement into a dimly lighted Las Vegas-style lounge. A bar ran its length, and she'd installed a sound system with a microphone. She liked to belt out a song or two as she belted down her boilermakers.

I didn't need to fret about attracting anyone's attention.

Currents ripped through the room. Something was up. Something in addition to Lana's skirt, that is. Bob's dazzling mother Lana posed on a bar stool in black lace slit to the kazoo to display her perfect legs and then some.

Her husband Don, the insurance guy, A.K.A. Dan or Mud, cursed quietly in the corner. He struggled through a web of plastic-coated wires to find the single bulb that shorted out all the lights on the aluminum tree.

Roy sat on the first barstool with his belly resting on his thighs and guarded the potato chips and Lipton onion-soup dip.

Bob, looking pained, fidgeted on a stool between his cousin Teddy, and Teddy's roommate, James.

Rita, always as ravishing as her sister Lana, embellished her cleavage with a plunging black bustier and a diamond pendant. She sat at the far end of the bar next to Mr. Super-stud, who was a dead ringer for Paul Newman. He swilled what appeared to be bourbon on the rocks and cast admiring glances toward Lana's kazoo.

Rita cringed behind the daiquiri blender and tried to divert Vi's wrath.

"Mom, it's not like Sam sells *used* cars." Her plea did not sway Vi.

"We'll settle this later, and sure as hell you're not wreckin' this shindig with your drama crap. And get them matchbooks from your hotel hookup outta my collection bowl. Just rubbin' Hank's nose in it."

"Merry Christmas," I said. Vi turned my way.

"You finally made it. We was worried." She swooped over to give me a hug. A red velvet rendition of her signature muumuu swirled around her ankles, and she tottered on gold platforms. Diamonds sparkled from her earlobes, encircled her neck, and flashed on her fingers—big ones.

"Sorry I'm late, Vi."

I handed her the shopping bag of gifts I had brought. Bob's was a specimen display case I ordered from Scientific American, and Vi's was a photo of her headlining at Bimbo's that I'd sneaked away to have framed.

"No problem, kid. Too bad you couldn't find nothin' to wear." She eyed my demure neckline. "Want to run up to my boudoir?"

"Thanks, Vi, but I'm okay with what I have on."

I expected Bob to acknowledge me with a hug or kiss or something, but he didn't even have the courtesy to get up. *What was his problem?*

"I can't stand these people," he groused to Teddy.

"Lighten up, man. Rita's my mom, and I could give a rat's ass if she screws up and screws around. Who cares?" Cousin Teddy slid off his stool. "Here, Amy. Take this one next to Bob."

"Come share mine, Teddy," said James, patting his seat.

Suddenly Vi swiveled on her platforms and bellowed up the stairwell.

"Get your buns down here, Hank. It's time to open the presents, and then I want to sing. I think I'll do *I'm In the Mood for Love*." She gave me that wink.

Hank had seen the roof of Roy's Cadillac. Apparently wary of a similar reprisal, he obeyed and staggered down the stairs, bottle in hand.

"Roy, you're Santa. Pass out the loot." Vi sounded impatient.

"I can't bend over far enough to reach under the tree." He mumbled through a mouthful of chips.

"I'll do it," Teddy offered. "Ho-ho-ho. Here comes Rudolph." His words were cheery, but his voice was tight with anxiety. He sat down on the floor next to the tree that now blinked on and off like a defective traffic light. Teddy reached under the branches, pulled out the packages and began passing them out.

He handed me a heavy rectangular box, the size used for shirts or sweaters. The gift tag read, "To Amy from Bob. Surprise." My mind leapt to the obvious conclusion. Bob had devised a deceptive maze of boxes.

Not so. Inside the box was a Happy Holidays Special Makeup Assortment by Avon, whose cosmetics Rita bought wholesale and pedaled as a pastime. Nor were Bob's accompanying words those of my imaginings.

"Now maybe you'll fix up your eyes right."

The *gall*. I was livid.

"Thank you so much, Bob." He thought I meant it.

Rita peered cautiously around the blender. "I hope you like it, sweetie."

Ah. I got it. This was the stocking-stuffer. *Don't lose your cool.*

"Love it." I smiled at her and gave a tiny wave.

"Weird. This tag reads, 'To Bob from Bob,'" Teddy looked puzzled and then handed Bob a small package.

Bob snatched it, slid off his stool, and said, with uncharacteristic animation, "We all have to go outside for this surprise."

Vi caught my eye and winked again. A moonlight proposal on the patio?

The surprise was parked behind the oleander bushes, and Bob wheeled it out lovingly. He'd bought himself a black and silver motorcycle, and the box contained the ignition key.

He didn't deserve to live. I felt my anger morphing into the scaffolding for a backbone.

"Look at that baby!" Sam Super-stud exclaimed.

"A Triumph Tiger 500 cc." The spider-freak crowed.

"It's cold as shit out here. Get your asses inside," Vi barked. She'd abandoned all refinements in her disgust.

Leaving Bob and Super-stud to kick tires and punch each other's biceps, the rest of us mobilized our rears and followed Vi as she wobbled back into the house.

"There's one last present here," Teddy said. He called out to Bob, "Thanks for picking this up for me."

Teddy stretched his arm way under the tree branches and plucked out a fancy little package wrapped in Give Me Gold's signature paper.

"For you." Teddy handed the gift to James.

James carefully removed the wrappings to reveal a black velvet jewelry box. He slowly opened the hinged top. Tucked inside were two identical metal bands.

Teddy's chest expanded with pride. "James and I are now engaged," he said.

Mind you, no one in the entire country was out of the closet, except for Liberace. No protocol or etiquette existed to fall back on. The silence shrieked.

Vi lined up half a dozen tumblers, grabbed the Courvoisier bottle from Hank, and poured bartender style straight down the row.

"Son, you don't have to do this jush to punish your slutty mother." Hank slurred, groping the edge of the bar to keep from falling off his stool.

"Teddy, you wouldn't be screwed up like this if my sister raised you right." Lana, puffing on her cigarette, preened like a princess. Her spirits were as high as the slit up her thigh.

I had no doubts—Lana was certain Vi would knock Rita out of her will for poor parenting and, even worse, for cuckolding the golden goose.

Rita's retort was immediate. "If you raised Bob so perfect, why did he turn out stingy? Imagine giving Amy that stocking-stuffer makeup kit instead of a ring. Selfish and insensitive." The significance of Teddy's announcement flew right by her.

"I can't stand these people," Bob sputtered to Super-stud.

"Vi, I'd better go home now," I managed to say. "Thank you all for having me. It's been a lovely evening."

"Merry Christmas, kid," she said with an odd glint in her eyes. "Don't worry. I'll fix things up for you. Both Bob and Teddy are gonna get a talkin' to—and then some. *Fu-fu, my ass.* Brian, hook up that mike. I'm ready to sing."

This would require more than a little fix.

*   *   *

When I arrived home, Mom was on high alert at the kitchen window. She threw open the door and said, "Where is it? I waited all night."

"So did I," I replied. "The ring is on Teddy's finger. And another one is on James's."

"What?"

"It's a long story, Mom. This was my gift from Bob." I showed her the cosmetic kit. Then I opened the side-door and flung it in the trash.

Roar. Putt, putt. Bob had arrived next door.

"Is that a motorcycle I hear?" She was completely flummoxed.

"Yes, that is Bob's present to himself. You'll have to ask him about it, because I am never speaking to him again."

"Good grief, what a mess. I'll straighten things out tomorrow."

CHAPTER SIXTEEN

"**B**ob's sorry."

Mom finished stuffing the eviscerated carcass of yesterday's Christmas turkey into a big pot and pointed to the kitchen table.

"He apologized to me from his heart of hearts and promised to make up for it on Valentine's Day. See, he even brought you a bouquet."

A bunch of dyed-blue carnations, wrapped in one of Safeway's cellophane funnels, sat in a vase on the table.

It's a wonder I can withstand this sweeping gesture.

Disgusted, I picked up the flowers, opened the side-door, and flopped them down on top of the garbage can so Bob would be sure to see them when he parked his shiny new motorcycle.

Wallowing in cold fury, I refused to leave my room when Bob putt-putted in next door and raced over. He knew I'd be home because of the rare Monday holiday. I'd dodged him all of Christmas day and intended to do so in perpetuity.

When I wouldn't budge, Bob left and began a cascade of phone calls which frazzled Mom had to field because I wouldn't answer the phone. Too little, too late. He didn't care about me—he was desperate to safeguard his bond with adoring Mom.

I guess the nerd finally got it, because he pulled out all stops, humbled himself, and recruited Vi.

Mom knocked on my bedroom door. "That tramp of a grandmother you like is on the phone." I listened as she stomped off, and then I picked up the extension.

"Hi, Vi," I said.

"Bob's a wreck, kid. 'Big emergency' he says. 'Amy's real mad. Maybe she'll listen to you.' Come on over after work tomorrow so's I can talk some sense into you. It's okay to park in the driveway. Brian's car is still at the detailers. And bring along that make-up stuff Bob gave you. I wanna see it."

*   *   *

I dug the cosmetic kit out of the trash, and the following day I left the office about six and drove straight to Vi's.

Her wrath was formidable, so I opted for curbside parking. I didn't want my VW under the kitchen window in case she was irked that I had dumped Bob.

"Door's not locked," she hollered down when I knocked on the side door. I followed her voice up the back stairs, carting along the cosmetic kit.

"Hi, kid. See these here new Melmac dishes Brian bought me," She held up a mustard-colored, daisy-rimmed plastic disk as I entered the kitchen.

"Nice, Vi." I hoped she wasn't going to fling it like a Frisbee.

"Let's cut the crap and get down to business."

Vi pulled a bottle of Lancers out of the refrigerator, reached for two wine glasses from the cupboard, and hitched up her muumuu. We sat down at the table. She poured the wine, and then she talked sense.

"Kid, Lana blew it big when she dumped Bob's father. He had a bundle. Now Rita's messed it up with Hank. Listen up. I don't want you screwin' up.

"Bob likes them bugs better'n he likes people. He's a little snot around me and don't pay enough attention to you. You can do better. When I said I'd fix things up, I meant *you*. Hand me that make-up box."

*   *   *

"I guarantee *all* my girls is winners. How about goin' for it, kid?" Vi asked as she took a substantial swallow of wine.

It took me ten seconds to decide—for once, I wanted to feel like a winner.

"I'm all yours, Vi. As long as there's no perm."

She raised her wine glass in salute and then drained it.

"I knew you was gutsy, kid, so I got my stuff ready. Don't panic none 'cause I know what I'm doin.' First, we got to put real blonde streaks in your hair. Good thing I had bleach left over from when I done mine."

A half-empty bottle of peroxide was sitting on the counter. Vi poured it into a Pyrex bowl, mixed in the contents of another bottle labeled Clairol's Golden Highlights and stirred a bit.

Vi slapped a bath towel around my neck, anchored it with a clothespin and shoved my head under the kitchen faucet. She shampooed and towel-dried my hair. Then she steered me back to my chair, poured some of the bleach mixture on a comb and ran the comb through my hair several times.

"Too much trouble doin' it like the box says so's I figured out this here shortcut. Now we time it for 20 minutes. Got to let it perk awhile." She turned on the oven timer.

Oh God. I think I might have a stroke. What have I got myself into?

My brave façade was dissipating rapidly.

"Vi, may I have a little more wine?" I asked, hoping to quell my tremors.

"Sure, kid. I'm ready for another nip myself. It'll keep me goin' 'cause I got a hell of a lot more work to do."

She reached over for the bottle of Lancers and poured us each another glassful.

"Cheers, kid." She took a big gulp.

Then she picked up a pair of tweezers and attacked my eyebrows.

"Ouch, Vi," I protested.

"Need more arch," she muttered.

The timer went off, and Vi thrust my head back under the faucet to rinse out the bleach. Then she wrapped my head in a towel.

"Color come out good. I'm finishin' up the hair after I pierce your ears," she said.

"What?" *More wine.*

Vi had me numb my earlobes with ice cubes, heated a fat needle on a stove burner, and punctured both lobes. She handed me more ice to stop the bleeding, rubbed on a little Polysporin, and inserted what looked like diamond studs.

"Roll these around for a few days so the holes heal up right," Vi said.

"I'll return them as soon as I get my own." I was proud that I only yelped twice during the procedure.

"Don't bother none. They're just rhinestones. Now I'm workin' more on the hair."

Another shampoo, conditioner, and a partial blow dry.

Next, Vi opened the kitchen catch-all drawer and pulled out a pair of hair shears. My nerves were shot, and I drained my wine glass.

"You got the straightest hair I ever seen, and we're gonna show it off. I'm just trimmin' the ends so it'll fluff some. Partin' it different, though—makin' it swoop on one side. Sexier that way. Then I'm gonna cut some off the other side so's you can tuck it behind your ear sassy-like."

My face was her next target. She rifled through the box of cosmetics like a Renaissance master choosing colors for the ceiling of a cathedral.

"Pinks and peaches should turn out good. Smokey brown eye shadow. Black-brown eyeliner. Black mascara. You got young skin, so's you don't need no foundation. Here goes." She was armed with half-a-dozen little brushes.

The suspense was excruciating. Eyes, eyelids, eyebrows, cheeks, lips. Finally, she stepped back.

"Done." Vi pulled a mirror out of the bottomless catch-all drawer. "Have a gander."

I snatched the mirror, took a deep breath, and looked.

Was this me?

Framed by perfectly arched eyebrows, my eyes were rimmed by dark eyeliner, and the eyeshadow somehow transformed their brown-green color to a dreamy hazel.

Flirty mascara covered my eyelashes, my cheeks were peachy and my lips a pouty pink. And my hair? Streaked and styled to a perfection worthy of *Cosmopolitan's* cover.

But did I look like a tart? Not quite. Just a hint, a suggestion—*come hither and find out.*

Three hours of tension and torture had transformed me from okay to *wow*—not red hot, but close.

From the time I was five years old, I had been dragged down by a negative self-image so crushing that even my Wonder Woman bracelets had been powerless to overcome it.

In my fantasies, I was never the princess or the queen. I wasn't good enough. Instead, I was the nanny, and the Austrian prince would discover me charmingly tending his motherless children. Or maybe Caesar would chuck conniving Cleopatra for me, his devoted maidservant. I was always in the shadows, always second best.

But now, as I looked in Vi's mirror, I felt layers of self-doubt slipping off.

I'm okay, I realized. Better than okay. Perfectly capable of playing the hand I'd been dealt. No need to hide, or crouch in back rows, or date dweebs. Or to cower in Mom's shadow. Sure, Mom was a force, but it was my defeating self-perception that held me captive.

I felt free—swept by a wave of confidence I had never known before.

"Vi, I can't thank you enough." I teared up.

"No need." Vi blinked fast. "Showbiz. Learnt all kinds a handy tricks backstage. Kid, you was pretty before, but I'm thinkin' you didn't know it. Now you got *real* pizazz, so go for it. Ditch them peter-pan collars and baggy dresses.

"Strut your stuff. You're gonna catch you a prize. But if any guy gives you trouble, check back with me. I sure as hell know how to handle a man."

She sure did.

CHAPTER SEVENTEEN

I bolted to the office on Wednesday, impatient to do good and to show off Vi's handiwork to my colleagues—three snarky guys who, from day one, resented my existence.

Would they be dazzled by the new me?

Forget it. Those turkeys never noticed my transformation, or if they did, they wouldn't acknowledge it. They were still angry because I had invaded their all-male stronghold.

When I walked in, pudgy Webber, who usually ignored me, looked up from the case folder where he stored his latest issue of *Playboy*.

I thought he might comment on my snazzy appearance, but instead, he asked if I'd gotten the rock out of my shoe. Fancy-pants Moroni busied himself admiring his reflection off the glass facade of the coke machine, and morose Anders stared at a Peace Corps application.

My entrance into their world had been shaky from the start. Four public agencies accepted my job applications, and I sailed through their written exams. But the subsequent oral interviews derailed me. During the first one, I froze with terror and even forgot my name.

Excruciating.

Convinced the grim-faced interrogators had focused on my limp, I gripped my handbag on my lap to hide my shaking hands, but the tremor in my voice gave it all away. All eyes bore down on me. *Please, let me evaporate.*

The interviewers placed me at the bottom of their lists or outright flunked me, and all four panels agreed that I wasn't assertive or tough enough to handle the work.

The rejections hurt—big time—but after the fourth humiliation, a woman named Mabel from County Social Services called. Lucky I was home because my mother would never have given me her message.

"Are you Miss Archer?" she asked.

"Yes." My heart did a cautious little jig.

"Well, a guy we hired yesterday quit before noon, so Major Rampart told me to call you even though you're last on the list. Be here at 8:30 tomorrow. Bye."

"Wait a minute, please. Who's Major Rampart, and where do I go?"

"He's the big boss over the Human Resources Department. We're on Broadway, near Jack London Square. Look for the creeps on the stairs. Bye." Her yawn was audible.

Would I be hired? Mom doused my excitement.

"Worthless welfare scum," she said through clenched teeth.

*　　　*　　　*

Dress your best, I told myself the following morning. My navy-blue pencil skirt, matching Eisenhower-style jacket, and lavender-flowered blouse should be perfect. Straight from the display window at The Little Daisy, my favorite shop.

Steeled for another torturous interview, I arrived half an hour early. The building, a brick relic from the 1930s, faced

Broadway and a few scraggly men sprawled on the front steps.

Chains blocked the main doors, but I followed a woman around back to the employee's entrance, read the directory, and punched the elevator button for the fifth floor.

Stand up straight, try not to limp, and remember your name.

I exited the elevator and approached a laconic clerk propped up on the reception counter.

"Hi. I'm Amy Archer, here about the position," I said.

"I figured. Mine's Mabel. Your name's not Ann?"

"No."

"Damn. I spelled it wrong on everything."

I handed her my birth certificate, college transcript, and inoculation verifications.

Mabel grasped my documents with her inch-long red acrylic fingernails, spent 20 minutes in a lethargic search for a staple remover, fumbled around at a huge clunky copy machine, and produced the copies.

"Is someone going to interview me?" I asked when she wandered back to the reception counter.

"Nope. Major Rampart called this morning. He busted his denture on a prune pit, so I'm supposed to give you this stuff and send you down to the third floor. A surprise—I thought you'd be dumped in the Pasture."

"Where?"

"The Old Age Department. It's just over on Franklin Street, but we call it the Pasture. Burned-out workers and wimps who can't tough-out the streets in Oakland are parked there."

She handed me a make-shift blue booklet titled *Agency*

Standards, Deportment, and Discipline and a green pamphlet labeled *Mandatory Dress Code.*

"The Major said to tell you 'don't screw up.' And I'll clue you in right now—you can't wear tight skirts. When you get off the elevator, ask somebody where Mrs. Maisie Li is. Her name looks funny, but it sounds like 'Lee.' I spelled it wrong on everything, too."

It sunk in—they *hired* me. The expression on Mabel's face squelched my excitement.

Why was she smirking?

*　　　　　*　　　　　*

The elevator doors opened onto a vast open room crammed with desks, file cabinets, and frantic people— absolute chaos.

Phones rang, typewriters clacked, and loud voices pierced the din.

I stopped a man pushing a cart piled high with thick brown folders—case records, I assumed.

"Where can I find Mrs. Li?" I asked.

"Over there, by the water fountain. She's the one drinking the Pepto Bismol." A flash of sympathy crossed his face, and then he said, "Lots a luck. You're gonna need it."

Geez. Something's way off, but what?

I plowed through the bedlam to the desk of a small, plump Chinese woman studying a four-inch thick case folder.

"Mrs. Li? How do you do. I'm Amy Archer." I extended my hand and addressed the top of her head. Her sleek black hair was blunt-cut, and when she looked up, a pink Pepto mustache rimmed her upper lip.

"Welcome to Purgatory. Call me Maisie," she said and moved a stack of cases off of a chair so I could sit down. A box was underneath her desk because her feet didn't reach the floor.

"Here's the deal." Maisie reached for the pack of cigarettes on her desk. "We work in units. One supervisor, two clerks, and six workers.

"Right now, we're at half-staff. One clerk and three workers—Moroni, Anders, and Webber." An eye-roll accompanied her recitation of each name.

"Plus, we have three uncovered caseloads. Yesterday, a new guy showed up, and I gave him the desk between Moroni and Anders.

"Two hours later, he's gasping for his life with an asthma attack. Moroni's cologne and garlic breath are awful enough, but the smoke from Anders pipe did him in. The guy quit on the spot. I'll put you next to Webber. He's a black hole of doom, but he doesn't smell too bad—although that's a matter of opinion."

"How many cases will I have?"

"You'll have 120. We cover the housing projects and a few stray streets in West Oakland.

"What do I do with the cases?" I asked, still clueless.

"You visit each family every two months to make sure they're eligible for welfare. No income, assets, or man under the bed, and then you refer them to whatever services they need."

"How would I know if a man is under the bed?"

"Look for shoes. When the boyfriends dive for cover,

they forget their shoes. *Shit.* Here comes Moroni. Watch out. He's a letch."

A knock-out waft of Old Spice assaulted my senses as a fortyish man with dark, thick, razor-cut hair swaggered over. A pencil mustache underlined his Roman nose, and he preened in a hand-tailored jacket, crisp trousers, and leather loafers.

"New clerk?" he asked Maisie, blatantly sizing me up.

"No, Moroni. This is Amy Archer, our new worker," she replied.

"Holy shit," he exclaimed.

Moroni turned toward a lumpy, unkempt, Viking-sized man who was tipped back in his chair with his huge feet plopped on top of his desk.

"Do you believe it, Anders? This tasty little pullet will be gobbled up by noon." Moroni snickered as he smoothed the lapels on his jacket.

Scruffy Anders put his feet down, shifted the mass of his body forward, and nodded in agreement.

"Jesus. The Major must have had a stroke," he said. "First, he sends the runt to supervise us, and now he hires a greenhorn WASP to invade the ghetto. Take a gander, Webber."

A third guy stuck his pudgy-faced head over the newspaper he was reading and took a whack.

"Did you fall off the homecoming float, dear?" Webber asked.

I sat, frozen, and clutched Mabel's papers while the three of them laughed in my face.

Please let me disappear.

Maisie interrupted their guffaws. Gathering her 4 feet, 8 inches, she stood almost tall.

"I've *had* it with you bozos. Don't call me a runt and knock off the put-downs. Now that Archer's on board, I'm making a caseload change in the housing projects. Moroni, you're reassigned to Cypress Gardens, and Archer will take over Harbor Homes.

Moroni's face flamed with anger. He slammed a coffee cup, coated inside with months of caffeinated brown residue, on Maisie's desk and exploded.

"You can't jerk me around like that. Harbor Homes is badass territory—off limits for candy-assed females. This little prissy will need three squad cars of cops to cover her back."

He glared at me and expelled revolting blasts of garlic with every word.

Maisie's eyes shot lethal daggers at Moroni.

"I heard what you said about Mary Jo Johnson's anatomy last week, and I won't let you demean a client that way. You're out of Harbor Homes and Archer is in.

"What I said wasn't demeaning. Man, her bazoomers are beauties. I was overcome with admiration."

"Moroni, you don't have a clue. You're out, Archer's in. End of discussion."

Astonished, the men went silent.

Then Anders muttered, "Hitler was a runt, too."

All three stood up and stomped to the elevator. As the elevator doors were closing, stubby Webber turned to Moroni.

"What the hell's a pullet?" he asked.

"A young chicken ripe for plucking. Webber, you got no culture."

*   *   *

Imagine—*me*, with a real-life caseload. Elated with the prospect, I was none-the-less puzzled by Moroni's outburst.

"Mrs. Li, what was that tantrum all about?" I asked. She didn't answer my question right away.

"I meant it when I said to call me Maisie. Otherwise, everyone else here goes by their last name. I don't know why. As for clients, if a woman has a bunch of kids, address her as Mrs. If you're not sure, just mumble Miz."

"Okay. What about Moroni's outburst?" I asked again.

"Enormous loss of face. The tougher the territory, the more prestige for the worker. The city is clumped ethnically. East Oakland is mostly Hispanic, City Center is Asian, West Oakland is Black, and each has chunks of poverty.

"The Housing Authority gives the projects fancy names so the politicians can pretend they're charming suburbs. High Street Haven, Fruitvale Meadows, Cypress Gardens— and Harbor Homes, the farthest point west. According to bighead Moroni, it's the most dangerous ghetto this side of Chicago, so the reassignment smashed his colossal ego." She snorted.

I was fascinated. Protected by my invincible belief in goodness and justice, I had not one qualm as I listened to Maisie continue her rundown.

"Moroni's such a braggart, I'm not sure I believe him, but when you're ready for the field, we'll go slow. I could have reassigned Webber or Anders, but that would have created a bigger uproar. As it is, those three have ignored, belittled, or sabotaged every move I've made."

She took a bottle of Pepto Bismal from her desk drawer, poured more into her coffee cup, and continued.

"When the Major stuck me with those three chauvinistic stooges, I was furious. 'Why me?' I asked him.

"'Because you're the least senior. All the other supervisors have tenure, so I can't make them take the assignment. You don't have tenure, and if you mess up, you're out. Shape the renegades up, Li,' he says like he's commander-in-chief and I'm the latrine cleaner."

Maisie chug-a-lugged the last of the Pepto Bismol and sighed.

"Moroni's an egotistical womanizer, hot-head Anders hates the Agency, and Webber retired at his desk 10 years ago. If those guys don't do me in, DeVoe will."

"Who's DeVoe," I asked.

"My boss, the Department manager. Watch your back because she'll skewer anyone who crosses her. If you go to the restroom to scream, be sure to check under the stalls first. She always wears pointy-toed shoes.

"And you'd better get yourself some Agency-approved duds fast before she calls you out."

*   *   *

Fancy-pants Moroni primped, grubby Anders ranted, and I settled in next to semi-smelly, grouchy Webber to observe hefty DeVoe from afar. I couldn't figure out how she crammed her sturdy feet into bitsy high-heeled pumps with arrowhead toes.

DeVoe skulked behind file cabinets with incredible stealth, pouncing on anyone breaking the rules enumerated in the Major's blue book.

Fortunately, she wore her hair ratted up in a dyed-too-black beehive. The poof on top of her head was visible over the top of the files, aborting many of her scouting missions.

"*Mayday.* Tower of terror approaching," Webber warned, but he was too late to save Moroni, who'd just swallowed a chunk of chocolate donut before official break-time—a serious breach.

"Insubordination," DeVoe roared.

Moroni's esophagus went into spasms, but his coughing subsided after Anders smacked his back.

Webber expressed disappointment. "Damn, if you croaked, your estate could have sued the county and the bitch for big bucks."

*   *   *

I struggled to learn the content of four manuals and the logistics of making all those home calls while remaining invisible to the stalking demon. I'd pawed through the sales racks at Capwells Department Store and found five drab dresses to rotate through the work week, hoping to escape her evil eye.

My friend Lynn was of no help because she forgot the bathroom protocol, failed to check out the stalls before trash-mouthing DeVoe, and was reassigned to the Old Age Pasture within the hour.

Lynn and I met in the park on December 28th for lunch

and to commiserate over her transfer. She wasn't too distressed over DeVoe's spitefulness.

"That bitch is inviting a lawsuit, and she's going to get it. But look at you. *Wow*. First you dump the geek, and then score with a makeover. Just in time," she said.

"In time for what?"

"My old classmate from middle-school, Matt Willis, moved back up here from L.A. a few weeks ago. He's good-looking, a hotshot salesman, and single. Up for grabs. We're having lunch at Dalke's Haufbrau tomorrow, the 29th, so you can join us. And my mom is planning a big New Year's Eve party. You'll be his date. Perfect."

"What if this Matt and I don't hit it off?" I asked.

"That's silly. He's cool, now you're hot—well, close enough—so what could go wrong?"

A vision of Mom's face roared through my head.

Lynn chatted on, delighted to arrange other people's lives even if her own wasn't so enviable. She too had failed in the collegiate scramble for a mate, and at age twenty-two was dating the seventeen-year-old who washed her mother's car on Saturdays. Lynn was on iffy legal grounds, and his parents were threatening to sue her for statutory rape.

"What a crock. Pete's a big boy," she insisted.

"Maybe that's the point his folks are trying to make. He's still a boy," I pointed out, but she was not open to reason.

"Why didn't you mention your mom's party before?" I asked.

"Because you might have brought Bob. If you were throwing a bash, would you want the spider-freak skulking around?"

Fair enough.

CHAPTER EIGHTEEN

"I guarantee *all* my girls is winners."

Vi inspirational words were riveted into my brain, and I intended to make her proud at my twelve o'clock lunch date with Lynn and mystery-man Matt.

Perfection was my goal. I'd set my alarm clock for an hour earlier than usual on the morning of the 29th to allow ample time for styling my hair and lathering on makeup. The most attractive outfit I could come up with, given the Agency's dress code, was a camel-colored, dropped-waist shift dress. Not a knockout, but at least somewhat fashionable.

Looking good, I reassured myself as I grabbed my trench coat and left for the office.

*   *   *

When I sat down at my desk, I was surprised. Surly Webber, scrunched over in his indelibly creased polyester pants, usually ignored me and read the newspaper when DeVoe was not on the prowl. But this morning he actually acknowledged my existence.

Webber put the paper down and leaned over chummy-like. Was he awed by my glamor? No.

"Sister, I got this stiff who's holed up in a hotel. He's

ditched me for months. If you dig him up, I'll teach you everything about this frigging job."

Why does he have that sly look?

His chubby fist shot out to hand me a psychologist's evaluation describing the stiff, Clarence Holmes.

A somber assessment. Agoraphobic recluse. Borderline Personality Disorder, minimal coping skills—potential suicide, the report stated.

How profoundly sad, I thought.

"Are you afraid something awful has happened to him?" I asked.

"Hell, no. I just need to knock him off my overdue-log so that bitch DeVoe will get off my back. I'm on the top of her shit list. You want the deal or not?" He brushed chocolate Hostess cupcake crumbs off his chin stubble.

"Of course," I said, awed by his years of experience. Wasn't I lucky that he would help me? And I was sure his hard-boiled attitude covered a genuine concern for Holmes.

Well, I would locate the missing Holmes, endearing myself to Webber, and I would also, with infinite compassion, find a fix for Holmes's mental disorders.

At last, I was a *real* social worker.

*   *   *

"No big deal." Webber took pains to reassure me as I threw on my coat, grabbed my pristine field-folder, and took off for the Hotel Will Rogers in my VW.

How was I to know it was a flophouse, subsidized for those who would otherwise be sacked out in a train station or under the bushes in a park?

The morning fog was thick and sticky. The gray gloom made it hard to see the outline of the dilapidated building until it popped up right in front of me.

I pulled the car over to the curb and nosed it into a parking space next to the entrance.

Empty pint bottles, shattered glass, and debris littered the sidewalk.

A chipped cornerstone commemorated the hotel's opening in 1931 as Oakland's finest—fourteen stories tall, in architectural defiance of California's earthquakes. Its first and only coat of paint had been white. What little remained almost thirty years later was filthy, peeling off in straggly strips.

As I sat in my VW looking at the decayed structure, an inescapable sense of menace overwhelmed me.

You can't back out. You've got to prove yourself, my inner voice urged.

Rigid with fear, I forced myself to get out of the car, stepping over the bottles and shards of broken glass.

I pushed open the creaking entrance door and reeled. The stench of stale cigarette smoke, urine, and the reek of bodies all hit me. I squinted while my eyes adjusted to the dim light.

"What you want, bitch?" a belligerent voice called out. "Rooms is five bucks a hour, up front."

My heart tried to beat its way out of my body. The question came from a man with black hair stringy with oil. He sat behind a scarred reception desk with his feet propped up beside a nameplate that identified him as *Joe Cappo, Manager.*

"I'm not here for a room, sir. I'm from Social Services, and I need to find Clarence Holmes."

My voice quivered, and I was sure he could hear the wild thumping inside my chest cavity. I fumbled in my coat pocket for my laminated Agency I.D. card.

"How come?" he asked. His glare was fierce.

"No one's seen him for a while, and it's time to renew his housing voucher," I explained.

"Fifth floor, room number 6A. Elevator don't work." He jerked his head toward the warped staircase.

Why were his eyes so hostile? I reached for the tilted banister, pulled my hand back when I saw a cockroach, and climbed the stairs touching nothing. The threadbare carpet was crusted, and disgusting stuff crunched under my feet.

I counted the landings to the fifth floor and stepped into the murky hall corridor. The sounds coming from the paper-thin walls were horrifying. Whimpers from little kids and cries from babies mingled with retching, flushes, loud curses. *Why were children in this ghastly place?*

Then something ran over my foot. I didn't see what it was.

Be careful. Don't panic.

I crept along the corridor and struggled not to gag. The faded door numbers were hard to see in the dim light from a single bare bulb in the ceiling. I couldn't find #6A, but I spotted an unmarked door next to #6 that looked like it might be a linen closet.

Stop. Don't move. I sensed something and froze in front of #6, rooted with fright.

Whap. Before I knew what was happening, Cappo had sneaked up behind me.

"Screw you and your vouchers," he snarled and shoved me, hard.

Flying headfirst into a filthy room, I came face to face with a naked woman. She was so drunk she could hardly stand. Suddenly, she whirled around and lunged for the open window, but she smacked into the windowsill and fell to the floor.

I heard a click. Cappo had locked me in with her. The wretched woman rolled over, saw me, and crawled across the putrid carpet straight at me.

Oh God, no.

She attempted to right herself by pawing up my legs. Halfway up, she gained enough momentum for another lurch toward the window but again flopped to the floor underneath.

Drool. Tears. Rolls of fat flesh. It was a horrible blur. What if she made it over the sill? I saw a cord near the bed and followed it to a phone under a pile of smelly clothes and empty liquor bottles.

Desperate, I called police emergency.

"A suicide is underway at the Hotel Will Rogers—a window-jumper on the fifth floor, room number six. I can't stop her," I blurted.

I sat for a moment on the edge of the sagging bed and realized too late that wine and worse had saturated the mattress and was now seeping into my coat.

Within minutes, I heard heavy stomps in the hall and a key in the lock. Two policemen flung the door open, flattened me behind it, and tackled the woman. A fireman and two medics followed, grabbed a sheet off the bed, wrapped her up like a mummy, and tossed her on a gurney.

I peeked around the door, grossed out, and watched the convoy rumble down the hallway.

A lump was rising on the back of my head, and I hoped for a concussion to erase what I had just seen from my brain.

I felt for blood, but there was none. Holmes remained missing, I was still alive, and I refused to retreat in ignominious defeat. My mission was to locate the man, thereby winning Webber's respect and undying gratitude.

Shielded by an illusion of invincibility, I held my nose, drew a deep breath, and knocked on the unmarked door.

It swung open, and I had guessed right. The room measured about six by eight feet. Shelves lined the walls, stacked high, not with linens, but with hundreds of cans of cat food.

An emaciated man, wearing coveralls and a Go-Bears tee shirt, lay on a cot that filled the floor space. I thought he was dead, but he abruptly sat up and stared at me with palpable indignation.

"Who the hell are you?" he asked.

"My name is Amy Archer. I'm from Social Services, and I need to find Clarence Holmes." I hoped my voice wasn't as wobbly as my knees.

"What for?"

"Mr. Holmes needs to sign a form to have his housing vouchers continued."

He thought awhile. "If I'm him and put my moniker on your God-damn paper, will you go the fuck away?"

"Yes, but I could arrange for you to have a better room."

"I asked for this space, so keep your fucking nose out of my business."

Numbed, I opened my field folder, pulled out what I hoped was the correct voucher form and handed him a pen.

He scrawled his name diagonally across the whole piece

of paper and put my pen in his pocket.

I grabbed the form and ran out of the closet and down all five flights of stairs, ignoring the jolts to my flimsy right leg.

No. Please no. Cappo was waiting at the bottom. Another ambush?

"Why did you throw me in that room?" I gasped.

"Damn county stuck that rummy bitch here, and I told that guy Webber I wanted her out. Door or window, it don't matter none. He didn't do nothin'. 'Not my case,' he says, so I put it on you." He oozed contempt.

"Lousy drunk wrecked my best digs." *Bam.* His fist hit next to a hole in a sheet-rock wall, and the cockroaches raced for cover behind the bare studs. He pointed to his feet.

"Damn fuzz messed up my carpet bad. Gimme vouchers to fix it, or I sue big time, gimp."

CHAPTER NINETEEN

Cappo's cruel words *shattered* my fragile self-esteem. Stunned, confidence demolished, I stumbled out to the street, unable to endure another toxic moment.

I stood on the sidewalk and groped for the aspirin bottle in my handbag. My head ached, and the repulsive smells of the hotel stuck in my nose worse than a roadside skunk's.

A single resonating peal from the clock at the top of the Tribune Tower startled me.

One o'clock. An hour late for meeting Lynn and her friend Matt for lunch.

Emotionally battered, physically drained—the likelihood of dazzling him with my newfound glamor and perky conversation was nil, but I couldn't stand them up.

I gingerly stepped through the debris on the sidewalk, climbed into my VW, and drove to Grand Avenue while my mind tumbled wildly through the horrors I had just survived.

Mercifully, a parking spot was open near the side-door of the haufbrau. I managed to steer the car reasonably close to the curb and between the parking strips without taking out any pedestrians. I slipped out of my coat, which reeked, and left it in the VW.

You'll simply have to soldier through this, I told myself as I exited the car. I took a deep, resolute breath and willed myself to approach the entrance. As I reached to push through the swinging doors into the restaurant's clatter, Lynn charged out with a tall, slender guy in tow.

My heart, which had been running a pounding marathon of fear and anxiety, took a leap—and then it soared.

*   *   *

This was Matt?

An Adonis—or Julius, or Marlon, or whoever. He was the ultimate. No kidding.

Close to six feet tall, fair, blue eyes, dark blonde hair framing his chiseled features. Preppy crisp in a suit, starched white shirt, wing-tip shoes—straight out of Esquire.

He was too much to take in all at once.

God, I'm a mess. That pitiful woman's crawl up my legs shredded my stockings, and my seat felt damp—the Thunderbird had soaked through my coat. And I was freezing.

"Lynn, I'm sorry and embarrassed to be this late."

I extended my hand to this stunning guy and said, "You must be Matt. So glad to meet you."

"What happened? You look like you got run over," Lynn blurted.

"My pleasure, and I think you look terrific." Matt interceded, clasping my hand in both of his.

What a courtly save.

"Let's go back in to get you lunch," he said.

"I'm out of here. You two are on your own." Lynn waved goodbye and galloped down Grand toward her car. A meter maid stood next to it, scribbling in her official book.

Now I need to reimburse Lynn for the parking ticket.

Inside, Matt claimed the only two spots available at one of the community tables, pulled out two stools, and asked what he might order for me.

Half a dozen busboys, the youngest of whom looked to be about 70, darted between the tables, tossing empty glasses, chipped plates, and bent utensils into metal bins. The clamor unnerved me.

"Some tea would be wonderful," I suggested through my chattering teeth.

"You're cold," he said. "Here, put this on." He slipped off his jacket and placed it around my shoulders—warm and cozy and protective. How considerate of him, and how good it felt. And smelled. A scrumptious blend of aftershave and maleness.

"How about a turkey sandwich?" he asked.

The thought of food was repulsive, but I didn't want to dismiss his offer.

"Maybe we could split one?" I watched him as he went up to the counter to place the order. Six feet tall for sure, and he had that physical ease about him that athletic people often display.

Please, please let me sparkle. But my aching head kept ricocheting between the terrors of the hotel and the splendors of this man.

Matt wove back through the tables balancing a tray with an all-white-meat sandwich, two dill pickles, a mug of tea, and a coke.

"Hope this will do." He slid onto the stool next to me.

"Perfect." I wasn't referring to the sandwich. *Don't sit here staring like a star-struck dolt. Talk. Start a conversation.*

"Lynn told me you just relocated from Los Angeles," I said.

"A real hassle. My new job opened up unexpectedly three weeks ago. No time to find an apartment, so I'm crashing at my parents' place in Berkeley. I'm twenty-six years old and feel like a fool living with my mommy and daddy, but it was the only way to get the show on the road."

"Well, I live with mine because I don't make much money."

"Lynn told me you guys loved your work."

"I've not been at it long, and it has its ups and downs. So *many* people are in awful circumstances and can't find a way out. Plus, the regulations are mind-boggling. But helping someone navigate the bureaucratic maze and find a few resources is a huge reward."

Did I sound like a sanctimonious twit? The morning's trauma at the hotel roared on replay in my head. Still stunned, I found it hard to focus on the conversation.

What would become of that pathetic woman? And those helpless children?

"Are we on?" Matt asked, interrupting my tangle of thought.

My mind grappled with the revulsion of the hotel, while I stared into the most beautiful blue eyes I had ever seen— light crystalline blue rimmed by dark navy.

"Sorry, I'm a little spaced. On for what?"

"For the New Year's Eve party Lynn's mom is throwing." He flashed a dazzling smile.

"Absolutely!" *The guy is irresistible, and Webber's treachery will not screw this up.*

I conjured up a vision and, sorry as I felt for her, I pushed the naked drunk woman out of the hotel window. For good measure, I had her land on and squash Webber on the sidewalk below.

A very therapeutic mental exercise, and my head cleared. I would deal with Cappo and rescue the kids later.

Now I was toasty warm, and Matt was certifiably hot.

I borrowed a pen from him and wrote my phone number and address on the back of a takeout menu. Too traumatized to eat much, I wrapped the rest of my half-sandwich in a napkin and stuck it in my purse.

Charming to the end, Matt insisted on picking up the check. Skinflint Bob also always picked up the bill to examine every item before announcing the amount of my share. To the penny.

"I'll walk you to your car," Matt said.

I shriveled. He would see my hideous Quasimodo lurch, so viciously underscored by Cappo, and lose all interest. But he didn't seem to notice.

"What time shall I pick you up?" he asked, ushering me into the VW.

Another shiver of apprehension engulfed me.

He would have to meet *her*.

"About 7:00 if that works for you." I reluctantly relinquished his jacket.

"Perfect. I think it will be a very happy New Year."

"So do I. And thank you."

I created another vision, shoved Mom into her garden shed, sprinkled her with aphids, and chained the door shut.

CHAPTER TWENTY

"Where the hell were you? Did you fall down a sewer?"

When I walked into the office, Maisie's questions startled me. I had put my coat back on and it still reeked.

"Sort of." I hedged. "I did a favor for Webber, a woman clawed at my legs, I sat in some wine, and I couldn't find a parking place." Best to omit mention of the extended lunch hour.

"But at least I found him," I announced, so proud of myself.

"Found who?"

"Clarence Holmes. He's living in a closet." I whipped the renewal voucher with his scrawl from my field folder.

"Webber sent you to the Hotel Will Rogers?" She looked startled. Then her eyes narrowed.

"Yes." *How much should I say? If I carry on about the revolting place, she might think I'm not up to the job.*

"The hotel wasn't very pleasant. A woman alcoholic tried to off herself, and I heard little kids crying who shouldn't be there."

Maisie shook her head. "Webber can't dump his garbage on you. From here on, you go only where I send you. Also, we vouchered Holmes for a room, so if he's in a closet, that subsidy's going to be chopped by two-thirds. And I'll take care of Webber."

My day wasn't over yet. She peeled the red band off a pack of Parliaments.

"We don't have time to deal with the alcoholic or the kids now. Pull yourself together because you need to go back out. The District Attorney's Fraud Investigators are ready to arrest Sissy Grimes, but they want her to sign one more affidavit to nail her."

"Why?" I asked in disbelief.

Maisie had been handpicking easy cases for me—single moms not willing to jeopardize their eligibility to fool around. Sissy Grimes was one of those clients. A soft, sweet woman, she had two girls in elementary school and an adorable three-year-old boy named Lamont at home.

"Because she claimed Jesse Jones was the father of her kids," Maisie responded. "Jones said, 'no way' and took a blood test. The fraud investigators got the kids' medical records from the County hospital, and they prove he's not their father. She perjured herself."

"Was it legal for the detectives to get those reports without her permission?"

"How would I know? Also, they want you to deliver this $20,000 invoice to her to repay all the welfare money she's gotten for the kids."

"What?" The whole thing was horrific. Worse yet, I would be the pawn carrying out the family's destruction.

"Why aren't those fraud guys doing their own dirty-work?" I asked, still incredulous over the viciousness of the system.

"Don't know and can't ask. DeVoe said we had to do it, and I'm already on her shit list." Maisie opened a roll of Tums.

*   *   *

I walked to my car and agonized. How was I going to tell this woman her life and her family were about to be ripped apart? Awful. Simply *awful.* I had begun stuffing my pockets with wrapped candies because the toddlers at home seemed terrified of me. When one little girl shyly asked if she could touch my hand, I finally got it. She wanted to know what my skin felt like. I held hands a lot after that, but a ton of candy was not going to fix this.

I drove to the crumbling Victorian house on Myrtle street where Mrs. Grimes lived, left my putrid coat in the car, and knocked on her battered door.

"Mama, white lady here!" Little Lamont called out, peeking from behind the splintered wood. He wasn't afraid of me anymore, mostly because his mama had accepted me as a benign and well-intentioned presence, and he loved to hold hands. Now his mother would hate me.

Just how terrible was her lie? She might have honestly thought Jesse Jones was the daddy. Worse yet, she had no relatives. Arrest her and three traumatized children would be dumped into foster homes costing four times more than her welfare check. I felt sick to my soul.

"How come you out this late, Miss Archery?" Her broad smile was cordial.

She opened the creaky door for me to come in and

motioned for me to sit down at the kitchen table. When I did, Lamont climbed onto my lap.

You've got to tell her. There's no way out of it.

"I have bad news, Mrs. Grimes. You're supposed to sign this paper that says Jesse Jones is the father of your kids and swear to it." I pulled the affidavit out of my field folder.

"Okay. You got a pencil?"

The little boy squirmed on my lap, happy with the Tootsie-Roll I had tucked into my folder to give to him. I couldn't stand it. The police would come, haul them off—*monstrous.*

I took a deep breath and spat out the whole gruesome scenario.

"The District Attorney's investigators have proof that Jesse isn't the father of your kids, so they want to arrest you for fraud. Also, I'm supposed to give you this bill for $20,000."

We sat on the kitchen chairs with the broken spokes on the backs and stared at one another across the rickety table.

"Holy Jesus, they be after me. What to do, what to do?"

She sat paralyzed. Fear possessed her entire body, her face was frozen, and she could not move.

This is cruel. I have to help her, but how? A thought broke through the fog of my own emotional turmoil.

"You need to go to Legal Aid fast," I said. "Please don't tell me anything because I have to report whatever you say. Don't sign any papers until you talk to a lawyer. Also, ask if it was legal for the D.A. to look up the kids' blood types at the County hospital without you knowing about it."

"Where's the lawyer?"

"On Seventh Street, next to Mi Rancho Market."

It was 5:35 p.m., and the store-front office closed at 6:00. It was impossible for her to get there in time unless I gave her a ride.

The Major's blue book included a list, pages long, of prohibited activities and dire consequences for violators. Rule #3 was clear.

Do not, under any circumstances, transport clients. But I imagined little Lamont being tossed in the back of a police car and delivered to sinister strangers.

"Let's go," I said.

Had I got myself into as much trouble as Mrs. Grimes? I wasn't sure, but maybe those interviewers were right.

Was this job too tough for me?

CHAPTER TWENTY-ONE

"**D**amn, *now* what have you done?"
Maisie's greeting shocked me when I arrived at the office the following morning.

The question blind-sided me. I'd spent the night dreaming about eyes. Cappo's squinting daggers, Mrs. Grimes's frozen with fright, Matt's reflecting the exquisite light blue of Artic ice.

Snap to. What was wrong? I was champing at the bit to rescue alcoholics and helpless children. Maisie was on her soapbox and steaming.

That whining, manipulative client on Christmas Eve came to mind instantly. She must have snitched about me giving her the money. Or Webber blabbed about my dress.

"I'm sorry, but that was the only way I could get rid of her," I said.

"What was? Who are you talking about?" Maisie pushed aside her ashtray and emptied a bottle of Mylanta into her coffee mug.

"I gave five dollars to a client on Christmas Eve. Also, I wore a red dress, but I kept my coat on all day."

"I don't think those are the problems. You need to go to the Major's office. He won't say why, but for him to break rank and bypass both DeVoe and me to handle it himself means it's bad."

"Do you have any tranquilizers?" I asked, groping for another aspirin in my bag.

"I already took all the Miltown," Maisie answered, rising to escort me back to the elevator.

"So long." She shoved me in and punched the button for the fifth floor.

*   *   *

My panic was under control as I approached Mabel, propped at her counter. She shook herself out of her torpor and pointed an orange nail toward the door labeled *Major Rampart, Human Resources Director.*

"Go right on in." I saw a spark of malicious interest in her ordinarily vacant eyes.

When I entered the office, a man, presumably Major Rampart, was seated in a brown Naugahyde office chair with his back to me. He was concluding a phone call.

"I know nothing about your voucher for Mr. Holmes being cut, Mr. Cappo, but if you're not happy with Mrs. Li's explanation, I suggest you duke it out with her supervisor, Ms. DeVoe. You'll lose. Good day."

He hung up the receiver, swiveled his chair around to face me, and rose, rigid and stern, from behind the polished wooden desk. He gestured toward one of the two armless straight-back chairs directly in front of it. His posture was perfectly military, and "Major" was clearly a genuine title.

"I'm sorry to meet you under these circumstances, Miss Archer. We had high expectations for you. Sit."

The Major's eyes were steel, and they terrified me. I sat.

"Are you aware of the penalties for collusion?" he asked.

"No, sir. And I know I shouldn't have given Mrs. Grimes and Lamont a ride. But I drove carefully, and we weren't in an accident."

His expression was peculiar. Something between puzzlement and disbelief.

"I said collusion, not collision."

"Oh. No, sir. I'm not familiar with the word or the penalty."

"Let me explain this another way. The D.A. is claiming you're in cahoots with Grimes and wrecked their case against her."

"Well, I didn't think it was right to trick her, so I took her to Legal Aid."

Did he have to sound so patronizing?

"What else?"

How did he know there was more?

"I wore a red dress and gave five dollars to a woman on Christmas Eve." My embarrassment was agonizing.

The Major's eyes locked into mine. Then he punched the intercom and barked at Mabel.

"Call Lieutenant Swathmore. Tell him I've completed an extensive internal investigation. The suspect is in my custody if he wants to come over and interrogate her."

My mind splintered. *Suspect. Lieutenant. Interrogation.* Would I be arrested, or fired, or both? Fear paralyzed my throat, so my question was a whisper.

"Please, who's Lieutenant Swatmore, and what's he going to do?"

"It's Swathmore. He's in charge of the D.A.'s Internal Fraud Investigation Department. And he hates welfare. A crooked worker makes for big headlines."

Oh, God. What if my name and face were all over the Tribune? *A public disgrace.* Dad would unfold his newspaper, clutch his chest, and fall over dead.

The intercom buzzed. "He's on his way." Mabel snickered.

A siren wailed briefly outside and minutes later the Major's door was thrown open by a large, beefy man whose clothes might have fit forty pounds ago. A gun stuck out of a holster on his hip, and the outline of another one, slung on a shoulder strap above his fat middle, was visible under his jacket.

"Where's the perpetrator?" he demanded.

Major Rampart pointed at me.

The Lieutenant attacked. He grabbed a side chair, turned it around to straddle it, and leaned in way too close to me. I clutched my handbag tightly, so he wouldn't see my hands shake.

"*You* conspired with Grimes to defraud the public." His fist was in my face. "I demand the truth—spit it out. All of it. Full disclosure."

Would anything come out of my mouth?

Yes. Vi would never have stood for this guy's bullying. I sat up straight, found my sprouting backbone, and spoke up.

"Well, sir, I didn't think it was wrong to take her to Legal Aid for advice. I shouldn't have given her and little Lamont a ride, though, and I'm sorry I wore a red dress and gave five dollars to that woman on Christmas Eve. If I get out of this, I'll not break any rules."

Oops—full disclosure.

"Also, I gave Lamont a Tootsie Roll."

The Lieutenant was incredulous and as flummoxed as the

Major had been earlier. Then his face turned to purple fury.

The Major beamed.

"Caught yourself one hell of a subversive, Swathmore. Want to feature this nefarious scammer on the front page and send her up the river for a Tootsie Roll violation?" His sarcasm was withering.

Swathmore glowered at the Major.

"You lucked out this time, Rampart, but I'll bring down your house yet. Bleeding hearts bleed taxpayers." He snarled, glared at me, and stormed out. I tried not to notice that he'd split his pants during his Columbo imitation.

"Am I fired?" I asked.

"No," the Major said, "but from here on out watch your p's and q's because Swathmore's got a big axe to grind. Strange. Swathmore's a turkey, but that's the first time he's smelled like one."

Careful. Be more careful. Thank God I hadn't told that woman to scalp a food voucher for cash.

As I left the Major's office, I tossed the crushed remains of yesterday's turkey sandwich into a trash can.

CHAPTER TWENTY-TWO

New Year's Eve loomed the following day. Here's how things stacked up.

I'd made a complete fool of myself at work and was now branded as a stumbling newcomer of questionable competence. Hours of self-flagellation did not change that reality.

My mind had dismissed Bob, aided by an imaginary giant scorpion swatting him with its venomous curly tail. But in real-life, he had stationed himself in the kitchen with Mom.

And all my rampant, glorious speculations about Matt's possibilities were about to be trashed—he hadn't called.

Maybe he's just a gorgeous, flaky salesman.

I hid in my room and listened until I heard the front door open and close.

"Is Bob gone?" I called out.

"The poor dear had to leave to work on a special project—something to do with earth worms. Why he's putting up with your snit is beyond me, missy." *Thwack*—the unmistakable sound of her knife attacking an unsuspecting root vegetable.

"It's not a snit, Mom. He's history," I again retreated to my room to brood in morose solitude.

The phone rang.

Bob thought he was so smart, sneaking home to call and trick me into speaking to him. No way.

But what if it was Matt, and Mom picked up?

I snatched the extension.

"Hello?"

"Amy?" It wasn't Bob.

"Hi, Matt." *Oh, the relief.* I could breathe again.

"Sorry I didn't phone earlier, but I wasted all afternoon looking for an apartment. No luck. Is 7:00 still good for you tomorrow night?" he asked. His voice had a husky, low-pitched quality that had been overshadowed in the noisy restaurant. Enticing, as was everything else about him.

"Perfect," I said, lowering my voice to a more seductive range as recommended in Cosmopolitan magazine

"Do you have a cold?" he asked.

"No, just a touch of allergy now and then." The phony phone posturing was impossible for me to pull off. Forget it.

"Can't wait to see you," Matt said before hanging up. He always seemed to say the right thing.

What a spin his call put on the evening. I put the phone back on its stand and opened my closet door. The cocktail dress I bought to wear to a multitude of parties celebrating my engagement to Bob languished next to my four abandoned bridesmaid dresses.

Not for long.

I snatched the dress off the hanger and held it up to me in front of the mirror. Fabulous. Black crepe, sleeveless, short skirt flared at the hem, high-cut bodice, low-cut back. Think Audrey Hepburn, the icon of contemporary style.

Shoes were another issue. A 1½ inch heel was all I could manage, so I was condemned to old-lady suede pumps.

The question was, could I rise to the level of the dress, do my hair and makeup, and obscure the repugnant footwear?

I wasn't certain I could replicate Vi's handiwork, so I called her.

"Hi, Vi. I have a date for New Year's Eve, and I need to look good. If I came straight from work around 5:00 tomorrow, would you be able to fix me up again?"

"Way to go, kid. You got the moxie. Bring over what you're wearin' and the makeup kit. I guarantee you're gonna be a stunner."

"Are you sure I'm not interrupting your plans?" I asked.

"Not no more. Me and the dud was goin' to Vegas, but poor jilted Hank got so riled up over Rita, he canceled the contract on her fancy new convertible. Then, that there gigaloo car salesman got *his* dander up and dumped her.

"Rita's a mess. I'm stickin' around 'cause I might pull off a reconciliation here. Hank's pretty easy, and I know how to handle a man."

"I wish I did."

"You got smarts and you're gonna learn, kid. Specially by listenin' up to me. When you get here, use the side door and come up to the kitchen. Don't forget the makeup."

I dug out the Avon kit and practiced, copying a Revlon ad in Cosmo.

Mom accosted me over her chopping board when I made an emergency Coke run to the refrigerator.

"Why are you all gussied up when Bob's already gone home? And what were all those phone calls?" She split a yellow onion with one mighty hack of her forged steel weapon.

"I'm rehearsing. I need to look smashing tomorrow night

because I'm going to a big New Year's Eve party with Matt Willis."

"What? She froze, incredulous. "You're going where? With who?"

"A friend of Lynn's, Mom."

"That shameless cradle-robber couldn't possibly know anybody who's decent." She resumed her attack on the onion, her eyes tearing from fumes and frustration.

"This is nonsense. I told you. Bob apologized to me, and he'll do something about the ring on Valentine's Day. You're going to end up like your spinster aunt."

"I'd rather be single like Aunt Jane than stuck with Bob. Forget it, Mom. He's clueless. Would you like to accompany him to Mount Diablo State Park to observe the annual tarantula migration? I sure don't."

"You should be ashamed of yourself, hurting his feelings this way."

She washed off her hands, flipped on the porch light, grabbed her gardening trowel from its hook, and stormed off into the night.

Please, someone kidnap her.

*   *   *

I knew Mom would screw up the works. She was priming to take on Matt, and my only hope was to have her gone when he came to pick me up.

Could I get her out of the house? I suggested to Dad that he take her out to dinner. "She likes the Sea Wolf on the wharf," I reminded him.

"I tried, Amy, but she said we had to stay home in case

you got into trouble with Lynn's no-good shiftless friend."

Since it was impossible to get rid of her, I'd have to be ready to leave as soon as Matt arrived.

Predictably, I was designated to cover the office on the 31st, but Lester, the guard, was taking no chances on my limited confrontational skills and evacuated the public at 4:30.

"Bomb threat," he insisted.

"Good grief, have you called the police?" I asked.

"No, it was only a paper bag, but you can't be too careful."

"You opened it yourself?"

"My lunch came in it."

*   *   *

So, I was at Vi's by 5:00. I toted the makeup kit and my garment bag through the side door and upstairs to the kitchen.

Vi, wearing a startling pink muumuu, heaved herself up from her chair to give me a big hug. I think she was more excited about my date than I was.

"Kid, we're gonna pull this off. Show me what you got."

I zipped open the clothes bag and took out the dress.

"*Oh*, nice," she exclaimed. "Real classy." She nodded her approval.

"Vi, it goes the other way around. The front is high, and the back is scooped."

"*Shit.* It's too late to fix it. What about the shoes?"

I pulled the dismal geriatric comfort pumps from the bottom of the clothes bag.

She gasped.

"Okay, kid. I'm takin' over this show. First, the damn ugly shoes. We got to dress them up, but not too much, because we don't want nobody lookin' at them."

She opened a cupboard and took out a jar filled with loose rhinestones, found a bottle of Elmer's Glue in the kitchen junk drawer, stuck a few of the shining stones on the shoes, and they looked just right.

Then she started on me, and when she finished, my eyelids were aglitter, sparkles highlighted my hair, and I felt like a princess.

"Now we got to jazz things up with accessories," she said. "You put on the dress, and I'll be right back."

I slipped into the dress while Vi plodded upstairs and returned carrying a jewelry box.

She picked out a rhinestone choker and matching hoop earrings. Then she attached a rhinestone broach to the dress just over my left hipbone—a sassy surprise.

We climbed the stairs together to the full-length mirror in her bedroom for me to see the total production. Another fabulous transformation.

"Vi, I'm speechless. You've turned me into royalty. How can I thank you?"

"By keepin' me posted. I wanna know if this guy is the real deal. Okay?"

"Okay."

"Now what perfume you gonna wear?"

Oh, *no*. I hadn't given it a thought.

"We're not allowed to wear perfume at work, Vi, so all I have is some cologne called Windsong that I bought at the drugstore."

"Listen up. You gotta smell good And expensive. Men got noses that can tell. Nothin' too sweet or heavy, though.

She sat me down on her vanity stool in front of a dresser tray crowded with fanciful bottles.

"Shalimar's old lady sticky sweet. Tabu's gonna knock him over, and there's somethin' cheap about it. I say Chanel #5 or Arpege. Stick out your wrists and we'll go with what works on you."

Arpege did the trick. Just a touch, and I was immersed in a light, slightly sensuous cloud.

"Vi, what would I do without you?" I asked her, grateful beyond words.

"Showin' you the ropes is my pleasure. Makes me happy I still got my touch.

We trooped back downstairs to the kitchen, and I gathered up my gear.

"Break a leg, kid," Vi said, giving me another hug as I was leaving.

"Now I got business with Hank and Rita. Things is still iffy. *Damn* that girl. I taught her better."

*   *   *

I was home from Vi's by 6:30. When I let myself in, Dad was folded into his faux leather La-Z-Boy recliner. He peered over his newspaper.

"Wow, Amy, you look great. Far too good for that crybaby Bob."

Whoa. Either Mom had died, or Dad had hit the bottle for him to dare say anything negative about moaner Bob. Or were backbones becoming contagious?

*　　　　　*　　　　　*

Mom wasn't dead. At 6:50, she positioned herself in the living room, perched on the edge of her Ethan Allen flowered-chintz throne—a medieval queen about to order a beheading. The chair swiveled so she could keep an eye on everyone.

My chest felt tight and my nerves gave off that scritchy chalk-on-blackboard feeling. I knew she was going to mess me up again.

At exactly 7:00, the doorbell rang. Dad folded his newspaper, pushed his tortoise horn-rim glasses up on his nose, tilted his chair to upright, creaked out, and went to the door.

He opened it, and Matt's entrance was perfection. Slim, graceful in a navy blazer, and impossibly handsome. I felt my face flush. He extended his hand to Dad.

"Mr. Archer, I'm Matt Willis. A pleasure to meet you, sir. And Mrs. Archer." He turned to her with his wonderful smile.

"Now I know why Amy's so pretty. And I couldn't help but notice your beautiful garden on my way in," he said.

Would his good manners and the compliments disarm Queen Harriet?

She forced a tight smile while Matt eased my bared arms into my black velvet holiday wrap.

"Thank you," she replied and shot him the evil eye. "I keep my garden free of slugs by pouring salt on every one of them. They shrivel up and dissolve."

CHAPTER TWENTY-THREE

Utter *mortification.* I wanted to evaporate.

How could Mom have been so deliberately rude?

Matt took my arm and steered me up the brick stairs bisecting the garden. Mom's camellias were in gorgeous bloom—red, white, and pink—and two months early for the season. She'd been busy with her saltshaker, and the leaves and flowers were untouched by undesirable crawlies.

The floral abundance did not distract from or lessen my embarrassment.

Matt had parked his car, a light blue Impala convertible, on the street at the top of the stairs.

What's with men and convertibles? I thought. At least the top was up.

He opened the door for me.

"You look *fabulous,*" he said as I slid in.

Maybe the evening was salvageable.

"What a lovely car. It smells new." I sniffed and smiled.

"It is. I'm a salesman, and first impressions open doors. It's important to look like a winner from the get-go. And I like to win."

"You mentioned at lunch that you sell office equipment." I hoped my shredded stockings and disheveled state at Dalke's restaurant might fade from his memory.

"Yep. That's where the big money is right now. But I switch companies and products if I see a hotter opportunity."

He turned the key to start the engine, gripped the largest steering wheel I'd ever seen, and eased the car down winding Snake Road to the entrance to Highway 13 going toward Berkeley.

Chatter was a distraction, but an elephant filled the back seat. The beast had Mom's face, framed by enormous tusks, and was growing exponentially. The creature's trunk slipped around my neck and began to strangle me.

What happened to your newfound spine? If you let this fester, this will be over before it's begun. Go head-on. My words burst out.

"Matt, I hope you'll forgive my mother's behavior. She's got a few hang-ups, mostly about control."

"No sweat, Amy. My work's competitive, and conflict is the norm. That's why I love what I do—to challenge, spar, and come out on top. My dad's an attorney, and I grew up with kitchen-table debates.

"I was on track to get a law degree, but the legal process is a stodgy bore. Who wants to wait months or years for a payoff? I like every-day fireworks. Your mom's testy? Bring her on."

He reached across the seat, took my hand, and squeezed it. We looked at each other. He grinned, and I smiled the biggest smile of my life.

"I have one question. What's a slug?" he asked.

"A gigantic snail that has no shell. Slimy too," I said.

Then we both burst out laughing.

I think he may be my ideal man.

*   *   *

Lynn's mom had decorated the family's 1920s Berkeley mansion to the hilt. Wrought-iron reindeer pranced on the lawn, and lanterns with glowing candles flickered on the steps up to the wreathed front door.

In the foyer, a towering Christmas tree almost touched the peak of the cathedral ceiling. Hundreds of silver-glitter bubble lights sparkled on the tree's branches, and their beams danced in the beveled windowpanes. Green garlands accented with red holly wound up the banisters of the grand staircase, and a fire roared in the living room fireplace.

Fairy-tale perfection. And Matt moved about creating his own magic.

"Champagne?" he asked. I wanted to swim in the crystal blue pools of his eyes. He was more handsome than I remembered. Fine features, not spectacular like pretty-boy Bob's, but clean. Similar to a young JFK.

We sat close on a plump sofa in what Lynn called the music room, sipped from elegant Baccarat flutes, and talked. He smelled deliciously of faint musk, a scent I hadn't noticed in the leathery car. I hoped the Arpege was having a similar effect on him.

Words tumbled out easily for Matt, and his enthusiasm was infectious.

This guy's a born salesman, I thought as I gazed at him with rapt attention. When I blinked, my mascara-coated eyelashes looked alarmingly like spider-legs.

Our party talk flowed from books (he liked le Carre's spy stuff) to movies (more spies for him with *The Manchurian Candidate*, while I sniffled through *West Side Story*).

Next up—football, and I zeroed in to sparkle.

Mom had always hated sports, so with the advent of

televised games, Dad and I immersed ourselves on Saturdays, Sundays, Monday evenings, and subsequently devoured Bowl games, pro playoffs, and reruns to drive her to the kitchen or garden.

"Man, that NFL playoff game on Sunday was something else," Matt said.

"Lombardi's play-calling puzzled me," I said. "Green Bay should have won easily." I sipped a bit of champagne.

"You know football?" Matt stared at me, astonished.

"Basketball, too. I was still at Cal Berkeley in 1959 when Pete Newell coached the team to the NCAA championships. I never missed a home game. It's my second favorite sport."

Matt sat there, speechless and seemingly transfixed.

But before I could display my full mastery of the Sporting Green, which included baseball and hockey (Dad and I needed cover for all seasons), Lynn's mom interrupted.

"Excuse me, dears. Matt, I know you two are getting acquainted, but I need a favor. That flaky combo I hired is still setting up in the ballroom. Would you play a few numbers to keep things rolling? I'll only steal him for a few minutes, Amy."

She led him to the baby grand piano in the corner, and Matt sat down on the bench. He patted it and motioned for me to join him. Just sitting beside him gave me flutters.

His fingers glided over the keyboard, filling the room with soft, classic ballads—"It Had to Be You", "As Time Goes By," "Moonglow." Their romantic lyrics wafted through my mind.

Then Matt looked at me, winked, and began to play Elvis's "Can't Help Falling in Love with You."

My heart leapt, and my head was in a spin. His musical

choices completely flummoxed me, and so did the wink. Were they playful teases?

Be careful. Don't be a fool and read too much into anything.

Lynn's mom trotted over again. "Musicians, they call themselves. Finally have their act together. Thanks, Matt. The caterers just finished laying out the buffet, so help yourselves."

"I'm famished," Matt said to me. "Grab a spot on a sofa, and I'll get something for us to eat. And more champagne."

He left in a flash. I found a vacant place, and when Matt came back, he was juggling two flutes and a plate with a single hot kabob.

"Too crowded around the buffet table. Want to share?" he asked.

I nodded yes. He sat down next to me, cozy close, and offered me the first bite. I waved it away, knowing the cube of beef would fall off and roll down the front of my dress. Instead, it careened off his blazer, but he caught it on the second bounce. Minimal damage.

"How talented you are," I said, enchanted by his performance.

"At the piano or catching flying beef?" he asked. "I'm not great at the piano—pick it up by ear. Joined a little group in college that played frat parties and dances. I was okay on the saxophone, but I kept getting blisters on my mouth so I gave it up. Too much of a drag because I talk a lot. In the sales world, I'm known as 'silver-tongue.'"

"Have you always wanted a career in sales?" I asked.

"Pretty much. I'm hooked on the rush that comes with closing a deal. In high school, I stumbled into a part-time job at Hinks Department Store demonstrating the pianos. My buddy worked next door in the luggage department and sales were lousy, so one day I walked over and started tap-dancing on the Samsonite.

"I sold out all they shuffled in. I loved the challenge and the adrenalin charge. A switch from law to a business major in college was a simple decision."

This guy was *not* a flaky salesman. Handsome, smart, fun—and not afraid of Mom.

Could it get any better? It did.

"Shall we dance?" he asked.

"Oh, I love *The King and I*." My head was still into his music.

"No, I meant would you like to dance?"

Could I? I knew basic swing from hours of watching American Bandstand with Lynn, but dare I risk making a spectacle of myself? Matt didn't perceive my ankle as an impediment, so why should I?

I swear I heard Vi's voice say, "Damn, kid, get off your buns and go for it."

"Delighted." I extended my hand. My cheeks were beginning to ache from so much smiling.

Matt took my hand and led the way to the ballroom. Huge oak doors opened onto the room, which was softly lit by half a dozen dimmed crystal chandeliers. Potted white Poinsettias graced the small cocktail tables that hugged the walls. White flocked wreaths dangled beneath shimmering wall sconces.

We paused in the doorway for a moment, captivated by the décor, and listened to the music the combo was playing.

My hand felt so right in his. *Don't let go.*

But he did—to swoop me into his arms and spin me onto the dance floor.

Oh, how we danced.

Whirling, dipping, holding, clinging. I think we were channeling Fred Astaire and Ginger Rogers because we owned that ballroom. I didn't know a waltz from a fox-trot, but I didn't need to. Matt's lead was strong and sure, and I followed in a state of blissful surrender as we floated around the room.

Transfixed by his touch, overcome by his sensuality—I was flooded with joy. And anxiety. Two other songs came to mind. Was this only make-believe—too good to be true?

Hold me, keep holding me. Please don't let go, I prayed.

But the musicians switched the tempo. Instead of clinging, we were swinging to Duke Ellington and rocking to Bill Haley. Matt and I effortlessly found the new groove, but the Twist was a hopeless tangle. We laughed when my ankle wouldn't budge and fell into each other's arms so easily.

Never had I felt so whole or happy. I was head over my matronly heels. Completely smitten.

"I hope you'll have dinner with me next Saturday night," Matt murmured as we swayed to everyone's favorite slow dance, "A Summer Place."

"Of course," I said. Did the invitation mean he was feeling a little of the magic that had engulfed me?

Hope. Just hope.

All too soon, it was midnight, but the obligatory kiss didn't count. It never happened. Lynn's seventeen-year-old boyfriend Pete showed his level of maturity by igniting a string of firecrackers inside the furnace. The resulting heart-stopping explosion occurred just as our lips were about to touch.

But the kiss on the doorstep when Matt took me home

counted—big time.

We stood in the shadows, outside the reach of the porch light. Our lips met, and our bodies melded into the exquisite oneness that we'd found on the dance floor. Neither of us wanted to let go.

Then Mom banged on the kitchen window with her trowel.

It's useless to hope for a kidnapping. The abductors would pay to give her back.

CHAPTER TWENTY-FOUR

New Year's Day dawned with a bright sun, but the air had a winter's chill. Dad immersed himself in Rose Bowl reruns in anticipation of the game the next day.

"The Huskies don't have much of a chance," he speculated. "Minnesota is top ranked and merciless."

So was Mom.

"I hope you got that foolishness out of your system, missy. Flouncing off with a flashy schmoozer while poor Bob is pining."

"Forget about Bob, Mom. I had a fantastic time with Matt, and we're having dinner Saturday night."

"Where—Luigi's Pizza Palace?"

"No, that's one of Bob's favorite hangouts. He gets excited when he's there because sometimes he can spot silverfish squirming in the molding. If you're lucky, he'll invite you to go for a slice after the parade of the tarantulas. Matt and I are going to Sanfords."

Take that, Mom. Sanfords, in a toney part of the Oakland hills called Montclair Village, was touted as one of the finest restaurants in the East Bay.

Mom glowered on her flowery chintz throne, creating a cold front that permeated the house. Dad roused himself from his recliner to check the thermostat and grabbed a sweater from the hall closet.

I refused to let her wet blanket extinguish my glow and returned to my room to call Vi.

"Hey, kid. How'd it go?" she asked. She listened intently as I described the wonders of Matt and the charm of the evening.

"This guy might be a keeper," she said. "Too young to have a big stash, but a go-getter. A looker, manners, and he don't mind spendin' the dough he's got. That's a ritzy restaurant he's takin' you to. Play a little hard-to-get, though. Make him *win* you. You got options.

"The dud and I are goin' to Vegas this weekend, so I'm gonna have Rita fix you up with her hairdresser. Guy's fruity, but he does hair and makeup and nails good. Don't take no chances and don't skimp. A man's gotta feel proud you're on his arm."

*   *   *

My head descended from a Matt-infused cloud and the glow expired when I arrived at work the next morning.

Maisie sat at her desk, surrounded by a mountain of cases. Her desk faced toward us workers, and ours faced hers—a floor plan designed by DeVoe for maximum surveillance. A pile of case records afforded the only privacy for any of us.

Wet-blanket Webber grumbled behind his newspaper. Maisie had told messy Anders to keep his monster shoes off the desk-top, so he sat gathering strength for his next rant with his size 15 feet shoved in the bottom drawer of his desk. Freshly pressed and starched, Moroni was buffing his nails.

A puff of cigarette smoke rose from behind Maisie's mountain.

"Amy, come over here. I need you to make a home call to the Garcia family. Their papers are way overdue for County Aid."

I walked over to sit in the chair next to her desk, with my back to the men, and she handed me a folder. I glanced through it and turned to the accounting ledger.

"This doesn't make sense. Two adults and three children are living on less than one woman with one child," I said.

"That's because Mr. Garcia is in the home. If he wasn't part of the household, Mrs. Garcia would be eligible for Federal assistance, about twice as much. But the Feds won't pay if the father is with the family. So even though he's disabled, all they can get is local money, and the County is bare-bones stingy.

"What?" No wonder fathers had to sneak around or split for their families to survive. I was about to howl my indignation when a wave of horror distorted Maisie's face.

I turned, and DeVoe had swooped out of nowhere to position herself in front of Webber. He tried to crumple and hide the newspaper, but it was too late.

"Webber, Clarence Holmes's renewal rolled off the overdue list. I noticed because it's been there for months, and I was going to order Li to write you up for it. Now I find out that you took it upon yourself to send Archer to the Hotel Will Rogers. Can't handle your own cases?" She sneered.

DeVoe was just warming up, and she leaned forward into cringing Webber's face.

"You are not a supervisor, and this was a serious breach

of protocol. I'll let you weasel out this time, only because there's a hiring freeze. Pull something like this again and you're out of here."

Then she whirled on those chunky feet, squashed into dainty heels, to confront Maisie.

"Li, are you incapable of keeping these so-called professionals in line? Your supervisory skills appear to be minimal. And, since Archer navigated the Hotel Will Rogers and survived, there is no reason not to send her to Harbor Homes, although I doubt that she can hack it."

She stalked off with an expression best described as a grinning grimace.

We all sat there, stunned. Diminished, insulted, humiliated—all five of us.

Anders pulled his feet out of his drawer, stood, and snarled. "*God-damn chicken-shit bitch*. I'm going to the men's room to yell and curse."

Moroni stared for a moment and then threw himself across his desk and pounded it with his newly manicured fists.

"The damned sadist. God, I wish I could find a rich woman."

Sullen Webber, resigned to the worst, unfolded the spreadsheet on which he kept his retirement calculations and addressed Moroni.

"Moroni, you think you look like Clark Gable with that silly mustache, but you got as much chance of scoring with a babe at the Ali Baba Ballroom as an ice-cube in hell. Don't feel too bad though. Shit, I can't even get myself fired."

*   *   *

"Why is she so awful?

I ripped the cellophane off the tuna sandwich I'd snatched from the machine and posed the question to Maisie as I joined her at her desk for lunch, hoping to ease the sting of DeVoe's hateful words with some support.

We liked each other, and if I wasn't meeting Lynn in the park, Maisie and I often spent the lunch hour huddled together. We needed to pretend we were having case conferences so DeVoe wouldn't penalize her for fraternizing with an underling.

"I don't know." Maisie said, still despondent from the humiliating dressing down. "No one knows anything about DeVoe except the woman's been here twenty-plus years, and she's mean as hell."

"You're a good supervisor," I told her. "She shouldn't have attacked you that way. These guys are set like concrete in their ways, and they're not going to listen to anyone. Do they care at all about the clients?"

"Anders does. He's outraged by poverty, politics, and bureaucracy, but in his heart he's a rescuer. If a client shows promise, I assign the case to him because he'll open doors. Anders has three women finishing their GED's, and he found one star who he's guided into winning a four-year scholarship to Merritt Hospital's nursing school. She'll become a full-fledged R.N.

"The guy's great in the field and then storms in here and raves like a mad-man. He hates this place. Promised his girlfriend he'd fund her while she did a voluntary stint overseas with the Red Cross. He didn't know she signed up for five years."

"What about Moroni?"

"He's okay if you don't mind a narcissistic womanizer. Forty-two years old and still lives with his mother in the Italian section of North Oakland. Mama Moroni worships her only baby and stuffs him full of garlic meatballs to ward off the floozies he meets at the dance clubs around town. I assign him grandmas raising grandkids to keep him out of trouble. He has no filters when it comes to young women."

"And Webber?"

Maisie took a chomp out of an apple and a swig of Mylanta.

"Don't get me started. Lazy, indifferent, and his only interest is in collecting his pension."

"I thought he was a war veteran. Webber keeps throwing out comments saying how terrible Korea was," I said.

"The dead-beat got drafted, but he knew how to type and lucked out with a clerical post at the Alameda Naval Air Station nine miles from here. Spent the entire Korean conflict shuffling papers as a file clerk. Never saw one day of combat, gets full benefits, and qualified for this job because of extra veteran's points on the exam. I assign him the dead-end cases that are going nowhere."

"Like that pitiful alcoholic woman at the hotel—what will happen to her?"

"The cops 5150'd her."

"What's that?"

"It's the law code that police use to commit someone 72 hours for psychiatric evaluation. Depending on the assessment, she might be sent to a state hospital because of the suicide attempt or end up in the county jail to dry out."

"What about those little kids at the hotel?"

"I made a referral to our Child Welfare Department.

They'll send out a specialized worker to do a health and safety check."

Maisie finished the apple and tossed the core into her wastebasket.

"You'd better hustle out to the Garcias before DeVoe can launch another assault," she said.

"Do they speak English?" I asked. "The only Spanish I understand is what's on the menu at the Mexicali Rose restaurant."

"I doubt it. You'll have to wing it."

*   *   *

When I returned to the office two hours later, I went straight to Maisie's desk and flopped down on her side-chair. I now understood why Moroni called it the confessional chair.

"I think I stumbled into big trouble," I told her. My instincts were right.

By the time I finished describing the home call, Maisie had groped through her top drawer, pulled out a bottle of Pepto, a pack of Parliaments, and was fumbling with a matchbook.

"Couldn't you have just stuffed the kid back in the attic?" she asked. "Now I need to go tell DeVoe." She sighed, rose, and trudged off toward DeVoe's office.

"What kid, what attic, and what's the big deal?" Webber butted in, eavesdropping as usual. He always smelled blood. And Moroni's ears also began flapping.

"The Garcias hid their Downs Syndrome daughter for five years. They're legal, but she isn't. They brought her down from the attic while I was there on a home call," I explained.

"Jesus. Didn't they feed her?" Morbid curiosity prompted Webber's question, rather than concern.

"Of course, they fed her. The Garcias aren't abusive. They were afraid she'd be deported and were trying to protect her. Theresa's almost twenty but acts more like their five-year-old. They put her in the attic when outsiders were around."

"So now Miss Goody-Good is part of the family. Warms my cockles. Isn't that sweet, Moroni?"

"Brings out the crocodile tears." Moroni sniggered. "Where's my hanky?"

I needed the hanky. Maisie plodded back and said, "I tried to save you, but she wants to hear it first-hand from you."

Ignoring the guys' sarcasm and shrouded in doom, I walked over to DeVoe's office, a corner cell devoid of human traces. No photos, mementos, or knick-knacks relieved the starkness or gave a clue as to its occupant.

All anybody knew about DeVoe was that she reveled in power, put-downs, and punishment. She left her office only to stalk or spy. The woman didn't speak to anyone on a personal level, refused to attend potlucks or to contribute a nickel toward a celebratory gift. She scoffed at the suggestion of signing a kindly intended card.

The door was open, and DeVoe motioned me in. I sat down in her grilling chair and squirmed, feeling the way I did as a sixth grader being admonished by Principal Boswell.

DeVoe was leaning back in her chair, and her pointy-toed feet poked out from underneath her narrow, battered metal desk.

"You found who?" she asked. Her scornful intonations were petrifying.

She knows very well who. Maisie just told her the story. What's her game?

I took a deep breath and said, "I needed the little girl to interpret for me. She was very shy, so I admired her parrot, hoping to make her more comfortable. She and I began playing with the bird, and Mrs. Garcia left the room. I thought she'd gone to get the bird's cage, but she came back with Theresa."

The pointy-toe shoes disappeared, and the black beehive tilted forward as DeVoe repositioned herself and leaned in for the kill.

"You must turn them all in to Immigration and Naturalization. If you don't, I will, and I'll bring you down for collusion, too. And you're not being paid to play, Archer." She dismissed me with a curt nod toward the door.

Geez, she is a piece of work, I thought as I retreated to my desk.

I dared not risk another encounter with Lieutenant Swathmore, and I would not dishonor that family's trust. What should I do—why not begin with the INS? That would appease DeVoe, and surely that agency would accommodate this exceptional circumstance.

"Webber, do you have a number for the INS?" I asked, slumping into my chair.

"Find it yourself." Webber grabbed his Rolodex and shoved it into a drawer.

"That's not very collegial. You said you'd help me."

"Listen, sister, I told you I'd help if you turned up the agoraphobic guy so I could get DeVoe off my back. You sneaked around, found the dude, and finked to Maisie. The deal's off, you little kiss-ass."

Anders had ambled in from the field, and he flopped his colossal body into his chair just as Webber began his diatribe. He listened, and when Webber shut up, Anders reached across the aisle to hand me a card with the number.

"I'm really grateful for your support, Anders. Thank you." I said, wondering if Webber might feel a twinge of regret for his churlish behavior.

Webber ignored my comment, ripped open a package of Hostess cupcakes, and stuffed one in his mouth before opening the case folder where he stored his Playboy magazines.

I called the INS number and spent the rest of the afternoon working my way through a chain of staffers who might have been spawned by DeVoe—devoid of any compassion. At last, I connected with a senior investigator who agreed that the family should stay intact.

"Absolutely," he said. "We'll haul the girl out of the attic and deport them all."

Now what? I called Legal Aid. "We're swamped and can't stop the INS. Your best bet is to appeal to a politician who has a Hispanic constituency—humanitarian intervention, and such. Probably won't work though."

God, the guilt. I had to tell the Garcías they were in jeopardy—because I was too *stupid* to keep my mouth shut about Theresa.

"Going back to the field," I told Maisie, grabbing my coat.

"At 4:45 on a Friday?" she asked.

"I have to. I don't feel right about this."

*　　　　　*　　　　　*

When I arrived at their house, Mrs. Garcia answered the door with a smile, worsening my apprehension. I struggled to find words she might understand, and she understood the message when I blurted, "INS, maybe pronto."

The smile disappeared, and disbelief, fear and disgust filled her eyes. I'll never forget the expression on her worn face—the woman had trusted me, and I betrayed her. She shut the door.

I couldn't undo what I had done to the Garcías, but I vowed to never again be cowed by threats to my job.

To do this work, I needed to be an advocate protecting clients not just from the perils of society but from those inherent in the welfare system. I had to know the rules and how far to look the other way without putting the client at risk.

Mrs. Dickson, my Latin teacher, had perceived honor as a black or white choice, so this was a big lesson in the gray nuances of integrity. Bottom line?

I ought to have left Theresa at peace in the attic.

CHAPTER TWENTY-FIVE

I wallowed in remorse, pounding myself without mercy Friday evening and into Saturday morning.

Then reality intruded. The García's were most likely tucked away in a safe house in Berkeley by now, and if I didn't knock it off, I'd look as if I had spent the night at the Hotel Will Rogers.

My appointment at the hairdresser's, thanks to Rita's intervention, was for 1:30, and I left Mom's deep-freeze early because I wasn't sure of where I was going.

The Salon de Alfonzo sounded fanciful and turned out to be a small, ornate shop on Lakeshore Avenue—close to the bustling traffic around Lake Merritt, Oakland's shimmering centerpiece in the middle of the city.

I parked in front of the building, stepped up over a steep curb to the sidewalk, and hesitated in the tiled doorway.

The door was flung open by a knock-out handsome man in his mid-forties. His brown hair, lightly frosted, was slicked straight back to showcase his bronzed face and pale blue eyes.

"Come in, my dear," he gushed. "You must be Amy. Rita told me how you ditched her stingy drab nephew and now you've got a hot prospect. We'll make sure he doesn't get away."

"Thank you for squeezing me in on a busy Saturday," I said.

"My pleasure. I love a challenge."

He ushered me in and steered me to a raised chair illuminated by spotlights. I sat down and stared at my reflection in a gilded mirror.

"I'm terrified of perms." My words spurted out.

"With that straight hair? It would be criminal. No, we're going to do a light frosting—subtle streaks, softer than what you have now. After that, I'll give you a fabulous cut. See this?"

He thrust a magazine under my nose, turned to an article featuring an innovative British hairdresser named Sassoon.

"His work will become the new wave, and you have the perfect hair for a geometric cut."

He opened a drawer and whipped out a rubber cap punctured with hundreds of tiny holes.

"Hang on," he said and yanked the tight cap over my skull. Next, he reached for a little pick and used it to pull individual strands of my hair, one-by-one, through the openings. I looked like an electrocuted mop when he finished poking and pulling. Then he mixed white goo in a bowl, picked up a flat brush, and painted the hair sprouting from the holes.

"Now, my precious, Amber will do your nails while the bleach is working. Then she'll rinse it off, give you a quick shampoo, start on your makeup, and I'll cut your hair. Every four weeks for a trim and color touchup. You'll be cutting-edge fantastic. Did you get it? Cutting-edge cut? Sometimes my wit astounds me."

"Thank you so much, Mr. Alfonzo," I said when I left three hours and half a paycheck later.

"Call me Mr. Al, dear. Now go break a leg."

If it didn't work out with Matt, I would spend the rest of my life living with my mother in semi-destitution, but it was worth it. My hair was gorgeously highlighted and cut to fall perfectly straight, just short of shoulder-length. And Amber was a wizard with nails and makeup.

The rest of my paycheck disappeared when I raced into Capwells and bought the tiniest bottle of Arpege Eau de Parfum I could find.

*   *   *

Thrilled with my slicked-up style, I was home by 5:30. I hurried to my room, ignoring Mom's withering glance. Dad peered over the sporting green section of the Chronicle. He gave me an enormous smile, a thumbs-up, and retreated like a turtle into his protective newspaper shell.

I changed into my second-best cocktail dress, a long-sleeved cream-colored crepe shift with little silver pearls lining the cuffs and the rounded neckline. My shoes were non-descript suede beige pumps and not worrisome because I could do nothing about them. And the final touch—a dash of Arpege.

My overriding worry—how obnoxious would Mom be when Matt picked me up? My fingers were coiled, and I dug my perfectly manicured and pink-polished nails into the palms of my hands to distract from my anxiety.

Dad, cordial as ever, answered the door when the bell rang at 6:30.

My whole being quivered when Matt, slender and striking in a dark navy business suit, made another dashing entrance. I dissolved at the sight of him.

"Good to see you, Mr. Archer," he said.

"No, Matt. Call me Henry. No 'sirs' either. Makes me feel old." Dad's smile equated to a thumbs up.

"Got it." Matt then turned toward me. His blue eyes sparkled.

"Wow, Amy. You are *stunning*."

I felt a flush rising through my entire body. *Vi called it right—make him proud you're on his arm.*

Then Matt glanced in Mom's direction. Her icy glare defied him to address her as anything other than Mrs. Archer, and she would have preferred that prefaced by 'Your Exalted Highness.'

How someone could be simmering hot and glacier cold at the same time was beyond me, but she pulled it off.

"Good evening, Mrs. Archer," Matt said. His smile was hopeful.

"At least you're punctual," she responded. Icicles dripped.

Matt wisely refocused on Dad. They rehashed the Washington Huskie's surprising win over top ranked Minnesota in the Rose Bowl while Matt helped me into my winter-white wool coat.

"You kids have fun," Dad said. Mom rose from her throne, Medusa minus the snakes, so we darted out the door before her petrifying gaze turned us to stone.

"My God, she's tough." Matt shook his head as he helped me into his car.

Has she ruined it again? The thought stabbed my heart.

Matt slid into the driver's seat, looked at me, reached over to take my hand, and grinned. I couldn't suppress a wave of giggles, mostly from nervous relief, and then the two of us were overcome with laughter, delighting in a newfound alliance.

This will be okay.

*   *   *

Miniature palm trees dominated the entry to Sanford's and surrounded the reception desk. As we slipped through the glass doors, Matt slid his arm around my waist and brushed my cheek with his lips. My knees went weak.

"Cocktails and dinner, sir?" a voice inquired through the foliage. Matt nodded an authoritative *yes* toward the fronds as I struggled to regain my composure and control my thoughts. *He's so worldly and attractive.* What does he see in simple me? How could this impossibly attractive, urbane man not be put off by the anomaly of my ankle?

I followed the maître-d as he led us to a candle-lit, semi-circular booth. Matt and I instinctively slipped around on the tufted faux-leather seat and snuggled thigh-to-thigh. Gardenias' floated in small containers at each place setting. Thank God I figured out they were finger bowls.

A waiter appeared, bearing three elaborately bound menus. He handed Matt two of them—one for cocktails and a dinner menu with prices quoted. The dinner menu he gave me didn't list prices.

"Do you need a moment, or would you like to order a cocktail while you peruse our offerings?" he asked.

"I think we'll order cocktails now," Matt said.

"Very good, sir. What would the lady like?" the waiter asked Matt.

"A dry Rob Roy, please," I murmured to Matt. Ladies were not to address wait-staff directly, according to Mom's social mentor, Emily Post, whose column in the newspaper she never missed.

I had no notion of what the cocktail was, but Bette Davis had ordered one in a movie in which she had epitomized sophistication.

Matt asked for a scotch on the rocks, and we waited while a busboy fussed with water glasses, a basket of croissants, and rosettes of butter in an iced dish.

"Special occasion?" the waiter asked when he returned with our drinks.

"Very special," Matt replied. My heart skipped. *Please, please like me.*

The waiter stifled an indulgent smile and suggested we try their prix-fixe dinner for two—a Caesar Salad, Beef Wellington, and Cherries Jubilee.

"Sounds great to me," Matt said. I nodded in agreement.

Matt was more intoxicating than the drink. God, he looked *so* good. Crystal blue eyes, thick brows, high cheekbones, square jaw. I couldn't stop admiring him through my spider-leg lashes. And to feel his firm thigh against mine—insanely distracting, as was his familiar faint scent of musk.

We talked sports, books, weather—anything to divert the potent chemistry that crackled between us. And not one word was about a bug or a carburetor.

The waiter reappeared with a rolling cart and entertained us for twenty minutes preparing the salad—lettuce torn into one-inch pieces, raw eggs whipped, anchovies mashed, garlic pressed, cheese shredded.

A grand production, and our entrée, filet mignon coated in paté and wrapped in a puff pastry, was delicious—but not what we were hungry for. Mesmerized by each other, we picked at the food and smiled promises to come.

Another cart appeared with the makings for the dessert, and somehow our conversation shifted to politics.

Oops. Potential disaster. Matt was a Republican into conservative economics. Not one of the raving John Birchers, whom Mom thought were voices from the heavens, but not on my leftist page.

The elephant peeked over my shoulder. *Let Matt know where you stand. If this is a deal-breaker, better to find out now.*

"I don't understand far right politicians who are always shouting about states' rights. What they're really doing is lining their own pockets while they slash programs to punish the poor," I said, voicing my indignation.

"How could anyone begrudge a person food, shelter, and a chance for a decent life?" I asked and stopped short.

No, no, don't go there. Shut up. You sound like Anders on a rant, and Matt will think you're a Berkeley nutcase. "Maybe you are," the elephant sassed before fading.

I visualized a 49er face-guard and muzzled my mouth.

Was Matt put off? He'd listened but not said a word.

Please, please don't be offended.

Then he broke into his irresistible grin.

"Of course, you have a liberal viewpoint—you're a social worker. I admire your compassion and commitment," he said, seemingly bemused.

Then he took my hand. He was neither put off nor

turned off. Our fingers laced, our eyes locked, and I would have voted for Richard Nixon.

I was completely overwhelmed by his nearness. A public kiss was unthinkable, so we sat entwined in delicious frustration while the waiter torched the cherries in brandy. My resolve to heed Vi's advice and play a little hard-to-get flew out the window. How could I do that when I was completely gaga?

Leaving the restaurant, Matt and I stole a moment behind a palm. He bent to take my face in his hands. I rose to my toes as best I could for my lips to meet his. An exquisite, lingering kiss. And on some unspoken level, we both knew.

We belonged together.

*   *   *

I dared to scoot over next to Matt on the way home, careful not to impede the turning of the hula-hoop sized steering wheel or the functioning of the formidable clutch rising from the center of the floorboard.

He parked in front of the house, and we indulged in another kiss. I tingled to my toes. And then a couple more kisses. The tingling evolved into undeniable lust, inhibited by middle-class propriety and the steering wheel. Plus the clutch was as constraining as an Amish bundling board.

Matt pulled himself together with commendable discipline. "Guess we'd better get you inside," he said.

"*She'll* be waiting down there," I cautioned. My racing heart suddenly became heavy and resigned to another humiliating scene.

"With her saltshaker?" he asked.

"And a tomato stake. Sometimes she spears the poor things."

"Yikes. Do you think they feel pain?"

"I think all creatures feel their own kind of pain," I said.

Matt smiled his entrancing smile.

"You *do* have the heart of a social worker." He slid out of the driver's seat and came around to open the car door for me.

The porch light was on, but I noticed another unfamiliar beam coming from somewhere as we started down the steps.

Suddenly we were assaulted by a blinding light. When I could see again, scowling Mom was standing in the kitchen window with her Eveready flashlight, scanning the garden to capture any sign of movement. She was not looking for bugs.

"Too much. Hold on," Matt said and turned to jog back up the stairs. He sprinted to the car, opened the trunk, and pulled out a large emergency roadside flood light.

He aimed it carefully at the kitchen window and flipped a switch to turn it on.

Mom was a deer in the headlights. Her eyes glazed, her mouth fell open, and her hair actually moved when she reared backwards and then lunged forward to close the blinds.

"I don't dissolve in salt, and she'd better realize that I'm not going away." He chortled.

The joy fluttered back into my heart.

CHAPTER TWENTY-SIX

When I walked into the office Tuesday morning, Maisie's desktop was a checkerboard of Tums. I took off my trench coat to hang it on the rack. The dry cleaner had fumigated it well.

"What's happening?" I sensed this was not the right time to ask if I could take on Harbor Homes. I obsessed over DeVoe's insult and wanted to prove I could handle whatever she threw at me.

"Shit. I don't want to talk about it. My mother and dumb-ass brother Georgie are coming for lunch at the Jade Palace tomorrow," Maisie said.

"A reunion or celebration?" I asked, surprised because she'd never mentioned her family before.

"More like the last meal before the execution. You think you have it bad with your mom? Mine is a total nightmare. I grew up in San Francisco, and Ma still lives there. She's the *Empress* Tang, breathing fire down Grant Street. My dorky brother lives with her, and he's her number one house-boy.

Maisie lit a cigarette and continued to vent. "We had a Mexican nanny, but Ma supervised all meals. She'd sit me on my booster seat at the kitchen table and yammer at me.

"'Empty rice bowl. Every grain not eat become pock-mark on face.' I was the fattest little kid in Chinatown. Then it was 'Fat girl. Fat girl. No get husband.' God, no wonder I ended up with chronic indigestion and Hubert Li."

Maisie seldom spoke of her husband, and when she did, she never called him by his first name. It was always "Hubert Li," as if to maximize a separateness and distance.

She paused and then said, "If you were my real friend, you'd come to lunch with me tomorrow."

I couldn't refuse that invitation.

"Well, okay," I answered, "but I don't even know your mother's name."

"It's Pansy but be careful to address the Empress as Mrs. Tang and bow a lot, because she'll freak when she finds out my best friend is a gringo. She's a bigot and hates anyone who's not Chinese."

"Then maybe I shouldn't go."

"Screw it. Ma will have to suck it up."

"How did she get a name like Pansy?"

"The family dropped their Chinese names when they came from China and picked new ones to be more American. Lily, Rose, Peony, Iris—I have a flowerpot of aunts. All the sisters do is play mah jongg, flash their colors, and one-up each other. My kiss-ass cousins are always after the colors—buttering up, hauling the old ladies around, flaunting their sticky, whiney kids."

"Colors?"

"Jewelry. Huge precious gemstones and gobs of apple-green jade they brought with them from China. Ma lives over Uncle Harold's jewelry shop, and he smuggled in more in the heels of his shoes for years. Now he's too old, and it's too risky."

Maisie had promoted me from a real friend to a best friend in short order, and of course I went with her.

*   *   *

The Jade Palace was the finest teahouse in Oakland's Chinatown. Maisie's mother and brother Georgie were to arrive early to claim a table at the popular restaurant.

They snagged the best one, next to the death-row fishtank full of crabs and lobsters, not because of their arrival time, but because of Mrs. Tang's stunning display of colors and the imperial presence she projected.

A tiny-boned bird-lady, she appeared fragile. It surprised me that the weight of her jewelry didn't topple her. The vibrant green emerald on her thin finger extended from knuckle to knuckle, and a double row of diamonds surrounded the gleaming stone.

She wore her graying black hair pulled back into a severe bun, so the matching earrings were in full view—so large they touched the top of her black brocade mandarin collar. Amazing how she kept her balance with all that hanging on her ears.

Maisie and I approached the table, and Maisie reluctantly muttered brief introductions to her mother and brother.

"I'm honored to meet you, Mrs. Tang." I spoke with what I hoped was sufficient deference.

Peering intently, her head framed from behind by doomed crustaceans, she put on a gracious face upon encountering my Caucasian one, nodded, and abruptly dismissed me with her shrewd eyes.

Then she turned toward Maisie and unleashed a brutal assault. Maisie didn't stand a chance.

"You smell—you smoke! Not good. Not suitable for wife to smoke."

Mrs. Tang paused her attack to commandeer a waiter rolling a three-tiered tea cart stacked with dim sum delicacies.

"Har Gow. Shiu Mai," she ordered, examining the plates. "No egg cup sweet. Make fat." She directed an evil eye toward Maisie.

"No lobster dumpling," she added, noting Georgie's longing gaze. "Cost too much. Eat lobster today, eat fish-heads and rice forever."

Mrs. Tang's scrutiny of the cart continued.

"Fun Gor no good. Too dinky. Puny, like Hubert. Sesame seed boy," she snorted.

What? I couldn't begin to digest that one.

Then she shifted her attention back to her bad seed.

"Why no babies?" the Empress demanded of Maisie, who by now looked more pitiful than the one-clawed crab on the bottom of the fish tank.

"Shameful you work. Wife should not work. You not smoke, dinky Hubert do better, baby comes. No baby, no colors."

Geez. My mom could do a number, but she wasn't in this league. Mrs. Tang's wrath might be diverted from Maisie if we focused on the food.

"You've chosen delicious dishes, Mrs. Tang." I picked up a sesame-chicken wonton with my chopsticks.

The Empress froze and then covered her face with her napkin and burst out in a Cantonese tirade. Then she stood up, placed the napkin on her chair, and left the table. And everyone in the restaurant was staring at me, not her.

"What's wrong? What did I do? What was she saying?" I asked, shrinking into my seat. My cheeks burned with mortification.

"It's all over for you." Maisie chuckled.

"Why?"

"You're a left-handed chop-sticker, a disgraceful social transgression in Ma's mind. At least you'll never have to eat with her again. I should try it."

"Ma called you a peasant, Amy. Sorry. I'll take her home," Georgie said.

He rose from the table and followed his mother to the entry door where she stood, the epitome of a martyred matriarch. Mrs. Tang steadied herself with a hand atop the bald scalp of a gold replica of Bhudda. A perfect backdrop to showcase her emerald ring.

Then the two exited with Mrs. Tang clinging to Georgie's arm as she fanned herself with a takeout menu. Georgie gave us a back-handed wave with his other arm.

Maisie and I remained seated, staring at one another.

"I wish this place had a liquor license," she said.

"You set me up for this, didn't you?" I asked, mildly annoyed as my embarrassment diminished.

"It was fun to see someone else pummeled for a change." She chuckled again. "You white devil squaws sure turn red when you're embarrassed."

"Have you ever done anything right?" I asked.

"No. Not from day one. Because I'm a girl, and girls are no good. Plus, the Empress had to have another kid to get a boy which was also my fault."

"How can you take it?" I asked, feeling so bad for Maisie that I split the last shrimp dumpling in half to share.

"I can't. Why do you think I married Hubert Li? When I was going to U.C. Berkeley I lived in a dorm, but after I graduated, Ma expected me to return home and live with her. The only way out was to get hitched. Why else would I be with that tight-assed little sesame seed? I seduced him in the back seat of his second-hand Chevy, and he had to do the honorable thing. The *sap*."

She ranted on.

"Georgie stammers because he was born left-handed. Ma would sit him in his highchair and tie a Porky Pig bib on him. Then she'd place a cup of Gerber's baby food and a baby spoon on the tray. He'd always pick up the spoon with his left hand, but she'd take it away and switch it to his right hand."

"'Clean plate. Pock marks,' she'd be jabbering at me. Then Georgie would stick the spoon in the cup and try to fling it sideways into his mouth. The mashed carrots were the worst. Orange blobs stuck in his black hair, in his ears, flying over his shoulder all over the kitchen."

"The nanny had to clean it up. Ma treated her like a slave, but Lola got even by teaching us every swear word she knew in English and her native Spanish. Ma forced Georgie to write with his right hand, so he almost flunked out of school, but to her a stammering ignoramus was better than a left-handed chop-sticker."

"Why was it such a big deal?"

"How would I know? Maybe because everyone sat at round tables and the left-handed person would be out of sync."

We left it at that.

CHAPTER TWENTY-SEVEN

The morning of Valentine's Day, I watched from the kitchen window as a florist brushed by Mom's camellias on his way down the brick stairs. He delivered a gorgeous bouquet of roses—the deepest red I'd ever seen.

I met the guy at the door, but he'd already rung the bell. Mom heard it and huffed into the kitchen. She stopped short when she saw the flowers. If I hadn't been home, I know she would have trashed every beautiful stem.

Mom was hell-bent on sabotaging every move Matt made as he orchestrated a beautiful courtship

"I don't like hot-house rose." Mom's hands were on her hips in her favored defiant stance. And her scowl would have withered a rain forest.

"Matt sent them to *me*, Mom," I said, enchanted.

"Too bad. There's not enough room in this house for my roses and his."

So, the following week Matt had flowers delivered to the office, captivating me, Vi a little, and Maisie not so much.

"Kid, don't be a pushover," Vi cautioned. "Might be he's all talk—it's too soon to tell. Smell them roses, smile pretty, and keep your eyes open."

Maisie thought Matt sounded flaky and that the flowers

were an over-the-top ploy. They annoyed her until she realized they also irritated the guys.

"Jesus Christ, where's the teapot and doilies? What's with the roses?" Anders asked. He stared at the vase on my desk filled with long-stemmed red buds and baby's-breath.

He'd just come in from the field, disheveled as usual, and threw his line-backer-sized body into his chair. Anders had a bland, Nordic-type face and might have been attractive if he wasn't so lumpy and sloppy.

"The pullet's got a new boyfriend." Webber paused over his retirement calculations to make the announcement. He sounded disgusted.

"What happened to bug-boy?" Anders asked.

"Guess she shot him down." Webber shrugged.

"God-damn women. They're all ball-busters like DeVoe, and they'll finish us off." Anders said.

He almost finished himself off. Anders sat down, tucked his huge feet in the bottom drawer of his desk, and rolled up his crumpled shirtsleeves. Next, he lit his pipe, leaned back, and pontificated.

Railing at the global plight of the working classes and the greed and callousness of the ruling elite, he knocked the pipe ashes into the metal wastebasket beside him.

When a flame shot up from the smoldering contents, Anders had worked himself into such a lather over the injustices to farm workers that he didn't notice the fire until the heat hit his elbow.

"*Augh*." Bolting reflexively, Anders might have escaped harm, but his right foot was wedged in the drawer, and he catapulted nose-first into Moroni's metal file cabinet.

"Fire," Webber shouted, starting a stampede to the elevators.

"No, take the stairs," someone with brains yelled.

"Webber, staunch the bleeding," Moroni called out as he raced to the far wall for the fire extinguisher.

Webber grabbed Moroni's Italian silk blazer and muzzled Anders' spurting nose, while Moroni struggled to remove the extinguisher from the niche where it had rested undisturbed for twenty-or-so years.

Maisie picked up my vase, plucked out the flowers, and soaked Webber's head as she poured the remaining water into the wastebasket. She later insisted she had to douse Webber to reach the flames.

DeVoe observed the spectacle from her office doorway, including the subsequent realignment of Anders' nose.

"Buffoons," she snarled before slamming her door shut.

Then she opened the door and stuck out her bee-hived head. "Archer, this is an office and I will not tolerate frivolity. Remember, you're on probation for an entire year. Have you been to Harbor Homes yet?" *Slam.*

*　　　*　　　*

I'll show that evil woman—I'm perfectly capable of handling this assignment.

Dark thoughts filled my head as the VW chugged over a raised ramp leading away from the populated fringe of West Oakland.

I started out the following morning with three objectives: to prove DeVoe wrong, to conquer Harbor Homes, and to locate Mary Jo Johnson, whose renewal application for Family Assistance was overdue.

A two-mile long overpass bridged industrial yards and dumps and merged onto a bumpy road—the only way in or out of Harbor Homes. It weaved along abandoned docks and dead-ended at water's edge.

What a stunning view, I thought, bringing the VW to a stop at the end of the road. Postcard perfection with the bay sparkling and San Francisco's skyline in the background.

I sized up the rest of the scene.

The housing project—constructed for shipyard workers during World War II—was an isolated cluster of decomposing barracks. Not a tree or shrub or blade of grass distracted from the ugly, dilapidated buildings. Dead weeds covered the dry dirt of the unpaved, littered parking area and choked the pathways.

I parked the VW and sat in the eerie stillness. No sound broke the silence, and not a soul was in sight.

Where is everyone?

Shivering with apprehension, I decided I had three choices.

Sit here and spook yourself out more, go back to the office and be stigmatized forever as a candy-assed female, or go find Mary Jo Johnson.

I got out of the car, slipped on my coat, and started up a thistle-choked path, plowing through the burrs.

Curtains moved behind broken windowpanes, and I knew eyes were following me.

Don't panic.

A sound—what was it? Movement.

I froze, petrified. Ahead of me, blocking the dirt path, were four menacing thugs who'd just come out of what appeared to be a shed.

Trapped and rooted in terror, I was afraid to go forward and afraid to turn my back on them.

A door opened to my left.

"Pssst. Girl! Get in here—fast."

I did, with my heart racing and pounding in my ears.

"What you be doin' out there? You crazy? Got no sense—just like my little sister Cassie," the woman scolded.

"Thank you very much for letting me in." Leaning against the wall to pull myself together, I looked around. I was in a battered rectangular cracker-box, about 12 by 20 feet, divided into two halves—a living area with stairs going to a second story, and a kitchen with a back door.

"I'm Amy Archer from Social Services, and I'll be taking Mr. Moroni's place," I managed to say.

"The Welfare send *you?* White folks is fools. I'm Alice Parsons. Have a seat." She gestured to a listing sofa and sat herself down with a grunt. A large woman, she wore a faded housedress and nylon stockings rolled to just below her knees.

"You got weeds stuck all over you, girl. Bad news, them hoods. They strips all the machines from the washhouse, and the gangs take over dealin' drugs. Can't do no laundry. If you got to come here, park over on the other side and cut through the back. And come early. They be lay'n up in the bed in the mornin'."

Bam. The front door flew open and three giggling little stair-step children charged through and out the kitchen door, chased by a lumbering woman.

"That be my sister, Cassie," Mrs. Parsons said. "Fell in a pond and almost drown when she eight. Not been right since—still a little kid in her head. They's all her babies and they's just playin.' I look after 'em, but I be tired out. Can't do no more a Cassies's kids after this last one. I tell Doc Jefferson he better fix things, and he say he already did. Hope so.

"I take the kids to Doc Jefferson for shots and stuff, but it be hard, 'cause I got to round up Cassie to go with us, and she sneak out on me. Same thing at school. Can't do nothin' unless I be the mama."

"There's something called a legal guardianship that might make things easier for you. Would you like me to check it out?" I asked. She nodded yes.

"Do you have kids, Mrs. Parsons?"

"I got one boy, Tyrone. Scrub a lot a white folk's floors so he go to St. Vincent's Day School. Nuns slap him upside the head and smack him with a ruler, and he be too scared to run the streets. He be outta here now—doin' good in the Army. Rest of us not gonna make it out, though."

As she talked, the smell of gas distracted me. I could see flames on the stove-top from where I sat.

"Mrs. Parsons, did you know you left the burners on in the kitchen?" I asked.

"Sure. Furnace don't work. Nobody's do. No other way to get warm."

The combustible potential of the tinderboxes was frightening.

"Won't the Housing Authority fix the furnaces?"

"Course not. And if you complains, you gets evicted. That's how it works."

"Are there any fire extinguishers around?" My question seemed reasonable. Her expression was quizzical, then resigned.

"Course so—and they parks shiny red fire engines on every corner, so we be safe and sound. You got no street-smarts, do you?"

"I guess not, Mrs. Parsons. Maybe you'd better show me the back way to get in here."

"I bet you lookin' for that Jezebel, Mary Jo. She vamp Mr. Morry outta all the vouchers and the rest of us don't get none," she said, heaving herself up and off the sofa.

Mrs. Parsons led me to the kitchen door and pointed out the rear pathway. She waved her arm, and I thought she was waving goodbye to me.

Then I saw several curtains moving and realized she was sending a message to her neighbors. Things were okay—I was harmless.

"Girl, watch your back," she cautioned in parting. "Anybody give you trouble, you come straight here. Any time. I'm used to lookin' out for folks that got no sense."

CHAPTER TWENTY-EIGHT

"**W**hat you doin' here, whitey?"

I'd found Mary Jo Johnson. She lived two buildings over, off a pathway snarled with more weeds and foxtails. The front door to her cracker-box was open, and strings of black beads hung Moroccan-style from the top of its frame.

Mrs. Johnson slinked behind the beads. Before I could knock, she had parted the bobbles to ask her belligerent question.

Hoping to deflect the waves of hostility coming my way, I introduced myself.

"My name is Amy Archer and I'm from Social Services. Mr. Moroni transferred to another job, and I'm taking his place."

"Shee-it," she said. She pulled aside the beads and let me in. "You got burrs on your knees. Your ass too. How'd they get up there?" she asked as I walked passed her into the dismal front room.

This *was* a rough place.

"I don't know." I shrugged off my coat and noticed foxtails embedded all over the backside. Had she meant her questions to be insults? Yes, she had. No mistaking her intent—or the reasons for Moroni's ill-advised fascination.

Gorgeous. That's the only word that did Mrs. Johnson

justice. A perfect nose between high cheekbones and enormous doe eyes. Lush hair that flowed to fall to her shoulders. Cocoa skinned, sultry, and her hot pants and halter overflowed. Vi might have made her a star, except she was only eighteen and already had three children.

She stared at the potato sack I was wearing. The dark beige shift resembled a brown-paper grocery-store bag, but I had to follow the Major's dress code until I was off probation.

"Ugly. Nobody gonna be lookin' down that," she said, her voice full of scorn. "Not that there's somethin' to see. Maloni kept droppin' his papers for me to bend over."

My ego deflated more than my front.

"Mr. Moroni was wrong to do that," I didn't know what else to say.

"Oh, I like it fine. Got me lots of vouchers. Not gettin' nothin' off no skinny white girl, though. Shee-it." She studied me with disgust—until a cagey look replaced the hostility in her eyes.

"I gotta get outta here. Maybe y'all *can* help." She motioned for me to sit on a tattered stuffed chair missing one foot.

Beads rained down from every door in the ratty apartment. The two toddlers were competing to see who made the most noise rattling them. I tried to focus.

"What do you have in mind?" I asked.

"I got a job counselor who keeps tellin' me to go to nurse-aid training or cosmetology school. Don't make no sense. Can't pay for no sitter if I go to school, and those jobs don't pay nothin' anyway. Got me another plan."

"Which is?" I inquired, noting her cunning expression.

"See, I go uptown and meet this guy in a club. Kinda old—thirty—but I hook him big."

Careful, please don't tell me too much.

"Lamar got a job, and he don't live in no project. Got a place almost to the hills. He say he marry me, and we all go live there if his mama like me. 'You come to her birthday party,' Lamar say, 'but you can't be lookin' like you struttin' the street.' See, his daddy be black, but his mama be white. Y'all look and talk like somethin' a honky mother'd take to."

I sifted the concept from the slam.

"You want to look and talk more like I do?"

Her distaste was palpable as she struggled to a decision.

"Only for the party. Can't take no chance. If his mama don't like me, Lamar be gone."

"When is the party?"

"Saturday."

It was Tuesday. Could she be toned down enough to get by honky-style?

"Okay," I agreed, "but you can't be angry if I make a few suggestions. This whole thing is your idea and might not work. All white people aren't alike and don't always think the same way."

"Well, y'all sure look the same."

*   *   *

The challenge was on, and we both tried, hard.

"What about putting your hair up or back in a fancy braid?"

She looked skeptical.

"How about some different shoes—more like mine?"

She was repelled. Didn't fault her for that—so was I.

"The shorts and halter won't work out too well. Do you have anything else, or could you borrow a plain dress?"

"How 'bout that brown thing y'all got on? Then I be cracker ugly all the way."

The loan of clothing was not on the Major's list of prohibitions, probably because he'd never thought of anything so preposterous. I was now as vested as Mrs. Johnson in her exodus from the flatlands as well as from my caseload.

"Sure. I'll bring it by on Thursday," I told her.

Mrs. Parson had given me lots to work on, but I made a quick trip to the field to drop off the dress, neatly hanging in a plastic bag, on Thursday morning.

Mary Jo Johnson opened the door, still in her baby-doll costume, but one of the several hundred cosmetology aspirants inhabiting the premises had braided her flowing hair into an intricate twist.

"Your hairstyle is lovely," I said.

"If y'all say so," she grumbled. "I got a girl-friend two doors down, and she loaned me these." She waved a wedge-heeled pair of bone-colored sandals at me.

"They'll be just right," I told her.

"I'm tryin' on that thing before you take off." She grabbed the plastic bag and stomped into the bedroom, causing another cascade of beads to rattle.

When she emerged, she had poured herself into the dress. It wasn't a tube on her as it was on me. Stretched tight across her front and rear, she could scarcely move her arms or bend over to pick up the baby.

That was as far as she'd go with the makeover.

"Any more and that man not gonna want me no more. Lamar be gone. You got a man?"

The question was part taunt and part pity, since she'd already dismissed this possibility.

"I'm working on it. Now, when you're at the party, try not to say anything unless you need to. Stick to 'yes, please' or 'no, thank you.' How about saying something nice, like 'what a fine son you've raised.'"

"You jivin' me?"

"No. You're the one who said you can't get him if his mama doesn't approve. Why don't you just keep your mouth full of cake?"

Would it work? Please, oh please.

*   *   *

Meanwhile, I had a lot of business to follow-up with for Alice Parsons.

I went back to Legal Aid for yet another consultation. Lynn was convinced that legal intervention was the only way to assail the appalling injustices we saw.

She planned to enroll in Hastings Law program as soon as her boy-friend Pete completed high school and college. (His disgusted parents decided that if Lynn was so hot for their son, she should finish raising and educating him.)

"A voluntary guardianship would do it," the law clerk told me. "Then the aunt would be able to authorize medical care and handle school business. I'll add her name to the list."

"This is urgent. How long is the list?" I asked.

"She'll be number 246. They're all emergencies, and no one has time to work on them except second-year students who help on semester breaks. We process only about twenty a year."

I couldn't find a quick fix for anything.

"Repair the furnaces at Harbor Homes? You must be kidding." This outrageous response came from the executive assistant to the director of the Housing Authority. "Fire extinguishers? The city's responsible," he said. "Pilot lights? Pacific Gas and Electric does that."

"An inferno if it goes up, but the Feds have to furnish the extinguishers," the city fire people insisted.

"We don't touch pilot lights at Harbor Homes," the gas company guy told me. "Those furnaces are shot, so they go out as soon as they're lit. Whole place can blow up, but it's all on the Housing Authority."

The buck was passed around and around without a single expression of concern for the plight or safety of the inhabitants of the miserable project.

Anders, who intended to avoid the field until the swelling went down and his nose could be identified, overheard my efforts and offered his opinion.

"Damn chicken-shit bureaucrats. The locals are indifferent jerks, but the big-time politicians are the real villains. The Feds have deliberately laid out the welfare regulations systemically to deprive blacks and keep them down.

"Look at the rules, Amy. Husband or boyfriend or father in the household? No welfare. Why? Oh, they'll just have more kids for the taxpayer to take care of, the party line goes. The real reason? To keep the men away so there's no family structure. No male figure for little boys to relate to— and the women have to go it alone. The same damned conditions that were forced on slaves."

His diatribe was impassioned, if a bit nasal, and gave me a lot to think about. Mom harped about women on welfare who had kid after kid for more money. For five dollars more a month? That's not what I saw.

*   *   *

The following week, I returned to Mrs. Parson's, dreading to tell her about the length of the guardianship list, but she met me at her back door and shrugged off her disappointment.

"Hope they get to me before the little one's growed," she said and shifted the conversation to hot news.

"You hear 'bout that Jezebel, Mary Jo?" she asked, nodding toward the Moroccan trail.

"No. What about her?"

"Movin' out. Uptown. Least she won't be hoggin' no more vouchers."

It was close to 6:00 p.m. by the time I worked my way to Mary Jo Johnson's door. She greeted me on the second knock with her original persona restored—red baby-dolls, stilettos, hair draped over her eye.

"How was the birthday party?" I asked, groping through the beads.

"Well, I do like you say," she said. "I eat a lot of cake. I tell Lamar's mama, 'you do good with Lamar—he good man. Cake's good too.' Know what she say to me?"

"I can't imagine."

"Girl, you pretty. But you dress so plain. You need stylin'. I'm gonna help you get fixed up."

She paused and then looked reflective. "She real nice. Got

white skin like you, but be talkin' like me. Give me a big hug, say to call her 'Mama' like Lamar do. My mama died when I was six. Left me with a man who say he my step-father."

Her eyes narrowed. She glowered. "He bad. Real bad. He be after me from the day she passed. When I be twelve, a preacher man and his wife take me in, but it be way too late."

And then a beautiful smile eased out the tension in her face.

"Y'all can cut me off the welfare. I be packin' up to move in with Lamar this weekend. Mama's gonna plan a weddin' for us."

I was awash in guilt again. She'd endured a horrible childhood of sexual abuse, which her highly seductive manor telegraphed, and I failed to pick up on it or to extend any empathy.

"You and Lamar are going to have a wonderful life. I'm truly happy for you," I said. My good wishes were sincere.

She smiled, nodded, and handed me my bundled-up dress.

"Sorry I busted the seams. Girl, y'all might could be fixed up some if you wasn't so flat."

CHAPTER TWENTY-NINE

"Look at this *stingy* little gold box."

Mom brandished the box of Godiva chocolates, the latest offering in Matt's courtship campaign. He never failed to phone, and thoughtful gifts kept popping up—a book, a card, a magazine—which Mom continued to diminish.

She removed the matching cord from the box and flipped open the top.

"And the candy's worse. Not a decent-sized bite in here." She popped the biggest one in her mouth, screwed her face into a sour grape, and all but spat it out.

"I don't like this chocolate. Too dark and bitter."

"He sent it to me, Mom."

"You'll get fat. Tell him I prefer See's candy."

When she realized her minor disparagements were not paying off, she went big-time.

Somewhere within the confines of Mom's narrow mind, the bigot-neurons fired up, and she shot off a favorite.

"He's Jewish," she declared.

"So why would that matter?" I asked. I understood her game as thoroughly as I had mastered the 49ers' offensive strategy and refused to bite.

"Don't you even *know*?" Her scorn was intended to shame.

"No, and I don't care." I imagined her in a synagogue filled with Hasidic Jews and watched her collapse into cardiac arrest. But the rabbi ruined the fantasy when he produced a defibrillator.

Determined to smoke out Matt's suspect origins, Mom invited him for the dreaded Archer family interrogatory dinner.

I relayed the invitation to Matt in the phone call that had become our evening ritual, a sure pathway to sweet dreams.

"She hates me. What's she up to?" he asked, puzzled by the outreach.

"No good, I assure you. Are you aware that you're Jewish?"

"How did she come up with that one?"

"Well, you don't qualify as Black, Asian, or Hispanic, so this was her next-best shot."

"I'll handle it." He chortled.

*   *   *

Matt stood in the doorway, impeccably dressed in trim navy slacks and a white, open-collar dress shirt. He held a paper bag in one hand and a sweet bouquet of pink tulips in the other.

"Hi, Matt. Come on in," Dad said. He'd opened the door at the first ring of the doorbell. Mom was at his side, exuding the cordiality of a stone pillar.

I stood behind them in the hallway, heart aflame at the sight of Matt. But my nerves shrieked at the prospect of another disastrous inquisition conducted by Mom.

"For you, dear lady." Matt smiled broadly as he handed

the bouquet to Mom. She had to unclench her fist to grasp the flowers.

"And for you, Henry," Matt said, handing Dad the paper bag. Dad reached into the bag and extracted a bottle of Manishevitz wine.

I knew it, Mom's face shouted.

"It's time to find out all about you, young man." Mom could not suppress the gleeful menace in her voice. She'd caught herself a Hebrew, and it was game-on.

She grasped Matt's elbow to shove him by me and down the hallway into the kitchen. No place in the living or dining rooms for the likes of him. The kitchen table was good enough.

Matt gave me a half-hug in passing, unable to escape Mom's rudder-like grip. "Trust me," he whispered.

The kitchen was divided by a mottled-yellow Formica counter. On one side were the necessities—the sink with Mom's large look-out window facing the garden, dishwasher, cooktop, refrigerator, double ovens set in the wall. The other half was intended to be a casual nook for eating.

Mom had a passion for Early American style maple furniture and had crammed the space with an oval table, a hutch, and four captain's chairs, leaving a maximum maneuverable distance of eighteen inches behind three of them.

Dad always sat at the far crest of the oval, nearest the door to the side yard where the garbage cans were stored. Technically, it was the head of the table, but in reality, Dad was pigeon-holed, exactly where Mom wanted him. She claimed the middle chair to his left, by the counter, and I was trapped opposite Mom.

The fourth seat faced Dad, and behind it, an archway led to the dining room, so there was lots of space for the occupant to move. Bob had been given the honor of this prime placement.

As we entered the kitchen, the tantalizing aroma of baking ham wafted from Mom's oven.

"Have a seat, Matt. How about a drink—bourbon on the rocks?" Dad asked.

"Sounds good, Henry. Thanks." Matt looked at the table setup and sensibly chose the location closest to him.

Bob's chair. Mom's face turned purple, and I thought a real coronary might be imminent, but she contained her fury and tightened her mouth into her pucker of disapproval.

Dad plunked ice cubes into two highball glasses, poured in some bourbon, and sat down at the table with Matt to talk football.

"How can I help, Mom?" I asked. My skin crawled with apprehension. I'd seen too many suitors bite the dust during this scene.

"Take the salad out of the refrigerator and put it on the table.

I opened the door to the fridge, and to my surprise found that she'd filled her best teak bowl with her shrimp salad—crispy lettuce, a ton of shrimp, slices of hard-boiled egg, avocado, light Louis dressing. A delicious salad usually served only on holidays or birthdays.

"Mom, this looks wonderful. Thank you for making something special for Matt."

"You bet I made it special for him," she muttered. "They can't eat it, you know."

"Who can't eat what?"

"Jews can't eat shellfish. I looked it up in the Encyclopedia. Some cockamamy nonsense about fins, scales, and hooves. Will you dish up the vegetables?"

"Sure." *And then I'll throw myself down the disposal.*

Next, she hustled to the oven and removed the pan holding the forbidden hunk of the unlucky pig. She placed the carcass, encased in a pineapple sarcophagus, on her carving board and sliced into it with her evil-looking Henckel saber.

I completed my task, scooping the boiled okra and mashed turnips into serving bowls. These were the veggies she prepared on the rare occasion of a visit from loathsome, draft-dodging cousin Buster.

Mom stood back, surveyed the table, and looked pleased as punch with the spread she had designed to out the infidel. We settled into our places and began to pass dishes.

I had to hold the bowls with both hands because I was shaking. I knew what was coming.

Sure enough, Mom attacked just as the turnip bowl reached Matt.

"Now, young man, just how do you make a living?" She leaned forward. Her wrists were on the table, a fork in one fist, and a knife in the other.

"I'm a salesman, Mrs. Archer. Right now I'm selling office systems." Matt scooped a teaspoon of turnips onto his plate.

"Staplers and hole-punches?" Mom scoffed.

"Not exactly." The platter of ham had made its way to him, and he piled several slices on his plate. "But I hate to discuss work, politics or religion over a fine meal. Look at this feast. *Ham.* What a treat. How did you know it was my favorite?"

She sputtered. Had he shut her down? No. Mom resumed her attack posture, drilling him with her eyes. She was determined not to be foiled by this fake Jew.

"I'd like to know all about your family." Her statement was a command.

"They're just fine. Thanks for asking, Mrs. Archer. How about yours?"

He had her number and deflected every intrusive question right back at her, while he chowed down two huge servings of ham and shrimp salad. Furious, she kept looking back and forth from Matt to her saber.

"Absolutely delicious. Excellent ham and fabulous salad. And the vegetables—how unique. I understand they're ethnic dishes popular in the Deep South. You have a broad culinary repertoire, Mrs. Archer. Thank you so much for a memorable meal."

Afraid to push his luck any farther, Matt graciously declined a piece of rutabaga pie, explaining we needed to leave to catch the 8:00 showing of the movie *Psycho,* for which he'd already bought tickets.

The choice of movie seemed appropriate to commemorate the occasion.

"Do you cook like her?" he asked, as we slid into his Impala.

"No. I can't cook at all. She's never let me in the kitchen."

"Thank God."

Why is he asking if I cook? Be still, I told my heart—and don't jump ahead of yourself, I admonished my head. Hard advice to take because I adored him.

*　　　　*　　　　*

"Trust me," Matt often said, and I did. I loved how he took charge and seemed unfazed by adversity. And his sense of humor, which adroitly camouflaged his single-minded drive to succeed.

"Amy, I can sell anybody anything. I'm just selling myself, whatever the product. It's the fun of making a cold call to a business and reeling them in that gets me going. What's neat about peddling office systems is the chance to evaluate a lot of companies. I enjoy working for this one, but if a better deal comes along, I'll grab it. I'm always on the lookout for new opportunities."

Maybe some of his confidence will rub off on me. I felt accepted and protected by him—as if he could manage anything that might go awry.

That was an over-reach.

"The exception is your mother," he noted. "She'll never buy into me, but I'm going to have a hell of a good ride baiting her."

My ideal man.

*　　　　*　　　　*

Whirlwind romances unfurl in novels, but in real life—and for me?

Yes.

It was as if Matt had snatched the fantasies hidden in my heart and was determined to make them come true.

Weekends were filled with enticements, so many that I began a journal so I would never forget.

San Francisco intrigued us. We strolled through Golden Gate Park hand-in-hand. Wandered through the De Young Museum enthralled with the Impressionists and puzzled by the Modernists. Stole little kisses behind the colonnades. Welcomed a pot of green tea at the Japanese Tea House.

The lush spectacle of flowers at the Conservatory led to a rash comment by Matt.

"Your mother would love this place. We should bring her."

I must have turned as white as the pristine lilies on display in front of us.

"A considerate thought, Matt, but do you want to be trapped with Mom in a car for a four-hour excursion?"

He turned whiter than me.

"Lost my head. Scratch that one. Let's catch a cable car to Fishermans Wharf." Crab-filled sour-dough sandwiches on the wharf, an abundance of pasta and garlic in North Beach, discreet kisses and cuddles when the fog rolled in—total enchantment.

And on the Oakland side of the bay, Sunday afternoon tea-dances at the Lake Merritt Hotel. Twice a month, big bands played in the Terrace Room overlooking the lake. A charming British couple gave complimentary ballroom lessons. We especially liked the tango where legs intertwined, and we were able to hold one another as tightly as decency permitted.

All the while, wherever we were, we were holding hands, laughing, cuddling, kissing—and agonizing in total physical frustration.

One Saturday afternoon, Matt wanted to check out Lake Merritt to see if we could rent a canoe. The guy at the boat house said it was too early in the season, but he steered us to a vendor on the dock selling food.

We bought our lunch from him. Shriveled salty hot dogs, stale buns, flat cokes, and we feasted—not on food but on each other. We sat on the grass under the branches of a huge old oak tree and cuddled up. Matt put an arm around me and reached over with his other arm to tilt my face toward him.

He kissed me. Scores of kisses had passed between us before, but this one was different. A soft kiss at first, but it grew firm, and I felt his fire and my own passion rose to match his.

We broke apart, but I *knew*. Matt was my man, and we would share a bed—soon.

Very soon.

"Will you spend next weekend with me in Monterey?" Matt asked as he helped me up off the grass. A green-headed, yellow-billed Mallard duck had waddled up for a handout with a mean glint in his little round eyes—sort of like the look Mom reserved for Matt.

I gave him my answer with another kiss, not the least bit subtle—pure passion.

*   *   *

Mom's reaction when I told her Matt had invited me to Monterey was a raw eruption. She was furious.

"I *forbid* you to see him." She stood at the ironing board, iron flailing. "I don't care what he says his name is. He ate all that ham, so he can't be Jewish, but I know in my bones—he's from foreign origins. Henry, stop her."

Dad was hiding behind the Sporting Green, ducking the flak with a shot or two of bourbon. To my surprise, he poked his head out and took a stand.

"Harriet, she's almost twenty-three and can do what she wants. Besides, I like him."

She slapped the iron down on the sleeve of a Pendleton shirt, steaming more than the iron.

"Missy, you're heading straight for disaster."

"No, I'm not, Mom. I'm heading down the coast with Matt."

*   *   *

Monterey was glorious—and the scenery was beautiful, too, what little we saw of it. The Pelican Inn was on the shoreline, just across the road from the beach. Our cozy, chintz-draped room was on the second floor, so we could see the bay sparkle in the pale winter sun.

That is, we noticed the view when we left the fluff of the downy bed long enough to look.

We couldn't stop touching one another. His skin was smooth and cool and hot underneath. I loved how he felt, and his touch, his smell, his passion. Was it magical because it was my first time? No, it was magic because of him.

I already loved him.

More weekends followed. We roamed up and down California's coast in a fog of infatuation and desire. I felt alive—completed at last, as my long-suppressed sexuality bloomed and layers of sensuality unfolded under Matt's seductive tutelage. I turned off the volume so I wouldn't hear an annoying voice in my head and refused to think about how he might have acquired his expertise.

The sensual was exquisite, but only part of our delight. Endless adventures of discovery. Carmel's trendy shops, kiosks serving delicate sand-dabs and fried calamari on the docks of Monterey's fairy-tale harbor, touristy cannery row and the John Steinbeck Museum, majestic Muir Woods. Knowing Matt would reach for my hand as we walked down a street, steal a kiss, sneak in a tender nuzzle.

Simply being in love.

*   *   *

One of our journeys led us to Point Lobos—a small, spectacular State Reserve edging the ocean with dramatic rock formations, groves of Monterey Cypress and Pine, and enchanting wildlife.

We wandered the trails, looking for otters in the kelp, barking harbor seals, and bellowing sea lions.

On our first visit, one path became uneven, and I explained to Matt that I had to stay on even ground because bumps, rocks and my ankle were a bad mix.

"Let's rest a few minutes." He found an enormous boulder for us to sit on.

"Tell me about your ankle," he said. So I did. He got the whole story sitting in a sea-side forest with gulls flapping above in the pure blue sky and the rippling ocean below rolling to the horizon.

I wasn't melodramatic—just matter of-fact—and ended the tale on an up-note.

"Mom and I made a follow-up visit to Dr. Whitecoat when I was about eleven. His starched coat still crackled, and he suggested, with absolute arrogance, that my legs might be uneven later in life, causing spine issues.

"'I'd like to shorten Amy's left leg as a precaution,' he said.

"Horrified, I looked at Mom, and for once, we were in complete accord. She grabbed my hand and pulled me out of that chamber of horrors for the last time."

When I finished my narrative, Matt leaned over and kissed my forehead.

"Tell me if anything we do is too much," he said.

I froze. A touching and sensitive move, yes. But alarming. Could this become *tsk, tsk, pity, pity*? I felt so whole with Matt. Had I ruined it all by being so open?

I faltered. What would Vi do? I heard her voice.

Kid, you know damn well what to do. You don't want sympathy, you want him. Go for it.

I turned to him, took his tanned face in my hands, looked into the blue pools of his eyes, and gave him a kiss that propelled us to a bed-and-breakfast in Carmel within the hour.

*　　　　　*　　　　　*

Matt spun the most awkward situations into something special. One weekend, we drove to Aptos intending to splash in the cold surf. But the tide was out, and I wasn't able to navigate the soft sand to reach the water's edge.

"I can handle this," he said when I explained the problem, and he swooped me up to carry and deposit me on solid sand compacted by the lapping waves.

No wonder I was afloat in a romantic blur. That's exactly where I wanted to be—in his arms forever.

CHAPTER THIRTY

"What's wrong?"

Maisie was sitting in a daze when I walked in Monday morning. The top of her desk was a checkerboard of Tums, a bad sign. The fellows, slumped at their desks, wore hang-dog expressions and seemed strangely subdued.

"Is DeVoe on her warpath? I asked, careful to glance behind neighboring file cabinets for the telltale beehive. I was still awash in a sensual glow from the weekend.

"The battle is over, and Moroni is the casualty," she said.

"What happened?" The vibe unsettled me.

"Moroni waltzed in this morning all spiffed up in a new sport coat. 'Vicuna wool,' he bragged. Then he went up to the lunchroom to get a bag of Fritos and spotted the new student intern on her way out. You know he has no filters, and he yakked about her rear end. 'Fabulous butt. Perfect bubble,' he says. DeVoe was patrolling the hall and heard him. The intern is Major Rampart's niece.

"The axe fell. Moroni is being sent to the Pasture. Transferred to Old Age Assistance, effective immediately, meaning right now."

I now understood the stigma of the Pasture. Thousands of cases from all over the county were 'banked' because the aged clients were comatose in nursing facilities and required minimal services. But others—primarily elderly women—functioned independently and required all sorts of help with housing, medical resources, and sometimes just someone to share a cup of tea and listen. This was where Lynn had been exiled, and she loved her assignment. But in no way could it be construed as a manly, chest-thumping endeavor.

The three guys, shattered by this devastating loss of face, continued to sit in morose, stunned silence.

Finally, Moroni emitted a pitiful sigh and fished an empty shoe box from a drawer in his desk. He was stoic as he packed his belongings—shoe polish, hair spray, Old Spice cologne, a bag of biscotti.

"What a bitch. Hand-holding whiney old broads in the Pasture," Webber said. Moroni winced. Even if well-intended, Webber could be counted on to say the wrong thing.

Dimly aware that he'd blundered, Webber reached over and handed Moroni the newest edition of Playboy. "Keep it as long as you like," he said.

"Buddy, meet Webber and me down the street at Clancy's Saloon at five," Anders chimed in. His nose had mended, but his blacken eyes had faded to yellow-green, giving him the appearance of an exotic owl.

"The booze is on us until six-thirty. Jesus, next that evil nut-cracker DeVoe will make you handle Santa's Work-shop." Anders rambled on, oblivious that his gaffe was equal to Webber's.

The seasonal organization of donated gifts and food baskets was viewed as the ultimate insult, reserved for the inept losers grazing in the Pasture. Moroni paled, and I swear I saw his chin quiver.

"How about a quick coffee-break up in the lunchroom?" Webber proposed. The gloom was too much, even for him.

"I've been banned from the lunchroom," Moroni said. Now his voice quivered.

"Shit. Let's go next door to the Health Department," Anders suggested. He judiciously removed his feet one at a time from his desk drawer. The three of them shuffled, heads bowed, to the elevator.

I'm such a patsy. I felt sorry for Moroni, despite his chauvinistic womanizing.

"How many condolence rounds can they squeeze in at half-price Happy Hour between five and six-thirty?" I asked Maisie.

"I don't see why they think Moroni has it so bad." She was spaced out and oblivious to my question.

"At least he's got a job, even though it's in the Pasture. DeVoe will fire me." Maisie took a swig of Mylanta. "

"Why?" I asked.

"Mabel sent me a notice. I have to do performance reviews for those two goons." She waived a piece of paper topped with the Agency's letterhead and sprinkled with numerous lumps of white-out. Unmistakably Mabel's work-product.

"Webber and Anders?"

"Yep." Big sigh.

"So?" I didn't understand the problem.

"I'm not a good writer, and DeVoe will crucify me. I envy how you can whip out court reports." She ripped open a pack of Parliaments.

"Want me to help?"

"You can't write up your peers. That's unethical."

And not without sacrifice. I had to break a date with Matt for Wednesday night in order to meet Maisie at her place.

"Amy, don't worry about it," Matt said when I called him, "Business is business. I literally got my foot in the door at Kaiser Aluminum today, and I can use the time to work up a proposal—but I'll miss you."

*   *   *

Maisie opened the front door that was flaking green paint and invited me into the tiny two-story duplex where she and her husband lived. The house was half a block off of Interstate 880, a major thoroughfare clogged with massive rumbling trucks and frantic honking commuters playing catch-me-if-you-can.

"You'll have to ignore the freeway noise. We rented the cheapest place we could find to save enough money to buy a house in the Oakland hills," Maisie said.

A short, slight fellow, with a scrunched brow and furrowed forehead, hovered behind her.

"This is my husband, Hubert Li." Maisie gritted her teeth and the corners of her mouth were turned down. A reluctant introduction if ever there was one.

Hubert Li had remained a mystery because she'd never said one word about him after our conversation at the Jade Palace. Her mother's description of Sesame-seed boy was right on. Puny.

"Happy to meet you," I said.

"Nice of you to help out my wife. She's a lousy writer."

This was not a love-match.

Hubert might not have been a supportive husband, but he was a perfect host.

"You girls need a little something if you're going to be at this all night," he graciously insisted.

Maisie and I sat on the sofa in front of the coffee table, while Hubert busied himself in the kitchenette. He brought two gleaming Waterford crystal goblets and a bottle of wine over to us.

"Hope you like Grey Riesling, Amy," he said.

"I've never tried any, Hubert, but I'm sure I'll enjoy it. Thank you."

He poured a couple of inches of the pale liquid into my glass and then leaned over to fill Maisie's glass. She deliberately blew two lungs-full of cigarette smoke in his face.

A two-inch-thick volume titled *Supervision and the Art of Positive Motivation* sat on the coffee table.

"This book is number one on the Major's reading list for supervisors," Maisie said.

I skimmed the contents and looked through the dismal examples while trying to acclimate to the whooshing traffic sounds outside.

"These samples are awful. Do you really want me to write formula garbage like this?" I asked.

"It's the safest way to go. DeVoe will tear apart anything I turn in, but at least I can say I followed the book."

Accent the positive, the manual stated. *Stress cooperation and team spirit*. Okay. I picked up the legal tablet I had pilfered from the office and scribbled out the tedious words of a first draft.

"Although reluctant to accept supervision, Mr. Webber's

strengths and skills indicate his potential to become a valuable part of the team."

A dead-end. We couldn't come up with a single strength or skill.

Meanwhile, Hubert, imbibing a carefully rationed Dr. Pepper, repeatedly filled our wine glasses despite choking on the blasts of cigarette fumes exhaled by Maisie.

As the evening progressed, I did my best to fulfill Webber's earlier prophesy of doom. The words, thoughts and revisions flowed easily after the second bottle.

"Although Mr. Webber is reluctant to accept direction, he seems attuned to the needs of the elderly. A transfer to the Old Age Department would resolve the supervision issue."

Take that, Webber. Think I forgot the Hotel Will Rogers?

We knocked out Anders's review on the dregs. This was a snap.

"Mr. Anders appears to have strong organizing skills since he has ample time to discuss minute aspects of every case and pressing societal issues at length throughout the day. He is an ideal candidate to head the annual Santa's Workshop project."

Want to call me a prissy WASP and laugh in my face again, Anders?

Those guys paid big-time for their guffaws and treachery, and Maisie and I suffered for our binge.

I weaved home on back roads. Soldiering through a blinding headache, I managed to go to work the next morning, but Maisie didn't make it in. I drank water all day Thursday and hid behind case folders, avoiding conversation for fear I would slur my words.

When Maisie dragged into the office on Friday morning,

she looked beaten up, literally. Something was wrong with her lip, and a scarf covered her head.

"Are you all right?" I asked, wondering if Hubert had one too many hostile puffs of smoke. She ignored my question and handed me an eight-by-eleven manilla envelope.

"I need you to give this to DeVoe. The performance reviews are in here, but I don't want her to see me."

"Okay. I'll sneak in her office and leave it on her desk when she goes on patrol. But what happened to you?"

"That damned passive-aggressive little Sesame-seed set us up. He knows I can't handle that much wine. After you left, I staggered up to my bed. The creep bunks on the futon in the spare bedroom, so I have the queen-size all to myself.

"Somehow, in the middle of the night, I fell out of bed and split my lip on the nightstand. And the crash shook the sparkles off the 1950 ceiling. They're stuck in my hair and I can't wash them out."

I'd just completed my furtive dash to and from DeVoe's sterile office to drop off the manilla envelope when my phone rang. Matt was on the line—with an epic proposition.

CHAPTER THIRTY-ONE

"Hi, Amy. Sorry to interrupt you at work, but my parents are bugging me to distraction. They're dying to meet you. How about coming for dinner on Sunday?"

My massive hangover had dissipated, but my head began spinning again.

"I'd love to meet your family, Matt. Sunday is fine." Could he hear my pounding heart?

When I hung up the phone, the realization sank in.

He's serious. An invitation to meet anyone's parents was no little deal. And I had one and a half days to gear up for what might be the most significant encounter in this relationship. I wavered between anxiety and hope.

Desperately needing to share this development with Maisie, I jumped up from my chair, but DeVoe had made one of her wraith-like appearances from behind Webber's file cabinet. I sat back down and waited while she jawed at Maisie and then stalked off.

The coast was clear, so I approached Maisie.

"How'd it go?" I asked.

"My God, I don't believe it. I thought DeVoe was going to annihilate me. But instead, she says, 'Li, I don't know why you look like a Hungarian refugee, but you nailed those suckers in your reviews. I didn't think you had it in you.'"

"Wow. A compliment from DeVoe, even though it was backhanded." I sat down in the confessional side-chair.

"You seem frazzled," she said.

"I am. Matt just asked me to dinner to meet his parents."

Maisie's eyes slit with suspicion. A few sparkles were visible in her hair where her scarf had slipped back. And a fresh schmear of Neosporin coated her lips.

"Hold on. This is moving too fast. What's his hurry?"

"It's only a dinner invitation," I said, but Maisie had again nailed it. Why the rush? I consciously suppressed my own puzzlement over the urgency I sensed from Matt. I needed to believe that he was besotted by my charms, and I didn't want to push open that defeating door of self-doubt again.

*   *   *

When I met Lynn for lunch, her reaction was the opposite of Maisie's.

"I knew this was a great match." She gloated.

"It's a simple invitation to dinner," I insisted, trying to focus on my tuna sandwich.

"Like, duh," she said, literally bouncing on the park bench.

*   *   *

Vi's response was measured when I dropped by her house after work. "Play it smart, kid," she counseled over a boilermaker at her kitchen table. "The stakes are high on this roll. If the guy's mother likes you, you got it made in spades."

*　　　　*　　　　*

Mary Jo Johnson's triumphant exodus from Harbor Homes had been contingent on the approval of Lamar's mama. Was my escape from Harriet Archer's household equally conditional?

Please, please let me sparkle.

But I was plagued with worry.

What to wear? After multiple wardrobe rehearsals, I settled on my cream-colored A-line skirt with a black sweater-set and black flats.

What to talk about? I spent Sunday morning reading Time magazine, Business Week, and the entire Tribune except for the obituaries.

Would my hair turn out? It did, and I went light with the makeup—*wholesome sophistication*, I told myself.

Was Mom going to make a scene? She was so peeved that she shut herself in her potting shed for the afternoon.

One less worry, but I still was a wreck by the time Matt picked me up at 5:30. Raw nerves and stabs of panic.

Nothing settled my jitters.

"What if your parents don't like me," I blurted as we settled into his car.

"How could they not?" he asked with that grin that melted me.

*　　　　*　　　　*

Matt drove down Ashby, turned right on Claremont, and wove along the backside of the university campus. Winding through narrow streets, we made our way to a serene cul-de-sac lined with trees gone bare for winter.

He parked curbside in front of a crispy white, green-shuttered colonial-style home and came around to help me out of the Impala.

"No space for me in the garage," Matt explained. "There's only room for two cars and a golf cart. My dad's an attorney, but his passion is golf. I've got a touch of the fever, but my younger brother Jack is as fanatical as Dad."

As we walked up the flagstone path to the house, I was so nervous that I forgot to worry about my limp.

"Fore." Someone yelled from inside the house, and a dog yapped.

Matt fished a jangle of keys from his pants-pocket.

"I'd better ring the doorbell, so we don't surprise any-one," he said. Just as he pushed the button, a fit, distin-guished-looking, thirty-years-older version of Matt opened the door.

"We heard you drive up. Amy, pleased to meet you." His smile was welcoming, and he offered his hand. "I'm Big Matt, the original, and this is Rose, Matt's mother."

A woman, whose wavy, prematurely white hair framed her pretty face, stood beside Big Matt in the entry hall. A cute little cocker spaniel trotted over to greet me with his nose.

"Welcome, Amy. Come in and meet our other son, Jack," Rose said. She wore a pale-yellow dress and exuded softness. "If dogs are a bother to you, I can put Arnie in the laundry area," she added.

"Oh, no, he's adorable. I wish I had a dog." The knot of my nerves loosened slightly.

A gangling teenaged replica of Big Matt, wearing a grey sweatshirt with a blazing red school logo, waved a golf club in greeting from the far end of the living room. Then he whacked a golf ball across the carpet and into a tipped-over highball glass in the dining room.

"Hole-in-one. Five bucks." He cheered, again brandishing the club, and little Arnie yelped.

"Jack, put that putter down and be civil," his father admonished. "Amy will think we're savages. I didn't see the hit, so it doesn't count."

A lilting voice called out from the kitchen doorway.

"Yoo-hoo, my dears. I'll join you in a moment."

Matt paled and looked as if he wanted to dissolve. A feeling I knew too well.

"Mom, you promised." His tone was accusatory. "You *know* how she blabs family business."

I'd never seen him so rattled. Were my nerves unnerving him?

Matt, Big Matt, and Rose exchanged uncomfortable glances, and Rose wrung her hands.

"I told Irma not to come for dinner tonight because you were having a special friend over, but she just showed up." Rose spoke apologetically to Matt.

Big Matt snorted in frustration.

"God, you know she'd jump on that. Good thing Irma's *your* cousin and not mine," he groused to Rose. "She'd be out on her rear."

"Well, I didn't want to hurt her feelings. I've set another place at the table and we'll manage. Now don't be mean to her. Please sit wherever you're comfortable, Amy." Rose motioned me into the living room.

I parked myself on a cream-colored sofa in front of a large bay window. As if on cue, a wiry woman sporting a cereal-bowl haircut bounded in, all aflutter.

"Oh, how exciting. Matt's new friend. How do you do, my dear? I'm Irma. You match the sofa. How clever."

She pushed passed Big Matt, stepped over Jack's highball-glass hole, and wedged in beside me on the sofa.

"Silly me. I thought *next* Sunday was when I wasn't supposed to come." Irma fluffed the skirt of her plaid shirtwaist dress.

"And all subsequent," the host muttered. "Ladies, how about a sherry? Would that suit you, Amy?"

"Very much, thank you." I could never handle Vi's boilermakers.

"Just a tad." Irma frowned and sighed in my direction. I caught a whiff. Bourbon, no mistake.

Big Matt handed Irma and me cordial glasses filled with an amber liquid.

"Scotch, Matt?" Big Jack asked.

"Fine." Matt looked at Irma with a wary expression.

"*Now* you're talking," Irma said. She drained her glass of sherry. "I'll have one of those."

Big Matt ignored her, so she got up, sashayed to the bar cart, and filled a double high-ball glass to the brim before squishing down next to me again.

"I understand you work in social services, Amy." Irma swallowed a lot of scotch and babbled on before I could respond.

"I'm the attendance clerk at Lincoln Middle School, and I hate it. All day long I put up with snotty punk kids. I can't leave because I'd forfeit almost twenty years in the system.

We single girls have to look out for ourselves, don't we?"

Girls? Good grief. She was ancient. At least forty, I was sure.

"Besides, Harold needs me." She sighed. "He's the vice-principal and a magnificent man."

Her glass was empty.

"Irma, I need your help in the kitchen. Right now, please," Rose called out. She sounded testy.

As she struggled to get off the sofa, Irma said to Big Matt, "I liked the scotch better than the sherry. I'll have another one of those." He pretended not to hear her.

"Irma!" Rose meant business. Little Arnie cocked his head, seemingly puzzled by Rose's abrupt tone.

"Harold's magnificent, I tell you. I'm coming, Rose." Irma pouted as she lurched to the kitchen.

Pong. Jack smacked a ball with the putter and drove home a straight shot the length of the living room, through to the dining room, and into the highball glass.

"Ha! You saw that one, Pops. How about my five bucks?" he asked.

Irma staggered in from the kitchen.

"Dinner's on the table, my dears. Where's that scotch?"

This time she forgot to step over Jack's hole and upended herself on the glass. She landed flat on her back and lay still for several seconds. Then Arnie trotted over and barked in her ear.

Startled, Irma sat up abruptly and cracked her forehead on the edge of the china cabinet.

The guys jumped up to assist, and Big Matt reached her first. He helped her to her feet and steered her to his chair at the head of the table.

"It has arms, so maybe she won't fall out. I'd better do a quick check for a concussion," he grumbled, reacting to her disconcerting blank stare.

Big Matt pulled out a chair next to Irma, sat down, and raised his hand with his index finger pointing up.

"Irma, I want you to tell me today's date, and then follow my finger with your eyes."

Her vacant eyes filled with annoyance. Then she spoke.

"If you don't know what day it is, you need help. And get your finger out of my face before I give you one of mine."

A burst of activity covered the awkwardness. Big Matt repositioned himself as far away from Irma as possible, Jack and Matt took chairs on either side of her, obviously fencing her in, and Matt seated me on his other side.

Rose hurried to the kitchen to improvise an ice-pack of ice cubes rolled in a towel for Irma to hold on the lumps rising on both the front and the back of her head.

Retreating to the kitchen again, Rose next appeared carrying a large stoneware casserole dish. She placed it on the table and sat down next to me.

"I hope the Spanish rice hasn't dried out. It's my specialty. Amy, with all this confusion, we haven't had a minute to talk. Your work must be very challenging. I'd like to know more about what you do."

What an incredibly gracious and composed woman, I thought.

Before two sentences were out of my mouth, Irma surfaced from behind the towel.

"Matt, dear, I hope *this* one's a keeper," she said.

What?

*　　　　　*　　　　　*

I was taken aback. *How many girlfriends have there been—am I a notch on a well-worn belt?*

Big Matt glowered, Rose muffled a gasp, and Matt shot a deadly look toward Irma.

"Putt, putt—*pow.*" Jack diverted our attention to his dinner plate, on which he'd aligned half a dozen olives in the rice to re-enact, with a celery stick, his afternoon on the golf course.

"We've got to map our strategy to win this weekend. No bogeys. I hate to lose," Big Matt said. He stabbed Irma with a terminal glare and snatched up his own celery stick.

All three guys piled more rice on their plates and reconstructed several troublesome spots on the fairways.

Rose sighed. "You wouldn't believe what they do with mashed potatoes."

*　　　　　*　　　　　*

While rice and olives flew, I collected my thoughts.

Of course, he's had girlfriends. Twenty-six, single, handsome—something would be wrong if he hadn't. And I was clearly benefiting from his prowess in the bedroom. Don't over-think this and screw things up.

I envisioned a grim, isolated convent atop a rocky atoll, swished the faceless forms of any predecessors to the inescapable retreat, and locked them out of my mind.

When the ninth hole olive bounced off Jack's plate and was snapped up by Arnie, I refocused and suddenly realized who Big Matt was—a prominent, big bucks torts attorney who won almost every case he touched, and whose triumphs were often touted in the newspaper. His intensity was a bit scary, but he clearly doted on gentle Rose and his sons.

I studied Rose, too—so composed behind her quiet facade. I wanted to know her, and I sensed we could become friends, given our similar demeanors.

Was the similarity what attracted Matt to me? Food for later thought.

Matt and Jack cleared the table, and I followed Rose into the kitchen to ask if I might help with something.

"Not a thing, dear. Do you cook?" she asked.

"No. My mom's territorial when it comes to her kitchen, but I'd like to learn. Where I work, potlucks happen all the time with everything from Filipino lumpia to Cajun gumbo."

"I'll be glad to give you a few tips. My standard old cookbook is *Better Homes and Gardens*, but I collect new recipes from magazines and newspapers. I have a brand-new book on order called *The Mastery of French Cooking*, by a woman named Julia Child who I saw on a talk show. I love trying out new dishes."

Rose's enthusiasm was contagious, and her attitude was the opposite of my mom's, who's repertoire came from Betty Crocker and tended to repeat itself every seven days.

Please, please like me, Rose. I'll master cookery from whatever book you recommend.

Jack excused himself to study for an exam, so Matt, Rose, and I returned to the table. Irma had dozed off in her chair under the towel. Big Matt remained seated at the table, shooting optical darts at his cousin-in-law. When we sat down, a flurry of charged glances flew—Rose to Matt, Matt to Big Matt, Big Matt to Rose.

I was sure this silent exchange was determining my fate, and a tumble of questions filled my mind.

Had I swayed Rose and Big Matt? Was I deemed a worthy match for their son? Did I fit?

This charming family captivated me. True, Irma was off center, but this could be an advantage. If I made the grade, perhaps her penchant for the bottle might offset Mom's predictable firestorm.

Please, oh please. I want Matt, and I want to be a part of you. Am I a keeper?

CHAPTER THIRTY-TWO

"How come you cut me off? Who gonna feed these kids?"

The fury that greeted me when I walked into the office displaced the suspense surrounding my future.

I wanted to grill Matt on the way home the night before, but Vi had previously counseled otherwise. "Never push. The guy's gotta think he's callin' the shots."

Hold your tongue, hope, and get to work, I told myself.

Monday mornings were bad enough, but it was also the first day of the month. A double disaster.

When someone's welfare payments were discontinued, a notice was mailed three days before month's end. The recipient found it, instead of a check, in the mailbox with no warning beforehand.

The system was cruel and, as Anders pointed out time and again, designed to punish. Even if a stoppage occurred in error, it was too late to avoid the bureaucratic hell of a three-month reinstatement process. No money to pay rent, buy groceries, or keep the heat or lights on—and nothing to fall back on.

Who *would* feed those kids? I wondered and worried.

The callers were angry, and their initial queries turned ugly fast.

Maisie had just returned from the dentist who'd fitted her

for a muzzle-like device to prevent further damage from teeth grinding. Her desk had a multi-line and receiver telephone setup, so I sat down in the confessional side-chair to help divert the wrath.

Imagine my delight when the third call I intercepted turned out to be Matt.

"Must be a madhouse there, Amy. It was impossible to get through on your line." He sounded exuberant.

"I sold the Golden Gate Bridge to a rich guy who's kind of a nitwit and wrapped up a huge contract. Instead of seeing 'Dr. Strangelove' at the Fox Oakland Saturday night, let's celebrate. How about dinner and dancing at the Claremont?"

The Claremont Hotel is a beautiful, sprawling white Victorian edifice in the Berkeley hills, reserved for landmark life events. My heart leapt. My head balked. *Don't get ahead of yourself.*

"Matt, you've spoiled me rotten—but congratulations on your deal. What a lovely way to celebrate."

Maisie eavesdropped and butted in when we ended the conversation.

"Speaking of nitwits, wake up, Amy. Matt's not celebrating a sale, he's planning to propose."

"Maybe, but I'm not sure. The Christmas Eve debacle with Bob was humiliating enough, and I don't want a repeat." I tried not to notice the occasional twinkle of a sparkly stubbornly sticking to her hair.

"But Matt isn't Bob, and he *will* propose. This is the part in the movies where Rock Hudson always does, and Doris Day simpers with delight. You should wear that dress with the pink sash. It's sappy romantic, just like you, and you can make goo-goo eyes like Doris." Maisie paused for a slug of Maalox.

"I've still got my suspicions about this guy," she said.

"Why?" Maisie's comments disturbed me, but I chalked them up to her disillusionment with Hubert Li. She'd never even met Matt.

"A hunch. Like I told you before, he's moving too fast, and you're too addled to think straight. You need to remember every detail for me. Promise? One of us needs a functioning brain to sort through this."

I promised, but later I skipped the parts that veered off-script. Maisie scoffed at movie make-believe, but I needed mine.

When I called Vi with an update, I caught her just as she was leaving for Vegas.

"Damn, kid, I'm bettin' this is it. We can't take no chances though. What're you wearin'?"

"The sleeveless dress with the swirl skirt and pink sash."

"*Shit*. Well, use a lot of glitter and hope for the best."

*   *   *

Mr. Al's greeted me with a gleeful grin when I arrived for what had become a standing Saturday appointment.

"Darling girl, it's not every day that someone gets engaged. Rita called me to let me know what you told Vi. I am *so* excited. Let's go glamorous today."

His concept of glamor emphasized elegance over seduction, which was fortunate because I just didn't have the nerve or equipment to pull it off the latter.

Wow. I felt like Grace Kelly when he put the finishing

touches on my hair, but I fretted all the way home. My dress, my awful foot-ware, my bag—had I got it right? My trappings were good enough, but was I?

The doorbell rang. Oh, *no*. Seven o'clock already? I shoved my feet in the least obnoxious shoes I was able to walk in and hurried from my room. Too late. Mom stood at the front door, blocking Matt's entry as effectively as a fired-up linebacker.

"H'lo, Harriet." Matt said. He was not in the least perturbed. Tall and distinguished-looking in his vested charcoal suit, he offered his hand to Mom.

"Good evening." Mom radiated distaste before extending hers for a reluctant, limp shake. She held a pickle jar in her other hand, and something moved in it—a huge, hideous spider.

Matt just stared.

"Mom, what are you doing with that awful thing?" I gasped. This debacle was my fault. I was fussing with my eyes when I ought to have been guarding the door.

"I'm helping my dear friend Bob with his studies by collecting specimens. He'll have a distinguished career in science. Unlike a dime-a-dozen salesman."

Oh, *God*. But Matt remained unfazed.

"Maybe you should keep it, Harriet. I can't imagine a more appropriate pet for you. Let's go, Amy."

*　　　　*　　　　*

Lanterns twinkled, lighting the gardens of the Claremont, and the sweet fragrance of night-blooming jasmine wafted through the soft air. A cocktail in the Terrace Lounge looking over the Bay to twinkling San Francisco, then a scrumptious meal—a shared Caesar salad and chateaubriand for two—in the elegant Garden Room that featured big band dancing on weekends.

True, we'd had a little pre-entrée skirmish over public funding for abortions. How had that subject come up? No matter. Back to make-believe, except it was real.

The parquet dance floor gleamed, and Matt tipped the bandleader to play a few romantic waltzes and foxtrots. Of course, he asked them to play our favorite foxtrot—Bobby Darin's "Beyond the Sea." Perfect for dancing, with its simple, lovely words and joyful lilt to the melody. But Etta James's "At Last" was *our* song. She'd captured so perfectly the longing, the waiting, the hope for that perfect love.

Floating in our own dream, we glided through the French doors that led to the gardens.

Matt took my hand and led me down a bower-covered path to a secluded bench. We sat and listened to the crickets chirping over the music drifting from the open doors. I tried not to scrunch the pink sash. Moonglow and moonlight. A few mosquitoes too, but I didn't flinch.

Then Matt knelt on one knee, my hand still in his, and I can't remember his exact phrases. He loved me, he wanted to spend his life with me, he'd never known such happiness. He spoke words of spun silver, but some were lost because of the pounding of my over-flowing heart.

"Will you marry me, sweet Amy?" he asked as he kissed my hand.

And my response came from the depths of my being.

"Matt, I love you beyond what I can describe. I can't imagine a life without you. Yes, of course I'll marry you."

He reached into the breast-pocked of his jacket and pulled out a small velvet pouch.

"This ring belonged to my grandmother," he said. "You can have any ring you want, but my mother hopes you'll accept this one."

The antique diamond engagement ring slipped onto my finger as if it had been made for me—well, not really. It stuck halfway, but we both pretended.

"Matt, it's lovely. I couldn't wish for a more beautiful ring."

The scene was story-book perfect.

"Before you say any more, Amy, there's something you have to know." He slid back on to the bench, took both my hands in his, and said,

"I've been married before."

My heart stopped.

What?" I asked him.

"I've been married before," he repeated.

The shock enveloped me in a wall of disbelief. My brain refused to process the words he was saying.

"What?" I asked again, trying to sort through the barrage of thoughts assaulting my mind.

"Why did you wait until now to tell me?" Overwhelmed by confusion and anger, I pulled my hands away.

"I know I should have, but I was afraid you'd dump me, and that would have been unbearable."

"You thought I wouldn't accept a previous marriage?" I challenged, incredulous and insulted.

"Well, it's not so simple. The reason I got married was because my girlfriend was pregnant. I was stupid and it shouldn't have happened, but once it did, there was no way out. No surprise—the marriage didn't work out, but she and her parents wanted to raise the baby. Her parents legally adopted the kid, so I don't have to pay alimony or child support. It's over and could have been worse. Twins ran in her family."

I thought my head would burst into tiny particles. How could he have withheld this from me—and for so long? It felt like deliberate deception, and it appalled me.

Did this signal a deficiency of character—a fatal flaw? What was worse: the sadness surrounding his marriage, his dismissal of a baby, or his failure to inform me?

And what was with Lynn—did she know when she hooked us up? Why didn't she clue me in beforehand?

Matt's *parents*. Were they aware he hadn't told me? Or had they been in on a plot to deceive? I remembered nervous glances around their dinner table, but I assumed everyone was uneasy because of Irma's antics. More likely, they were afraid she might blurt out secrets.

It was all a jumble, and I couldn't gather the scattered pieces to process any of it.

Matt and I sat next to each other on the bench, each in private misery, as the air cooled to a chill.

Quietly, he slipped off his jacket and draped it over my shoulders. The intoxicating scent of him enveloped me, and I saw tears glistening in his incredible blue eyes.

"I am so *sorry*, Amy. I ought to have told you. There just never seemed to be a right time. I didn't let Lynn know anything either. Sure, I've had girlfriends, but not one could hold a candle to you."

He reached for my hand and held it gently.

"I've never fallen in love before, Amy. You're the only

one to have my heart. Damn, I *do* love you, and I won't lose you. You deserve the best—a loving, committed husband—and that's what I'll be. Yours forever. For keeps. Please, will you forgive me?"

His tears and sincerity tore at *my* heart. I didn't think I would ever stop loving him, so how could I not forgive him?

I took a deep breath, willed myself to quell the cascade of confused thoughts, and then looked into those eyes that had held me captive from the moment we met.

"Of course." I dissolved into the comfort of his arms.

Blinking away my own tears, I slammed shut the portion of my mind struggling with this disturbing ethical lapse—and with the troubling doubts voiced by Maisie.

Matt and I loved each other, and everything would be okay.

CHAPTER THIRTY-THREE

Mom went ballistic.

My God, she shot denunciations like missiles. The garden had so many potholes from her vengeful digging that the gophers gave up and moved over to Bob's. She refused to accept that the engagement was a done deal.

Her litany was relentless.

"You can't marry him. He's no good—a fly-by-night salesman who'll never make a decent living." She sputtered, jerking open the kitchen spice drawer. Then she slammed it shut.

"He talks too much, and I don't believe a word that comes out of his big mouth." A clove of garlic rested peacefully on a cutting board, and she turned to whack it to mush with her meat mallet.

"I don't like his family. Who ever heard of serving Spanish rice to company?"

*   *   *

When Rose invited the three of us to Sunday dinner—a proper and hospitable gesture—Mom viewed the overture with the level of suspicion she reserved for people with Russian accents.

The fated day was cold and damp with drizzle. Dad drove with care, tuned out to Mom's non-stop harangues regarding Matt's deficiencies and his own navigational skills.

I agonized in anticipation of her behavior and turned off my ears. A pleasant fantasy drifted into my head. Dad would park the car, and Mom would step out into a pothole. The image morphed into a sucking sinkhole, swallowing her whole.

No luck. Mother Earth spit her right back up and out.

Dad guided Mom, bucking all the way up the path to the front door where Rose and Big Matt welcomed us.

After Matt took care of introductions in the entry hall, Big Matt ushered us into the living room where a cozy fire crackled in the fireplace. He immediately engaged Dad in a convivial conversation about football.

"Can I fix you a drink, Henry?" he asked, and relief flooded Dad's face. Soon the three men were enjoying highballs while speculating about the upstart AFL league and its potential danger to the NFL in the coming season.

Could I join the jovial trio? No, I had to sit next to belligerent Mom on the cream-colored sofa, doomed to witness the debacle about to unfold.

The snug, double-breasted navy coatdress Mom wore had a military look, which, when paired with the hostile glares she kept firing, established a one-woman war zone.

"Would you care for some sherry, Harriet?" Rose asked with an inviting smile. She looked soft and pretty in a pale-blue knit dress.

"Only water, thank you." Mom's arms, folded tightly across her chest, remained in their antagonistic position through-out most of the mercifully short evening.

Rose tried again. "I've just finished reading a new biography of Eleanor Roosevelt. She certainly is a woman of accomplishment."

"She doesn't know her place." Mom's evil eye shot round the room.

Optimistic Rose made one last attempt. "I hope you like the Spanish rice."

"I'm allergic to curry," Mom grimaced.

"There's no curry in Spanish rice. Just a little paprika." Rose had become testy.

"Then I'm allergic to paprika."

I wanted to throw myself into the imaginary sinkhole and never surface again, but somehow, we all made it through to the cherry pie.

Oh, please, please, let her not completely alienate them.

*   *   *

And the assault never stopped at home.

"Henry, you should have put a stop to this when he asked for her hand. Why didn't you just say no?"

"It was a courtesy, Harriet. And damn decent of him, I thought." Hide behind that newspaper fast, Dad.

"Why hasn't Mr. Mouth been in the service?" she demanded to know. This was the true measure of a man, according to Mom. She had that Eisenhower fixation, insisting he was the finest leader the country had ever had.

"Matt's lung has collapsed a few times," I explained. "The doctors can't figure out why."

"That's easy. He talks so much that all the hot air comes out."

Would she let up? No.

"Irresponsible propagator—I know he's no good. Look what happened with the other girl. What if you two have a baby and it grows up and marries another one of his kids? Who knows how many he's scattered around? Then they'll have a weird one."

Please pass the bottle, Dad.

And the persistent question, "What about Bob?" who now left the kitchen only for biological necessities.

At last, the epiphany came. One afternoon, as she patrolled with her saltshaker between the camellias and the Cecile Brunner roses, a moment of clarity hit Mom. She realized, for the first time, that she had a wedding to produce.

Mom evicted Bob from his semi-permanent maple perch in the kitchen, and when I arrived home from work, he'd already jumped the fence and was gone.

A thick volume, titled *Etiquette: The Blue Book of Social Usage*, and authored by Mom's favorite columnist, Emily Post, was propped on the counter. Three-by-five index cards covered the kitchen table.

"What's all this, Mom?" I asked.

"I'm organizing, and there's no time to be lost here, missy. I picked out your china pattern, so that's out of the way."

CHAPTER THIRTY-FOUR

om also designed my wedding dress.

Lynn and I sat in the park eating chicken-salad sandwiches, and I pulled out Mom's sketch, which she intended to hand-make based on a Simplicity pattern.

"It will be of sentimental value for generations to come," Mom said. No matter that she didn't know how to sew.

"You *can't* wear that." Lynn gasped.

Yards of nylon curtain lace swooped over an antebellum hoop, and the fabric was contorted into rosettes spaced six inches apart.

"Just hope you never have to eat off the china she picked out for me," I told her. "Pink and red rosebuds crammed over the entire surface. There's not one thing about this wedding we've agreed on yet, starting with whom the groom should be."

*　　　　*　　　　*

The next skirmish was about when and where the marriage should take place.

"May would be nice, Mom," I suggested.

"Too soon," she said. "I don't want anyone to think you have to get married. Besides, the church might not be available then."

"What church?"

"First Presbyterian." Her certitude was surprising since she'd never set foot inside. I hadn't either, but it turned out not to matter, because the arrangement didn't suit Matt—or rather Big Matt, to be precise.

"Uh-oh." Matt whispered to me over Mom's kitchen table. We huddled over her three-by-five cards, practically lip-reading so Mom wouldn't over-hear us from the garden. Every few minutes, her head would appear in the window, and she'd make a sour Olive Oil face at Matt as if he couldn't see her through the glass.

"Dad expects the wedding to be at Northbrae Community Church. He's not religious, but he puts a lot of bucks into that church to grease connections."

I had dreamed of a Unitarian service in a garden under a canopy of pale lilac-colored wisteria. But no one asked me what I wanted.

Why didn't I speak up and at least share with Matt my preference for a garden ceremony? My new spine appeared to be eroding, and comfortable old deference was slipping back in. But the stakes seemed too high to risk rocking Big Matt's boat.

"Her mind is set for First Presbyterian. She'll never agree." I mouthed the words, shaking my head.

"Sure she will. Watch this."

Matt walked out into the garden to the spot where Mom was kneeling over some geraniums. He came up behind her and mimed a kick to her backside. Then he tapped her on the shoulder and squatted down to look straight into her defiant eyes as she turned around.

"Harriet, we all want to start off on the right foot, so I

suggest a compromise. How about either Temple Sinai on Summit Street or the Baptist church on 10th Street?"

Big Matt reserved Northbrae Community Church for six p.m. on the second Saturday in July.

*   *   *

Matt and his father won that scuffle, but Mom was steaming and determined to call all subsequent shots. Every chapter in that blue book opened to a new battlefield.

Emily Post deemed wedding consultants essential, so Mom set out to find one.

She located three hopeful candidates and subjected them to interrogations reminiscent of those that terrorized my college admirers. Intent on making a grand social statement, she envisioned a reception worthy of Emily Post, Queen Elizabeth, and the entire British aristocracy. When they failed to share her vision, she dismissed them as incompetent no-nothings.

"Those silly party-organizers don't know beans about a proper event. I've taken control." She girded her apron and hurtled forward.

Her demands were fanatical but tinged with poignancy.

When Mom eloped twenty-plus years ago, she was only seventeen and missed out on all the frills. This reception was her wedding party. The sky had no limit and budget be damned. Dad revised his retirement plans.

Stay out of it, I told myself. Especially after Mom bristled and refused when we offered to help with the funding.

First, we needed a suitable venue for the reception. Matt and I had attended a cocktail party a few weeks earlier at a small country club in the Oakland hills. Perched atop a hillside and showcasing a sparkling view of San Francisco bay, we thought it was charming.

"Tell your mother the place turned me off. She hates me so much that she'll jump on it," Matt said.

He was right.

"Mom, if you're still looking for a venue, that party Matt and I went to was at the Hilltop Country Club. I thought it was a lovely spot, but he didn't like the place at all," I told her while suffering through one of her succotash creations at dinner.

"Probably too posh for his unrefined tastes," she said.
Now she's even sounding like Emily's book.

*   *   *

Mom met with the club's manager the following day and gave a full report at the dinner table.

"Timothy was a difficult young man to work with." She plunked a scalloped potato and pork chop casserole on the table. Mom was big on casseroles.

"I told him I expected access to the main reception hall, the patio surrounding the pool, use of the club's grand piano, the kitchen, and the cloak room. Also, I wanted catering, valet parking and janitorial services provided."

Dad put down his knife and fork and butted in, staring at Mom in disbelief.

"My God, Harriet, I just paid off the mortgage on this house. I don't want another one."

"Neither here nor there, Henry. Don't interrupt. So, this Timothy says, 'Mrs. Archer, if you want that much space, from 6:00 p.m. to 12:00 on a prime summer weekend, the rental fee is doubled, and if the piano is included, the charge will be tripled because we'll need to haul it out of storage and have it tuned.

"You'll have to hire your own caterer, bartender, and whoever else you want. We provide limited janitorial service, but if you make a big mess, you'll be billed for any cleanup.'

"The *nerve*. As if my guests would be uncouth ruffians. Well, I let him know a thing or two. Amy, if you didn't have your heart set on this place, I would have walked out."

No, you wouldn't, Mom. You hate Matt too much.

"Matt's will be unhappy about this," I said.

"I know," she replied, smiling.

"What was the final tab?" Dad asked.

"Triple, as I said, but I proved my point."

"Which was?" he asked. He rose from the table to fetch a tumbler and his bottle of Jim Beam.

"To let that whippersnapper manager know who's in charge of this event—*me*."

*   *   *

Caterers toppled as quickly as the wedding planners. Mom relayed her tales of frustration every evening at the dinner table, which she quickly converted into her command center when the dishes were cleared.

"I can't believe these food people. Wanting to serve pots of *French* melted cheese with pieces of bread stuck on long forks. And some sort of fancy beef stew."

"Beef bourguignon?" I asked.

"That's it. Well, I'll have no foreign foods served at *this* reception."

To my surprise, Dad brought her up short.

"Harriet, if you keep it up, you're going to be cooking for 200 people, so knock it off. And what about that piano?" Dad asked, sounding increasingly annoyed as he eyed the Pyrex dish in center of the table—a tuna-noodle concoction topped with crushed potato chips.

"What about it?" Mom retorted. Defiance flashed in her eyes.

"If we're being charged one-third of the cost of the venue rental for it, it would be nice if someone played it."

I decided Dad's confrontational courage was coming from the bourbon bottle, and I wanted to stop the discussion before he dug himself too deep a hole.

"Matt plays the piano beautifully," I said.

Mom snorted, pulled the telephone directory from the catch-all drawer in the kitchen, and flipped to the Yellow Pages. She engaged the services of a moonlighting music teacher the following day.

*   *   *

Mom's lists spawned more lists that cluttered the kitchen table as she worked her way through Emily's book.

One-by-one, she assembled her troops—a stationer for invitations, an ethnically and culturally cleansed caterer, likewise for the bartender provided by the caterer, a baker who specialized in wedding cakes, a florist, and the pianist who turned out to be timid, bespectacled, and totally cowed by Mom.

Eisenhower would have applauded the determination with which she rounded out her battalion.

And I chose my attendants—Maisie as matron of honor, and Lynn as bridesmaid, along with three of my college friends, each of whom had included me in their wedding parties.

Matt picked his brother Jack to be best man. Two friends from college, one guy from work, and Lynn's boyfriend Pete completed the roster for groomsmen.

Lynn was over-the-top excited when Matt included Pete, who'd been ostracized from adult activities after the firecrackers-in-the-furnace incident during her mom's New Year's Eve party. And she dismissed Mom's giant tutu bride's gown.

"I found the groom, so I should have some say-so. Amy, you need to buy your dress at the Gray Shop. It's the best bridal salon this side of San Francisco, and they don't carry dresses with pantaloons."

*   *   *

Aunt Jane had hovered in the background for weeks, overjoyed because not only had I found a fellow, I'd come up with one that Mom hated. When I called to invite her to go shopping with me at the legendary Gray Shop, she was ecstatic.

"Amy, this is the most important dress you'll ever have. I'm honored to accompany you. But what the hell did you tell your mother?"

"The truth, Aunt Jane. That I wanted to select my own dress. She started to throw a hissy-fit, but I told her she wouldn't have time to make the dress because of the terrible infestation of aphids on her roses. She flew out the door to the garden, and that was that."

Since we both worked in downtown Oakland, Aunt Jane and I met on our lunch hours for an initial look at what the store had to offer.

Skipping lunch, I caught the #15 AC Transit bus that ran up and down Broadway at 12:05 and darted off when it coughed to a stop in front of the store's entrance.

Aunt Jane had beaten me to it. Once inside, I found her floundering in yards of billowing white tulle. The bridal coordinator approached us as we pawed through the maze and introduced herself as Delores.

"Are you just browsing, dear, or have you caught a live one?" she asked me.

"A live one," I told her. "But I'm not sure these dresses will work. They're all so elaborate," I said, disappointed.

"I will not have my niece looking like a marshmallow on the most significant day of her life," Aunt Jane interjected. She fortified herself with a snort from her flask.

"Ah." Delores mused, peering through eyeglasses secured by a chain around her neck.

"Something not so frou-frou. I'll show you my favorite." She disappeared behind a mirror-encased pedestal and reappeared with one dress.

The simple white sheath was plucked from my dreams—sleeveless, pearls tracing the softly scooped neckline, an empire waistline from which shimmering satin fell straight to the floor. I *loved* it.

"Note the back," Delores murmured. "Just the slightest suggestion of a train—très élégant."

The bridesmaids' Georgette sheaths had the same lines. I chose a pale, blue-tinged lavender color to honor my now-defunct dream of standing beneath a pergola entwined with wisteria. Little matching tiaras completed the look. *Perfect.*

"A *smashing* success," Aunt Jane declared. Then she ran out of the store to hail the #15 bus going up to 20th Street. "I know that bastard of a supervisor is going to give me a note of reprimand, but it's been worth it," were her parting words.

Oops. I hadn't realized the time. I finalized my choices with Delores and left to catch the #15 on its round-trip heading down toward Jack London Square.

I tucked all the swatches Delores had given me in an embossed envelope. I could hardly wait to get back to the office to show them to Maisie, who reacted quickly when I opened the envelop to display the fabrics.

"*Why* are you marrying that ass?" she asked.

CHAPTER THIRTY-FIVE

Maisie was appalled that I would marry Matt. She detested him.

Slim Jenkin's bar on Seventh Street had become our after-hours conference site. The bar stools were tall—our feet dangled and flapped—but that's where we sat. Hardy men bellied up and ordered scotch. We fancied ourselves just as tough, so we drank Cutty Sark and soda, like it or not.

Happy-hour drinks were only a dollar off at upscale Slim's, so we never had to worry about running into the guys there. Webber and Anders met up with Moroni and the three men sauntered two blocks down Broadway to plebeian half-price Clancy's, leaving us to squabble about my future in peace.

"Matt's arrogant," Maisie claimed.

"He is not. He's just self-assured," I countered. What did she know? She'd only met him once for an abbreviated lunch-hour burrito binge at the Mexicali Rose.

"He blathers on and on and on." She persisted, picking all the cashews out of a bowl of nuts on the bar.

"Well, you could have contributed to the conversation if you hadn't been so absorbed pigging out on the Fantastico Burrito Grande. I love to listen to him."

"You're really too good for him."

"You sound like my mom."

That would end the discussion because nothing was worse than being likened to one's mother. Besides, I dismissed Maisie's objections as projections of her disgust with Hubert Li. Plus the aggravations generated by the guys. Maybe she just didn't like men too much.

Maisie also fumed because she would have to wear bridesmaid's gear.

"First you decide to marry that motor-mouth ass. Now I have to dress up like a f---ing gringo fairy. The purple dress is dorky enough, but then you tell me to put that ridiculous gismo on my head. Why not give me a wand so I can sprinkle stardust all over?"

"Matt's not an ass, the dress is pale lavender, and you're the matron of honor. You need to wear your tiara, carry flowers, and make sure I don't trip on my train."

"*Shit*. Why not go down to the courthouse like I did with Sesame Seed?"

"Are you crazy? My mother would kill me."

*   *   *

Mom would have preferred to knock off the groom.

"That huckster will never amount to a hill of beans." She huffed, slamming dishes into the dishwasher in a fury.

Matt had discovered her Eisenhower obsession and, polishing off a sizable slice of meatloaf, he declared World War III at her table.

"Harriet, the New Deal was brilliant. Eisenhower couldn't hold a candle to FDR," he asserted, sending her into apoplexy.

Her tirade shifted from Roosevelt's deficiencies to Matt's the moment he left.

"How can he support you selling staplers? You don't even have a place to live."

"Mom, he sells office systems and equipment, not staplers. And we've found a great place to live."

"Where? And why didn't I know about it?"

"Because we just discovered it late this afternoon. I haven't had a chance to tell you because you and Matt kept arguing about whether Mamie Eisenhower is an alcoholic."

"That lovely woman does not have a drinking problem. How could she, married to our nation's finest president?"

*   *   *

Matt and Big Matt *had* found a perfect place for us to live. They left me out of the decision loop, but I would not give Mom the satisfaction of knowing that Big Matt's approval preceded mine.

I left the office for the field first thing that morning to avoid possible encounters with evil DeVoe. The force of her wrath had increased tenfold because, according to the grapevine, she developed a severe case of hammertoes from those pointy-toe heels she wore.

Now she stalked in Hush-Puppies' Comfort Sneakers. Without heels, the top of her beehive hairdo was no longer visible as she crept through the maze of file cabinets. Ominous.

The ghetto was preferable, but a knock on any door in Harbor Homes resulted in an avalanche of wrongs needing to be righted. The strength of those stalwart women, trapped in the project and coping with countless injustices, inspired me to work as hard as I could for them.

Ida Mae Cole's black eye triggered the day's biggest challenge. She had become the target of a sadistic bully who worked part-time as a security guard. Terrorized by him for months, Mrs. Cole was afraid to file any charges, and Legal Aid couldn't help her get a restraining order unless she followed through with a police complaint.

I found her cowering in her darkened apartment, trying to hide her bruised face.

"Mrs. Cole, you've got to do something. This isn't right. Do you need to see a doctor?"

"No. And what good's a piece of paper gonna do? He got a gun from that phony security job, he crazy jealous, and I know he gonna kill me some day. Follows me day and night. Head always poppin' up in the window, and he shoves his way in to beat on me. No way to get away, Miss Archer. I'm livin' a nightmare, and I see what's comin'."

Her nightmare was real. Safe shelters for battered women were non-existent. Stalking was a phrase reserved for game hunters—no such word or concept even existed in law. It wasn't a crime.

And domestic disputes were not considered police matters. The precinct desk-sergeant made that clear when I tried to convince him of the danger to Mrs. Cole later that afternoon.

"Some guy beats up on his old lady? We don't touch it," The officer yawned in my face.

"But he's insanely jealous—a batterer who's threatened to shoot her with his gun," I pleaded.

"The gun's legit. The guy's got a license for it, and he needs it for work. What's the problem?"

"He physically assaults her, and she's terrified."

"Probably caught her steppin' out on him. Case closed."

*　　　　*　　　　*

I was worn out when I straggled back to the office after six. Maisie had taped a note to my phone—*Urgent. Call Matt.*

My mind leapt to the nightmare that haunted me. He couldn't take Mom a minute longer, and he was dumping me. I *knew* it. I steeled myself and made the call.

"Guess what?" Matt asked when he answered on the second ring. I dared not speculate, but he didn't notice my lack of response and rattled on.

"This is amazing. Dad wanted to practice putting, so I decided to go along and cut out from work early. We meant to take a shortcut to the driving range in Tilden Park, but got lost in the hills. Out of nowhere, a house popped up in front of us with a 'lease with option to buy' sign. The place blew us away, so I rented it and just picked up the keys. Meet me there before it gets too dark—it's in Shepherd Canyon, almost to Skyline."

No one ever asked me anything. My feelings flipped from anxiety over being chucked to hurt—deep hurt. Shut out and overlooked again. I flashed back to the pain I felt as a child, disregarded by the grown-ups in my world.

Couldn't Matt have let me see the place first? His father's opinion was more important than mine? And to top it off, I'd been of no help to Mrs. Cole, who remained in terrifying jeopardy. Tears welled, and I wanted to think about it all, but time was running out—the sun had begun to set.

I hurried to the VW, raced up Broadway Terrace, crossed the freeway, and followed a eucalyptus-lined road through a lush canyon filled with thickets of pines and laurels. An occasional house intruded through the dense trees.

Still upset, I sensed that strange elephant in the back seat of the VW again.

Matt's Impala was parked in the carport of a small, A-framed house on the downside of the steep hillside. As I pulled in beside it, a deer and two fawns looked on from across the street.

Charmed, I rushed down the stairs, crossed a redwood deck, and walked through the front door Matt had left ajar.

He *had* found the perfect place, and my pain flipped to joy.

The house was a chalet of glass and wood overlooking the wild canyon and a sea of trees. Its beamed ceiling soared, and windows ran the length of the open living space, broken only by a sliding glass door. A dining area was tucked in the far corner, next to a postage stamp of a kitchen.

Matt grinned at my obvious delight and extended his hand. We glided over the hardwood floors, and into what would be our bedroom, with its own sliding doors and deck. One large bath, a second, smaller bedroom, and a guest bath.

In my euphoria, I failed to note that the washer/dryer closet had been tucked two landings down in an unfinished basement.

"Let's dance," he said and folded me into his arms. We waltzed, whirling around and around, keeping time to the silent music within our hearts.

I'd never been happier. The two of us, in this enchanting chalet, the cozy seclusion of a tranquil forest, and *no* Mom.

"Matt, I love this place, but can we afford it?"

"Trust me. I'll just sell a bunch more bridges."

CHAPTER THIRTY-SIX

Multiple file boxes now competed for space with the lists covering the red-checkered tablecloth on Mom's kitchen table.

"Clever," Matt exclaimed when he first saw her layout. "Harriet, your ability to organize is remarkable, and these file cards are as sturdy as Vegas playing cards."

He picked up several stacks of cards and demonstrated with a rapid-fire shuffle.

"See?" he said.

I stifled my gasp. He had just commingled names, addresses, trendy appetizers and entrée options.

The response I expected from Mom would have led Matt closer to the coffin than the alter. But she didn't rise to the bait, substituting a calculated cold front for an apoplectic rage.

When Matt pretended remorse with two pounds of See's milk chocolate creams, Mom feigned forgiveness, but I *knew*. Retaliation was coming.

Revenge surfaced via the guest list.

"Those Willis people may invite twenty guests," she announced over the reorganized file boxes. She'd invested in new ones with little latch-locks following the shuffling episode.

"But you said you were planning for two hundred."

"I am."

"Mom, you can't do that. We don't even know a hundred and eighty people. You have to divide things equally."

"I do not."

The ensuing hour-long debate drove Dad to the bourbon bottle, and Mom gave in only after I threatened to elope.

"Who's on your list, anyway," I asked, now thoroughly suspicious.

"Mostly our beloved kin."

Her answer was way too quick. I waited until she got up from the table, and as soon as she stuck her head in the oven to see if the pot-roast was salvageable, I grabbed the file-box she'd been fiddling with. The latch was unlocked, so I flipped through the cards.

Wait a minute.

"Why is Bob's name here?" I asked, indignant.

"I'm inviting him." She slammed the oven door shut.

"Well, if you're including him, then I'm going to invite Vi."

"No way. That woman was a harlot."

"A what? That's silly. She's my friend, and I thought this was *my* day."

An even bigger brouhaha followed, and the pot-roast shriveled into history. Vi made the guest list, but I had to agree to three of Mom's second cousins, gross blights on her family tree.

"You've included your cousin Buster? You can't stand him," I said.

"No matter. Kin is kin." And that was that.

*   *   *

Maisie had almost fallen off her stool at Slims when she found out the guys from the office were coming.

"My God, you didn't invite those bozos, did you?" she asked.

"I thought it would be rude not to."

"All three—Webber, Anders, and Moroni?"

"Yes."

"They'll see me in that dumb-ass fairy dress and never let me live it down." She ordered a double Cutty Sark.

*   *   *

Mom was in her own orbit and hell-bent on knocking everyone else off theirs. Emily Post's blue book never left her hand. If it wasn't in the book, it didn't happen, and if it was, it did.

"You can't be serious," I told her. "Gift displays are for rich people and princesses. Who wants to look at Corning Ware?"

I guess she did.

"Your hair is different, Mom." I noticed because she looked good in her artichoke-bouffant helmet, and now her hair seemed weird.

"I'm letting it grow because I'm going to have a chignon for the wedding."

No one under the age of eighty would be caught dead in the style, but it didn't matter, because that's what the mother of the bride in Emily's book wore, so that's how it would be.

Her obsession even extended to her choice of attire—the lace dress she found at Capwells was the exact shade of blue as the book's cover.

The part of the book Mom ignored was the chapter

dealing with the honeymoon. She attempted to relieve the groom of that responsibility.

The four of us—Mom, Dad, Matt, and I—were seated at the kitchen table. Matt put on a brave face as he stared at the Brussel sprouts drowning in a bowl of Campbell's cream of mushroom soup.

"Tell Matt I've mapped out a lovely wedding trip." Mom said, addressing her comments to me. "First, we'll drive to Capitola for the begonias. Inland, though, because I don't like all those bohemians around Big Sur. Then down the coast to Hearst Castle."

Matt prickled.

"Harriet, I'm sitting here at your table two feet away from you. Why would Amy need to relay your message? And what do you mean *we*?" he asked. "Amy and I will plan our own honeymoon, for *two*." He never gave her an inch on the honeymoon or anything else.

*   *   *

But *we* didn't plan our own honeymoon.

Hawaii was my dream. I had stacks of brochures stashed in my desk. Palm trees, beaches, mid-night romps in gentle surf. Should it be Maui or Kauai?

Matt never asked me what I wanted.

"Dad's worked it all out," Matt told me. "He's loaning us his lodge at Tahoe for a week."

Left out of the loop again, and I dared not say a thing. Matt was pleased, so why risk offending Big Matt? Besides, I was too busy and too besotted to care—much. But it festered, and the elephant stirred.

CHAPTER THIRTY-SEVEN

"Hi, kid. What's up?"

Guilt, shame, and joy—all at once. How had I neglected Vi for so long?

"Vi, I'm so glad you called. I miss you, but so much has happened that I can't keep up with myself."

"Well, get over here after work tomorrow so's we can catch up."

"I'll be there. Would you like me to pick up some Chinese on my way over?" I asked.

"No thanks. I'm gonna send the dud for food so's he's outta our hair. Speakin' about hair, how's yours?"

"Mr. Al is working out fine. Tell Rita I really appreciate the referral."

"Rita and me's not talkin' right now. Big ruckus. Tell you about it tomorrow."

*　　　　*　　　　*

Vi's husband Roy, aka Dud, had parked his car on the street in front of the house, so when I drove up, I boldly parked in the driveway under the kitchen window.

I tramped up the back stairs, and when I opened the door and stepped into the kitchen, Vi greeted me with an enormous hug.

"Kid, you're lookin' damn good," she said, stepping back for an inspection. "Like the hair, and you got the makeup down cold. Still could jazz up the clothes though."

"I'm still on probation at work, Vi, so I'm stuck with the dress code on weekdays."

Her muumuu swirled—a tropical print featuring pink flamingoes—as she reached for wine glasses from the cupboard and took a bottle of Blue Nun from the refrigerator.

"Roy," she called out, "get goin' over to the Silver Dragon and don't hurry back. Amy and me got lots to discuss."

"H'lo Amy," he yelled, and then I heard the front door open and close.

*   *   *

"He don't mind cause he's gonna eat a whole dinner at the restaurant before he comes back here and scarfs down another one. Now, have a seat and tell me what's goin' on." She tugged the cork from the bottle.

"Vi, you were right," I said, pulling out a kitchen chair. "That weekend when you and Brian went to Las Vegas, Matt proposed."

I extended my left hand to show her my engagement ring. Vi frowned.

"Nice, kid. Pretty, but kinda dinky, don't ya think?"

"It's an antique, Vi. The ring was his grandmother's and his mom wanted me to have it."

Vi thought this over.

"Well, the sentimental part's okay, and you musta done

good with his mother. But I wanna know how he proposed—nothin' I love better'n a love story."

So, I described the enchanting beginning to the evening at the Clairmont Hotel. But then I came to Matt's revelation. It might have been the wine, but I choked up when I told her about the pregnancy, his marriage and divorce, and my dismay that Matt had withheld this for so long.

"It was a shock, Vi, and I'm still not sure what to make of it."

Her response was thoughtful.

"Kid, I seen plenty a shotgun-setups and they never work. He shoulda told you sooner, but men's men, and don't be surprised at nothin' they do." She snorted and shook her head before continuing.

"Now, I'm not bein' nosy, but you got that honeymoon glow, and I don't want *you* gettin' knocked up. Seen it time after time. Couple's in love, she gets pregnant, he gets cold feet, and she ends up on her own with the kid. Or she hides in one a them homes for unwed mothers, pops out the kid, and puts it up for adoption. Heartbreak all the way."

Vi was on target, as usual.

"Matt's been careful, Vi, but I have an appointment next week at Planned Parenthood to get the Pill, just to be sure."

"Smart, kid. Don't depend on nobody else to take care of business."

She poured us more wine as I rattled on about weekends with Matt, the wedding dress, Mom's obsession with Emily. Then I mentioned the chalet and red flags flew.

"Kid, listen up. If he says somethin' about buyin' the place, stall until after you're married. Remember what I told you. Make sure you got your name on the deed."

Yes, ma'am.

Our attention was diverted when we heard the front door open. Roy waddled into the kitchen, reeking of garlic and soy sauce, and placed a big paper bag on the counter.

"Good seein' ya, Amy," he said. He fished four super-sized cardboard containers out of the bag, opened them, and stuck serving spoons in each.

"Pork chow mein, egg foo yung, fried won-ton, and sweet and sour chicken. Help yourself, ladies. It's real good."

"Where's the spring rolls and potstickers?" Vi asked.

"They was tasty, too," he said.

Vi cast a disgusted look at his spectacular paunch, got up, opened a cupboard, and handed each of us one of her Melmac daisy plates.

"Mister, if you keep eatin' double, you're gonna need a wheelbarrow to cart around that stomach. Take your plate and go watch TV. Me and Amy's still discussin'."

Roy took a second plate from the cupboard, loaded both dishes, and shuffled off.

"Vi, you mentioned something about Rita," I said, approaching the cartons with caution. I figured the egg fu yung and a piece of the chicken would be enough to counterbalance the wine. Calories were a persistent enemy, and I had to fit into my wedding dress.

"Kid, it's messy," Vi said, sitting back down at the table with a hearty serving of her favorite, the pork chow mein.

"See, when Hank cancelled the contract on her fancy new car and the gigaloo dumped her, Rita bawled for days. Then she got mad and blamed Hank for the whole mess, even though she started it. Tossed him out of the house.

"Hank's beside himself. He comes to me and says, 'Vi, I

want Rita back, but she won't give me the time of day. Talk some sense into her.'

"I think on it a while, and then I tell him, 'Hank, she's not gonna listen to me. You gotta make her jealous.'

"'How do I do that?' he asks.

"Find yourself a snazzy-lookin' date, go someplace where Rita's sure to see you, and get all lovey-dovey with the date. I know Rita, and she's not takin' no backseat to nobody.

"'How would I find a date and where would I take her?' he asks.

"Hank, you got no imagination, I tell him.

"'That's what Rita always says about me,' he says.

"He's hopeless, so I take over. A good-lookin' woman, Luci, works over at the bank. Not in Rita's class, but pretty enough, and I know she's single. So, I go over to the bank to deposit some dividend checks—I already told you about investin' in blue chips, kid—and I lay out the deal to Luci.

"I'm upfront, tell her Hank's married to my daughter, Rita, but they're separated. He's still carryin' a big torch and needs to shake her up so's she'll want him back.

"Luci says, 'Vi, I been doin' your deposits for a lot of years, and you're a straight shooter. If it'll help you, I'll do it. Besides, I could do with a fancy dinner out. But I wanna meet this guy for coffee first, just in case he gives me the creeps.'

"Okay, I say. I tell Hank to take off his glasses, suck in his gut, and go over to the bank to meet Luci and take her out for coffee. It goes okay, and Luci calls me and gives me the green light.

"Now, Rita's favorite restaurant is Roxy's in downtown Oakland. I call Rita and tell her I got a cravin' for a good steak, but I'm not gonna go with Brian 'cause I'm sick a watchin' him eat. 'Don't blame you,' she says, so I call the restaurant and make two dinner reservations. One for Hank and Luci at 7:00 and one for me and Rita at 7:30. I figure that gives them time to settle in before me and Rita show up.

"It kinda worked, but not too good. Rita picks me up. We get to Roxy's right on time and walk in.

"Hank and Luci's at the restaurant, but not at a table. They was sittin' in a booth in the bar haven' a high old time. And I only seen Luci workin' at the bank and didn't know how good she looked gussied up. All cozied up, they was laughin' and smoochin' up a storm. Didn't even see us. Rita and me was non-plussed.

"'We're outta here,' she says. *Damn*. I didn't even get my steak. Rita bitches all the way home and says she's gonna give Hank the come-on and take him back."

"So your plan worked, Vi?" I asked, awed by her manipulative skills.

"Almost. I just didn't figure Hank and Luci would get the hots for each other. They're still whoopin' it up.

"Then Rita remembers seein' Luci when she took me to the bank and figures out I set it up. That's why we're not talkin'. Want a fortune cookie, kid?"

"Better not, Vi. Thanks for dinner. My mom's working on invitations and she's mailing them on this coming Thursday, June 1st, because her book says they should be mailed six weeks before the wedding. The date's July 15th.""

"Wouldn't miss it for nothin', kid."

CHAPTER THIRTY-EIGHT

"We're off schedule here." Mom hunkered over the multitude of file boxes and lists still littering her command post.

"What's off?" I knew that whatever the problem, Matt was to blame.

"You haven't even bought your wedding rings yet. That cheap huckster probably can't afford them. The nerve, sticking you with a used, leftover engagement ring. Sentimental antique, my eye. He most likely picked it up at a pawnshop. Bob would have presented you with a beautiful diamond from Give Me Gold."

"Mom, Bob would have given me a ring off of one of his pistons. Matt and I are going shopping on Saturday to get the rings and whatever else we'll need for the house."

"I thought flimflam man had furniture in storage."

"He had it delivered yesterday."

"I want to see it."

"Mom, *I* haven't even seen it yet. Matt dresses impeccably. I'm sure his taste is excellent, and his things will be lovely. I'm going over to the chalet right after work today."

The prospect of setting up our own household made me giddy with anticipation. When I was a little girl, my long-lost friend Penny and I spent endless hours furnishing our doll houses. Everything had to be just-so, and white wicker was my favorite. If a piece only came in colored plastic, I'd paint over it using a bottle of what looked like white nail polish that I snitched from Dad's desk.

I'd looked through Mom's McCall's magazines over the years and loved finding a room displaying plump cozy chairs and sofas covered in white and pastel fabrics. Those images became imbedded in my fantasies.

Someday, you'll find your someone and live in a quaint house filled with light and white.

Excited, and consumed with curiosity, I rushed to the chalet after work the following day—driving with care because of the abundance of deer in the neighborhood. I nudged the VW into the carport next to Matt's Impala and bounded out.

Down the stairs, across the deck, and through the un-locked front door. I came to an abrupt stop.

No amount of imagery could transform the leather couch that now occupied almost one entire wall of the living area. Big, brown, and ugly. I hated it at first sight.

All his stuff was big, brown, and ugly. A trestle style table—with four toasters still in their original packaging piled on top—benches rather than chairs, matching end tables shoved on either end of the couch, and an over-sized, overstuffed armchair. And a square little Motorola TV standing on spokes for legs.

Thank God I don't see any beanbag chairs.

"What do you think?" Matt asked, popping out of the bedroom with a cheery grin on his face.

"Well, everything's quite sturdy and very masculine," was all I managed to say.

"I know you might want to make a few changes. Have a look at the bedroom."

I looked.

Help.

Two fanged gargoyles peered at me from the corners of a roughly carved headboard, and a leering demon loomed in the center. A chest-of-drawers sprouted multiple pulls in the shape of smaller gargoyle skulls.

The little ones will fly like bats and whoosh over our heads in the night, and the big one is a drooling pervert. I'm never shutting my eyes or making love in their evil presence.

My reaction was instant and visceral. I jumped backward, landing on Matt's foot.

"You know, this bedroom set might not be so hot," he said, rubbing off the smudge I'd made on his immaculately shined shoe.

It certainly wasn't.

"Several years ago, I worked for a furniture manufacturer and the company went belly-up. Somehow their products never caught on."

No kidding.

"This stuff was all floor samples they wanted to ditch, so I took what I needed and never gave it much thought. How about we go shopping for a new bedroom set after we buy the rings on Saturday?"

"Can we afford to?" What a wonderful question to be asking. *We*, planning a future.

"Trust me," he said.

Not wanting to go near the tainted bedroom, I cautiously approached the couch for a first sit. *Poof* went my dream of intimate cuddles on a soft, inviting sofa. Hard as a rock, and so massive I felt like a Lilliputian. My feet dangled inches off the floor, and a foot-and-a-half separated my back from the couch's.

Packing boxes were scattered all over the living room, and I was afraid to look inside them for fear of what atrocities I might find. But curiosity about the four boxes stacked on the table that contained toasters overcame my hesitancy.

"You must like toast a lot." I eyed the table.

"Oh, *those*. I worked for a car agency before I took this job, and these were the prizes I kept winning for salesman of the month. My mom took a couple. They come in handy as wedding gifts.

"The whopping prize came when I won as salesman of the year. I got a huge discount on the Impala. But the dealership rules said I couldn't win the big contest more than once, so it was time for me to move on."

This will be an interesting life.

CHAPTER THIRTY-NINE

The Saturday shopping trip began at Give Me Gold. I knew Mom would harp to eternity if my wedding ring didn't come in one of their fancy boxes.

"Oh, this is perfect." I was delighted when the jeweler showed me a simple white-gold band sprinkled with a few small diamonds. Just right to complement the antique engagement ring without overpowering it. Matt chose a wide gold band etched with a serpentine design. He wanted to pay for both our rings, but I insisted that I buy his.

"I want you to have something special from me that will last forever." My gaze locking into his mesmerizing eyes.

"Well, when you put it that way, of course. I'll cherish it, darling Amy. Shall we have them engraved?"

The jeweler, who'd been standing by listening and suppressing eye-roles, cleared his throat.

"May I suggest that you have them sized now and inscribed after the wedding? One never knows, and I can't resell a ring that's already been engraved."

Awkward. Extremely awkward. Matt filled the silence.

"Appreciate the advice, sir, but we're in this for keeps."

No wonder I loved him.

We left the rings to be sized and inscribed, each with a simple *Forever*.

*   *   *

On to Breuners Fine Furnishings. The store was in downtown Oakland with its entrance and enticing display windows facing Broadway. We parked on 20th Street and walked around the corner.

Matt stopped to admire a huge, handsome piece featured in one of the windows.

"That's a stunning dining room credenza, but it's rather large," I said.

"No, it's not a credenza. It's an entertainment center—TV, stereo, turntable, speakers. The works, all in one place. Cool. But let's go find the bedroom furniture. Need to get a king-sized mattress. I hate that queen-size of mine."

He liked big things.

Matt took my hand and led us inside to the store directory. I *loved* it when he held my hand.

Bedroom furnishings were on the third floor. We took the escalator and stepped off into a multitude of mattresses.

"Try a few," the salesclerk urged. We bounced up and down several rows and came to the conclusion that Matt liked rock-hard and I preferred pillow-soft. We compromised with a medium so that each of us would share the discomfort equally.

"Are you sure a king-size will fit in our bedroom?" I asked. How I loved the sound of *that*—our bedroom.

"Trust me," Matt said.

The size of the mattress limited the number of suites to consider, because not all manufacturers made king-size headboards.

"Look at this set." I pointed to a mirrored dresser, a large chest-of-drawers with civilized pulls, and a sleek, unadorned headboard. The light, ash-toned wood appealed to us both. But the price was staggering.

"Matt, we can't afford this." I whispered so the loitering salesman couldn't hear.

"Trust me," Matt said. "Do they carry dishes here?"

"They have a department for fine china."

"Why don't you go choose something to replace that God-awful flowery mess your mother picked out. I'll finish up here and come find you."

*   *   *

The Fine China Department and Wedding Registry occupied premium space on the second floor, and the slow descent on the escalator allowed me a bird's-eye view of a vast array of table-trappings.

Hundreds of plates perched on grooved shelves on one wall, and an amazing number of crystal goblets and flutes sparkled on the glass shelves of an adjacent wall. Locked glass-topped counters held multiple setting of silverware.

Wow.

A matronly woman with a kind face, obviously a salesperson, was deep in conversation with an agitated customer waving a mangled utensil in her face.

"Madam, I'm very sorry for what your disposal did to your fork, but we are not responsible for the damage. I'll be happy to order you a replacement, but you must pay for it," the salesclerk informed her.

The customer huffed off wearing a sour expression, and the clerk turned to me.

"May I help you, dear?" she asked.

"I hope so. I'm getting married in July, and I think my mother might have registered me for a china pattern that I don't like," I told her.

"Let's check it out. My name is Bernice. What's yours?"

"Amy Archer, but my mom could have used hers, Harriet Archer."

"Happens all the time. Mothers get whacky. Let me sort through our files."

She sat down at a fanciful Queen Anne style desk and began flipping through the cards on a massive Rolodex-type file.

"Yes, here she is. Oh dear, whoever waited on her should have told her the pattern she chose has been discontinued. Had so many roses on it that people couldn't find their food. The silver she selected is still available, though. Grande Baroque."

"I'd like to start fresh, please," I said.

"We'll fill out a new card for you and get you registered. Now, all our patterns are displayed on the dinner plates lining the far wall. While you browse, I'll begin the paperwork. No hurry."

This will take forever, I thought.

Wrong. Within five minutes, I knew what I wanted. Lenox Weatherly. An almost translucent cream-colored bone china, softly swirled and trimmed in platinum.

"I found the perfect pattern, Bernice," I called out. She was beside me in a flash.

"Lovely. Now let me show you the glassware Lenox makes to go with it. Very simple water goblets and wine glasses also rimmed in platinum." She led me to the wall of crystal.

"I love these," I said, fingering the fragile stem of the wine glass.

"Next, you'll need silverware. Do you want solid silver or silver-plated?"

"Silver-plated will be fine."

I was drawn to a simple pattern called Morning Rose. The lines flowed, and one delicate rose tipped each handle. But I hesitated.

"My fiancé might find this too fussy because of the rose," I told Bernice.

"Let's set up a full place setting on our demonstration table so you can see how everything looks," she suggested.

Gathered pieces from the walls and cabinets, Bernice laid them out on a small damask-covered table.

We stood looking at the display, and I thought the entire thing went together beautifully.

"Shall I write up the patterns for the registry?" she asked.

"We'd better wait for my fiancé to see it, Bernice. He might not like it."

A voice from behind us said, "He likes it just fine."

We turned, and Matt was standing there with his irresistible smile.

The look on Bernice's face was that of instant adoration.

"The silverware isn't too feminine?" I asked him.

"I've lived with masculine long enough. It's time for a change. I knew you'd choose something wonderful. This has the same, understated elegance that you have, Amy."

In my entire life, no one had ever paid me such an extravagant compliment. I was completely flummoxed, and I thought Bernice was going to swoon.

I love this man.

CHAPTER FORTY

Hunger tore us from Bernice. Edy's Ice Cream Parlor and Luncheonette was two blocks down the street, so we walked over for a late lunch and serious review of our purchases and financial state.

"Did you buy the bedroom suite?" I asked as we settled into a pink Naugahyde booth. Color-coordinated menus were already on the table.

An aproned waitress appeared before Matt could answer.

"Have you looked at the menu yet?" she inquired.

"I glanced at it, but I know what I want," he said. Matt had a metabolism that burned countless calories within seconds of consumption.

I watched in envy as he ordered a triple-layered turkey, bacon, and cheese club sandwich and a three-scoop chocolate sundae with extra sauce, whipped cream, and cherries. And coffee.

My metabolism was similar to that of the slugs Mom exterminated, and my wedding gown had already been fitted.

"I'll have the lunch-sized Caesar salad with the dressing on the side. And one scoop of orange sherbet, please Also, an iced tea."

The waitress scribbled on her order pad and left.

Matt and I resumed our conversation.

"Yep. I bought it, but it took some maneuvering. I know

both the markup on furniture and how a salesman is evaluated not only on dollars per sale but on also on volume and rapid turnover. Roll those babies out the door. So, I offered him 25% over cost.

"He laughed in my face. Then I told him I wanted that entertainment center in the window, and that I'd pay 30% over cost for it."

I gasped.

"Matt, the price tag on that is more than my VW."

"That's regular retail. By now, the guy's interested, and he also wants to know what company I'm working for. He hates selling furniture. I gave him my card and told him I could arrange an interview with my boss.

"Then it was time to toss him a bone. 'Look, I'll pay 30% over cost for both the bedroom suite and the entertainment center, but that's my last offer.' The guy swallowed the bait and wrote up the sale on my terms. We're in, Amy—landed them both. What a great afternoon."

I now understood the term 'hustler.'

"May I change my order from the sherbet to a chocolate marshmallow float?" I asked the waitress when she returned with our coffee and iced tea.

Might as well live big.

*   *   *

Jittering with sugar rushes, we began our discussion of financial and household responsibilities. Simple, because it was all prescribed.

I had a joint checking account with Dad—single women were not allowed individual accounts—and the same rule applied to car loans. Once a month, I deposited my meager paycheck and wrote a check to Dad. A nominal amount for room and board and a sizeable sum to reimburse him for the payment on my VW. Two more to go and the pink slip would be mine.

Matt and I agreed that he would manage major finances. The man always did. But something didn't feel right with me handing over my entire paycheck for deposit into an account in his name alone.

How would Vi handle this? I asked myself, in the bliss of a sugar fog. Her voice roared through my head.

"Kid, keep the one you got with your dad. After you're married, the bank's gonna let you open your own. Have Matt open a joint account for household stuff, and you both pitch in—but he's earnin' the big bucks, so's he should toss in a lot more. Once he gets rollin' you shouldn't be puttin' in nothin'—a *real* man takes care of his woman."

I wasn't sure she and I had actually had the conversation or if I was channeling her thoughts, but when I suggested to Matt that he open a joint account, to which I would contribute modestly, he was in complete agreement.

"But only until I'm established in this job," he said. "You work so hard for such a paltry amount of money, it should be yours."

Thank you, Vi.

Monetary concerns were out of the way, so we turned our attention to other responsibilities. It was assumed and agreed that I would manage the household. The woman always did.

When the sugar high wore off, I realized that Matt's duties were to write checks, oversee car maintenance, and open jars.

Mine were to clean the house—vacuum, mop, scrub, dust, polish. Tend to the laundry—sort, wash, dry, iron. Shop for groceries and necessities—supermarket, drug store, and related errands. Cook—and I couldn't boil an egg. All on top of my forty to fifty-hour work week. Plus, I was to be a charming companion, a gracious hostess, a hot lover, and maintain a smashing appearance. And write all the thank-you notes.

A tall order, but in 1961, that's what was expected of a good wife. And I intended to be the best.

*   *   *

The new bedroom furniture was to be delivered Monday of the following week, but the entertainment center would not be ready for at least six weeks because someone in North Carolina was constructing it.

Matt began moving his stuff from Big Matt's house and tended to a myriad of details. Pacific Gas & Electric, water, garbage collection, and telephone service. We agreed that Mom would be given the wrong number.

Then Matt came up with a terrifying suggestion.

"How about we move my bedroom furniture to the spare room and turn it into a bedroom for guests?"

He scoffed at my insistence that the gargoyles would zoom around in the night and bite us, so I had to come up with something that would frighten him as much as the grimacing creatures that spooked me.

"Matt, if we set up a spare bedroom, I guarantee my mother will park herself in it."

That was enough, and he arranged for the Salvation Army

to haul the gargoyles away on Friday. I imagined the little ones hissing and the big one growling and spitting as they were tossed in the truck.

We also discovered, while unpacking boxes, that if even one bench was pulled out to sit at the trestle table, it was necessary to climb on and over the bench to access the postage-stamp kitchen.

"This will get old fast," Matt said, cracking his head on the overhead hanging light fixture.

When he explained the origin of the bruise on his forehead to his father, Big Matt came up with a quick fix.

"Your mother is on pins and needles waiting for that damned new cookbook, and now she wants to replace the table and chairs in our kitchen with something called Country French. Son, you can learn a lesson here. Happy wife, happy life. I'll buy Rose what she wants, and you two can have our old stuff. We'll loan you our card table and folding chairs for you to use in the meantime."

*   *   *

Big Matt and Jack brought over the card table and chairs on the Sunday before the furniture delivery from Breuners. The three fellows struggled, moaned and grunted as they maneuvered the trestle table and benches into the spare bedroom, now to be referred to as the office.

My office, where I was confined to write thank-you notes while the guys lolled on the deck recuperating from their efforts. Sprawled in the folding chairs, Matt and Big Matt drank beers, Jack had a Coke, and they chomped chips and talked golf. They graciously excused me so I could work on the notes.

Curiosity got the better of me. Now that the kitchen was accessible without a treacherous climb, I took a break to see what other provisions Matt had stocked. I flung open the cupboard and refrigerator doors, admittedly miffed at the unfair division of tasks.

In the fridge, I found Nation's hot dogs, milk, a cube of butter, a six-pack of Coke and two six-packs of Budweiser beer.

The cupboard contained staples: salt, pepper, French's mustard, Heinz catsup. Plus, Skippy peanut butter, a loaf of Kilpatrick's sliced white bread, hot dog buns and a can of Folger's coffee. Well, he'd certainly taken care of himself. I now hated peanut butter and never drank coffee.

But then I realized he'd segregated the shelves and filled the lowest one, most easily within my reach, with my essentials. Red Rose black tea, saccharin, canned white tuna, mayo, Del Monte sweet pickle relish, apricot jam and the most thoughtful of all, two cans of colossal black olives.

Was there ever a more considerate man? My heart melted.

*　　　　*　　　　*

The bedroom furniture was delivered Monday morning, as promised, and now that we had a bed, Matt finished moving into the chalet.

I raced over after work to check out the bedroom set. I loved it—so sleek and simple. The king-sized mattress was a trifle large for the space, making it necessary to shuffle sideways between the dresser and the foot of the bed, and the dresser drawers could only be opened part-way, but who cared?

We lined three shelves in the kitchen before a dash to the bedroom for a splendid inauguration of the Serta.

But we made a pact. I would not spend an entire night until we were married because I wanted to be snuggled with my husband the first morning I awakened at the chalet. And Matt was convinced that my mom would attack in the predawn hours if she discovered my overnight absence.

Besides, another issue had presented itself—we had forgotten to buy any king-size sheets. Matt's left-over queen-sized ones proved to be totally inadequate after one romp, but I suggested we hold off on a purchase because of the upcoming bridal shower.

"You never know what type of gift might turn up."

CHAPTER FORTY-ONE

How true.

When Lynn and her mom had offered to host a bridal shower, I was delighted, but Mom was ticked off when I told her about the proposed party.

"You'd be marrying Bob if that beatnik cradle robber hadn't interfered and set you up with a two-bit salesman," she crabbed.

She'd just finished scouring an unlucky frying pan with an SOS pad and plunked herself down at the kitchen table with Emily's book on her lap.

"Lynn's mother should be ashamed of her daughter for seducing that adolescent Pete."

"Mom, there's no way I would have married Bob, so let it go. I think it's lovely that Mrs. Westin is having the event at her house, and Lynn and Pete are none of our business."

"Who's on the guest list?" she asked. Not for a minute did she believe that anything was not her business.

"Lynn and her mom, Matt's mom Rose and his aunt, Irma...."

She interrupted me.

"That lush Irma will get drunk."

"That's hard to do on Hawaiian punch." I continued with the list. "Maisie and the three bridesmaids, four girlfriends from work, Aunt Jane, and Vi."

Mom's face resembled those of the gargoyles banished from the bedroom. "My sister will be swilling from her flask, and I will not associate with that low-class tramp Vi. Bob's told me all about her."

Enough. No way am I going to let her ruin this once-in-a lifetime event.

"Vi's been a great friend and mentor to me, Mom. I hope you'll come. But if you're going to sit in judgement of Vi, Lynn, and Irma, and most likely get into a fight with Aunt Jane, then it's best that you stay home."

I spoke bold words, something I was finding easier to do. Not speaking up had landed me in church and honeymoon locations, neither of which reflected what I had wanted, and I had only myself to blame. Enough of this cowardly dance on eggshells.

Mom looked shocked at my response.

"I don't know what's gotten into you, missy. It's not like you to be rude." Her jaw was set as tightly as her half-grown-out hair.

Stand your ground. Don't cave.

"I'm not intending to be rude. I just don't want what should be a happy occasion spoiled. Check out what your guru Emily Post says about the responsibility of a guest to be polite."

"I'm always gracious." She thumbed through the pages of Emily's book. "*Humph.* If those wild Berkeley people know any etiquette, they'll put on a proper English tea, with little watercress and cucumber sandwiches—although I wonder about that. Cucumber makes me burp."

*　　　*　　　*

The shower was on the third Saturday in June—a warm day, just right for me to wear my favorite summer dress—a sleeveless periwinkle cotton print with a bell skirt. Mom dressed for combat in her wool navy-colored military coatdress.

"Aren't you going to be too hot in that?" I asked her as we drove up to Mrs. Westin's splendid mansion.

"I felt a chill coming on. Why is that red balloon tied to the front gate?" she snapped.

"So people will know it's the party house." I maneuvered the VW into a tiny space at the curb.

"Typical Berkeley bohemian." She snorted.

"Would you prefer to wait in the car?" I was determined to not be intimidated.

Mom pretended not to hear me, opened the car door, and stepped out before I turned off the engine. She marched to the gate, apparently intending to charge headlong up the stairs, but she couldn't figure out how to open the latch.

Please, please don't antagonize everyone.

As Mom pounded on the gate, three bridesmaids dressed in summery pastels rounded the corner and joined us. Maisie was on their heels.

Some of Mom's steam defused in the flurry of introductions, and I knew how the latch worked, so we gained entry and trooped up the stairs together.

Mrs. Westin, svelte in a white linen sheath, stood at the door greeting everyone with sophisticated aplomb—a far cry from the feral Berkeley denizen Mom had envisioned.

"How lovely to meet you at last, Mrs. Archer. Hard to believe our girls studied together all those years, and we never met," she said, extending her hand. "Please call me Adele."

Mom hesitated a moment and then returned Mrs. Westin's handshake with a limp wrist. The acceptable protocol would have been for Mom to ask Mrs. Westin to address her by her first name.

Did she?

No, Harriet Archer did not, and I wanted to disappear. *She's screwing up the works, as predicted.*

Lynn, not so svelte in a crumpled yellow shift, was kept hopping because all the guests arrived within the next fifteen minutes and scattered into the muted tones of the main living room and adjacent music room. Their pink, yellow, and baby-blue summer dresses popped out like bursts of flowers.

Vi stole the show. She swished in, her hair obviously and expertly tended by Mr. Al, wearing a dramatic turquoise silk caftan. My girlfriends, awed by her star presence and gorgeous costume, flocked to introduce themselves and showered her with compliments.

Mom bristled, and my nerves jangled in fear of an outburst. But Lynn came to the rescue and herded everyone into the elaborate dining room.

"Mrs. Westin, this is fabulous. Thank you so much," I said, surveying the setup.

"My pleasure, Amy. I love to entertain, and you and Lynn share a special friendship."

She had laid out the long, rectangular dining table, draped with a white lace tablecloth, for a buffet. Crustless tea sandwiches—chicken, egg salad, and, yes, cucumber, were artfully arranged on Spode tiered plates. Molded aspect salads—shrimp and fruit—shimmered on platters alongside trays of cheese and sliced melons.

Sideboards flanked the table on either side. A gleaming silver tea service was stationed on one, along with additional tiered plates of glazed petit fours, finger-sized chocolate eclairs, and miniature cream puffs. *Yum.*

Two crystal punch bowls sparkled on the other sideboard. Embossed labels identified the contents of one as traditional Hawaiian Punch and the other as Long Island Iced Tea.

Mom scrutinized the lavish spread, and not even her jaundiced eye could find fault.

"The woman must have a copy of Emily Post's book," she said, refusing to acknowledge either Mrs. Westin's first or last name.

A brief fantasy flashed through my brain that involved a drowning, but neither punch bowl was deep enough to submerge Mom's head and big hair. Plus, there were too many witnesses.

The Long Island Iced Tea surprised me. Matt and I had gone to dinner at a restaurant called Trader Vic's that was noted for exotic drinks. The cocktail menu listed the ingredients for various concoctions, including Long Island Iced Tea, and I remembered the recipe because I couldn't quite believe the mixture—triple sec, gin, vodka, rum, and tequila, with a splash of coke.

"Lynn, is that punch the real thing?" I asked, puzzled that Mrs. Westin would be serving something so potent at an afternoon ladies' shower.

"You bet it is. My mom hates a stodgy party, and this is her signature ice-breaker."

*   *   *

Mom, hovering by the table, picked up a luncheon plate. Did she place any food on it? No. She turned it over to see if it was genuine Wedgewood.

Please, please don't humiliate me anymore, I prayed. Had anyone seen that? How could they have not?

Next, she reached for a linen napkin and began fanning herself with it.

"I'm too hot. I'm going to have the iced tea, although I don't know why it's being served in punch cups instead of glasses," she said.

Uh-oh.

"Mom, it's not really iced tea. It's straight alcohol with a little coke. You'd better try the Hawaiian Punch."

"Nonsense. Why would it be called tea without any tea in it?"

She picked up a cup and tossed down the contents like a glass of water.

"This coke is delicious," she said. "I'll have another."

"Not a good idea, Mom."

She snatched the punch ladle and refilled the cup.

I hesitated.

Wait a minute. This might be a fantastic idea. If she drinks herself into a stupor, she might shut up. Chug-a-lug, Mom.

Mom consumed two-and-a-half cups before she went down for the count.

Tottering into the music room, she abruptly sat down in a soft leather chair.

I placed some sandwiches (no cucumber) on a plate to take to her, but by the time I arrived in the room, she had nodded off—or passed out. I wasn't sure which.

So we all ate, drank, and whooped it up as Mom snored

quietly in the background. Aunt Jane, Irma, and Vi bonded while comparing their purse flasks, and my future mother-in-law Rose came down with the giggles.

"Who's going to be the recorder?" she asked, stifling a genteel hiccup. Custom called for someone to jot down comments as gifts were opened—and to read them back as possible wedding-night conversation. Whoever rendered the funniest line won a prize.

"I'll do it," Lynn volunteered.

The first gift I opened was from Rose—a hardback copy of Rombauer's *The Joy of Cooking*—which sparked a communal conversation about favorite foods.

Lynn handed me the next gift, elaborately wrapped in gold and white foil. I opened the box and inside was a filmy black lace teddy from Aunt Jane.

Wow. The subsequent exclamations of "oh" and "ah" were followed by tipsy speculations as to which of the previously mentioned foods were the most effective aphrodisiacs.

"Not none of them, girls. The best is oysters," Vi declared. "Get things goin' with a little champagne, and then dish up some fresh oysters on the half shell, some chocolate-covered strawberries, and a damn good red wine. Does it every time."

"Should the oysters be raw or cooked?" Irma asked. She was all ears and looked a bit cross-eyed.

"You can bake 'em in butter with breadcrumbs but don't get too fancy. If your man goes overboard on the eats, you're gonna have a flop on your hands."

Mom regained consciousness at the tail end of the discussion, noticed *The Joy of Cooking*, and misunderstood the topic. She thought we were talking about cookbooks.

"Well," she said, shaking herself awake, "I think Betty Crocker does it best. Follow her instructions and the goodies puff up perfectly."

The prize, embroidered tea towels, was divided between Mom and Vi. Mom had no idea why she had won.

*   *   *

Matt was flummoxed when he saw the two sets of sheets we had received as gifts at the shower. Plaid flannel from Mom, and red satin from Vi.

"I guess we either swelter or slide off the bed, he concluded.

God. One more task. Now, in addition to writing fourteen more effusive thank-you notes, I would need to exchange the sheets.

Matt wouldn't have time to run the errand because he was off to his bachelor party.

A shower was a multi-generational bonding experience for women, but a bachelor party appeared to be the opposite. Guests were Matt's contemporaries from work and college. Best-man Jack and groomsman Pete were underage, and Dad and Big Matt were over age, so the four of them were excluded.

I surmised that I would not be happy about whatever went on and chose not to learn too much about it—except that gifts were not involved, eliminating the need for thank-you notes. Men got all the breaks.

CHAPTER FORTY-TWO

One day before the momentous event, the wedding party gathered on the steps of the church in North Berkeley. Friday, July 14 at 5:00. The date more aptly might have been a Friday the 13th with a full moon.

I wore my baby-blue, flare-skirted Lanz dress—treasured because of its scalloped neckline.

Mom chose not to wear her navy-blue combat dress. She disguised herself in a summery flowered frock, so I was lulled into the hopeful delusion that she would behave. Foolish me.

Her nose was already out of joint because Big Matt had won the final say-so on the church. And it didn't matter to her that he and Rose were generously hosting a dinner at the quaint, historic Hotel Durant immediately after the rehearsal. He'd stepped on her toes.

Now Mom stood tapping those toes, arms folded across her chest, as the disparate horde of 16 participants crowded the stairs.

Bride-and-groom-to-be, both sets of parents, matron of honor Maisie, best man Jack, Lynn and the three other bridesmaids, and the four groomsmen, including Lynn's boyfriend Pete.

Forced alliances in an unfamiliar setting, and everyone milled in uneasy camaraderie.

"Just who are we waiting for?" Mom demanded to know at 4:03.

"The minister," Big Matt responded.

"Is that what you call the head of this cockamamie modern church?" Mom asked.

Maybe the God of this church will smite her.

Big Matt glared, but before he could formulate a retort, a spry 60ish man opened the stately doors.

"Welcome, folks," he said with a cheery smile. "I'm Pastor Tom. Let's go in and have a look at the chapel."

Dad grabbed Mom's arm, herded her away from Big Matt, and we all followed the pastor through a small vestibule and into the chapel.

A fine chapel it was—a simple space highlighted by stunning stained-glass windows. Brilliant colors lined the panels along the side walls, a cascade of panes in softer hues backed the nave, and the vaulted ceiling looked as if it reached to heaven. A beatific angel smiled down from one of the higher-placed panes.

Pastor Tom's countenance was kindly, but he took charge with a strong hand.

"We'll begin at the beginning. Who is going to escort Mrs. Archer to her seat?" he asked.

Pete fidgeted and shifted from foot to foot, radiating teen-age discomfort despite his manly size. Reluctantly, he raised his hand.

"Me. I lost the coin-toss," he said.

Mom shot Pete a slit-eyed missile, and Dad faked a cough to mask his spontaneous guffaw.

Pastor Tom carried on, directing everyone to their designated locations. Once he was convinced that everybody had at least a minimal grasp of what to do, he turned his attention to the actual ceremony.

Matt and I had already agreed on a few variations.

I was not an object and under no circumstances would I agree to be given away. Mom immediately protested when she heard my conversation with the pastor.

"You have to let your father and me give you away. That's how it's done," Mom insisted.

"Many brides choose to omit that portion of the proceedings." Pastor Tom's interjection was firm.

Mom simmered. The wrinkled frown on her face reminded me of a chrysanthemum's scrunched-together petals.

Then Matt and I rehearsed our spoken lines—the parts pledging to love, honor, and cherish.

"What about obey?" Mom demanded to know.

"Mom, I will not vow to obey my husband," I said.

"Just as well. It's all backwards, anyway. He should be promising to obey you."

As we left the church, the pastor pulled Matt aside and whispered something. In the car, away from flapping ears, Matt relayed the conversation.

"After one hour of your mother, Pastor Tom told me he'd be praying for me."

*   *   *

I couldn't risk waiting for divine intervention. My nails were imbedded in my palms, I was treading water through waves of anxiety, and I knew Mom had to be disarmed before she destroyed the rehearsal dinner.

Matt's face was stoic as he maneuvered the Impala across Berkeley, but the furrow marring his forehead telegraphed his distress. He had to be equally upset and apprehensive. I reached over the chastity clutch to take his hand.

"Matt, I'm sorry Mom's being insufferable, but she's not going to spoil the evening. I have a plan." I borrowed his line and said, "Trust me."

"You've hired a hit-man?" His amazed blue eyes danced at the prospect.

"That's Plan B."

*   *   *

The Impala was too big to fit in the hotel's underground parking garage, so Matt dropped me off at the entrance while he searched for street parking.

Heavy wood doors, carved and embellished with wrought iron in keeping with the hotel's Spanish design, guarded the entry. I struggled through them and into the lobby, determined to intercept Mom and limit the damage.

Rose, Lynn, and other dropped-off ladies began wrestling their way in and coaxed me to join them, but I shooed them on into the restaurant area on the pretext of waiting for Matt.

Sure enough, Mom thundered in wearing her buffalo expression. I reached out, grabbed her arm, hooked my elbow into hers in an unbreakable grip, and corralled her into the ladies' lounge.

"What's the matter with you—why am I in here?" Confusion replaced the defiance in her eyes.

"Because I will not let your bad attitude ruin this occasion. Knock it off, Mom."

"What bad attitude?" Her jaw jutted out as defiance burbled up again.

"I'm not arguing with you. Remember our talk before the shower? The stakes are higher this time. You have two choices—to behave like a civilized, appreciative guest, or to go home. I hope you'll pull it together. But if you stay and screw up, or choose to insult the Willises by going home, Matt and I will not attend the reception."

"You can't mean that."

"I do, Mom. I can't take it anymore, and neither can Matt. His parents are throwing this lovely party and they don't deserve to be disrespected."

Her jaw receded and her lower lip puffed out. Her pout of temporary surrender.

"But I don't like him or them." She was determined to have the last word.

"Tough. That's the way it is. I suggest you take one of Dad's Milltown tranquillizers or hit the bar."

"There's a bar here?"

"Yes."

"My God, where's your father? He'll get plastered and embarrass me."

If she hadn't darted out the door, I would have pummeled her to sawdust. My eyes went out of focus, and I literally saw red. When my fury subsided and I was able to see again, I hurried out to the lobby and followed the sign to Henry's Bar. A serendipitous bit of irony.

I located them tucked in a corner of the bar. Dad sat at a round cocktail table, fidgeting with a double old-fashion glass that was empty except for two melting ice cubes. I interrupted the whispered dressing-down Mom was administering to Dad and pointed to the hotel's small banquet room.

"March," I said.

*   *   *

A waiter, holding a tray of fluted glasses bubbling with champagne, greeted us at the arched doorway. I made a desperate grab, and my hand trembled as I raised the glass.

Matt is going to call it off. Why should he put up with this ridiculous, dysfunctional garbage?

The first sips settled a raw nerve or two, and I calmed enough to look at the room. Rose's magic touch was everywhere. Six round tables, dressed in starched-stiff white cloths, were each crowned with a bouquet of white roses and blue irises.

Extra seating had been added because the Willises magnanimously invited the spouses of the bridesmaids and groomsmen. (Maisie refused to inform her husband Hubert of the offer.)

Delicate swan-shaped place-card holders defined the seating and cemented my admiration for wise Rose. She eschewed the traditional head table, jumbled ages and alliances, and placed Mom and Dad at a table where they knew no one. A brilliant move because Mom had no history with her table-mates and thus had no territory to defend and no axes to grind.

And perhaps a bit of divine assistance had occurred. Irises happened to be one of Mom's favorite flowers. Mom took one look at the table displays, pinched a petal to verify its non-plastic authenticity (I hated when she did that) and immediately sought out Rose to engage her in a collegial and detailed conversation about growing a bearded variety of the species.

I could breathe. And Matt looked on in wonderment.

"What the hell did you do?" he asked. He clinked his champagne glass against mine.

"Something I ought to have done a long time ago." I broke every rule of public conduct to give him a kiss. He kissed back.

Keepsake menus, embossed with Matt's and my names, informed us that we would dine on the ubiquitous Caesar salad, a clever take on surf and turf consisting of prime rib and grilled prawns, and finish with a surprise confection—strawberry parfaits.

I pitied the folks at Mom's table as she continued her lecture on bearded irises, but otherwise, the evening was lovely. As the party broke up, Rose reminded everyone to take their swans as favors. Then she made another inspired move. Mom and Dad were standing by their table, readying themselves for departure. Rose walked over to them.

"Harriet, I insist you take one of the centerpiece bouquets," she said.

Mom's face reflected multiple emotions—surprise, suspicion, avarice—before she responded.

"I would love one. Are you sure, Rose?" She almost sounded sweet.

"Absolutely."

Mom beamed, and her thanks were sincere when she and

Dad took off. I had hoped that the gesture would have a lasting effect. *Ha.*

My thanks were also genuine and profuse, and I invited Rose to join the wedding-party ladies at the church the following day. She glanced at where Mom had been sitting, caught herself, and looked back at me before she shook her head no.

"Thank you, Amy. I think it's best if I just take my seat early on and enjoy watching the guests as they arrive. I don't want any apple-carts over-turned."

Gracious, insightful, tactful—Rose was going to be the perfect mother-in-law.

Poor Matt.

CHAPTER FORTY-THREE

The big day dawned. Saturday, July 15, 1961. Sunny, not too hot, and bound to be beautiful—except I was running on empty. *Totally* exhausted.

I dragged out of bed, threw on a pair of capris and a tee shirt, went to the kitchen, and made myself a cup of tea. I carried it out to the garden and sat down on the bench to reflect and regroup.

The last two months had been a blur of events, places, and decisions. Jousting with Mom, pleasing Matt, moving mostly out of Mom's and partially into the chalet, working 40-50 hours some weeks, and topped off by the social whirl of celebrations, each of which required the damnable thank-you notes. Diligent though I had been, I was still behind and owed at least 30 more.

And work had exploded, literally. Mrs. Parson's oven blew up at the beginning of the week, creating absolute havoc in Harbor Homes. I expected the Housing Authority to relocate Mrs. Parsons and her family temporarily while the stove was replaced and the kitchen repaired.

Instead, Mrs. Parson received an eviction notice on Thursday claiming she had damaged Federal property. My colleague Anders assured me he would follow up during my honeymoon week, but the initial burden of intervention had fallen on me.

*   *   *

"What in heaven's name are you doing out here?' Mom stuck her head out the door of her potting shed and startled me into spilling half my tea.

"Just thinking, Mom. What are you doing?"

"Organizing. I ran out of room on the kitchen table. If you're thinking about dumping that big-mouth huckster, we'll just skip the church part and turn the reception into a party. Bob's not coming to the wedding because he's going on a field trip to take a mosquito count in the wetlands. The *real* reason is because you broke the poor boy's heart. He'd be here in a flash if I called him."

"Mom, Bob likes bugs and you. He has no interest in me, and I am marrying Matt. Today. So get over it."

"Well, I tried." She huffed and sighed. "You'd better get it together, missy. There's no time to waste on thinking. What time is your hair appointment?"

"Mr. Al is doing the works—my hair, make-up, and nails at 12:30. Where's Dad?"

"He had to run some errands. And my hair appointment at Curl Corner is at 1:00. You and I have to be back here before 4:00 so the bridesmaids can dress."

Another sore subject. The maids and I had agreed that they would dress at their own places and go directly to the church. But Mom hadn't trusted them to arrive at the church wrinkle free. She bullied Delores, the bridal coordinator at the Gray Shop, hi-jacked all the dresses, and buried them in her closet.

"Mom, there would have been a lot less stress if the maids had dressed at home and met us at the church."

"Neither here nor there." She disappeared into her shed.

More tea. I made another cup and went to my room for a last-minute check-out. The gifts I had bought for Maisie and the maids sat on my dresser, wrapped in silver paper with pink bows. Limoges trinket boxes, each with a different flower motif. They were so delicate and pretty that I bought one for Mom, too, and hid it in a drawer.

My going-away outfit—a trendy summer suit with a slim, white lace skirt and a blouson jacket set off by a hot pink shell—was hanging in a garment bag and ready for transport. Matt and I were changing clothes at the reception and leaving straight for the wilds of Tahoe. My costume was totally inappropriate considering the destination, but it would make for a flashy departure.

I'd already packed my suitcase for the honeymoon, and I was feeling confident that I had it all together. A last-minute check of the bathroom dispelled that notion. Two drawers and the medicine cabinet were crammed with cosmetics. Because I kept the small bag I used for weekends at the ready, I'd overlooked countless necessities, including multiple lotions to restore my twenty-two-year-old skin.

I found Mom in the dining room, admiring Rose's centerpiece bouquet on the table. I thought she was going to say something nice. In my dreams.

She shook her head. "I can't believe that Willis woman served us Spanish rice for dinner when we went to her house." No grudge was too old for Mom to carry.

"Mom, forget it. This is an emergency. I need a make-up carrier."

Her defensive hackles sprang. "It wasn't on the bride's list in the book, and it's too late now. You'll have to use your father's duffel bag."

There had to be a better solution.

Matt and I were both spooked into honoring the custom prohibiting us from seeing one another until the ceremony. But how could a phone call jinx anything?

When I phoned him to explain my dilemma, Matt was not at all perturbed.

"No problem, Amy. I'll run over to Hinks. Maybe I can still get a discount. Guess what? I just had a call from Dad, and it worked. He got the judge to sign the papers."

"What papers?"

"Well, my divorce wasn't final. Dad and I didn't mention it because we knew your Mom would have a conniption.

CHAPTER FORTY-FOUR

"My *mom* would have a conniption. What about me?"

I tried not to screech, but I couldn't take it in.

"Don't worry. We'd have gone through with the ceremony, and Dad planned to fix it up later. But he drove over to the golf course this morning and found his buddy, the judge, who took care of the paperwork. I'll go get the bag you need now."

What—am I crazy? Matt had implied that his first marriage and the divorce occurred several years ago. I couldn't believe what I'd heard, and in seven hours I would be married to this man.

Or will I?

Jitters. Just jitters. Do not panic. My mind was mush. Another huge omission, deliberate deception, father and son conspiring and not in the least phased by the prospect of bigamy. What else had they chosen to withhold from me? And why?

I was aghast, but I could not stop the day from unfolding. I blocked every duplicitous occurrence from consciousness and refused to think. Mom was right. No thinking.

Blackout. I was so stressed that I didn't even remember driving to Mr. Al's. He'd highlighted my hair to perfection two weeks before, and today he was going to tease it into a mini-beehive and anchor on the veil. I sat in blank silence as Amber, his nail and makeup wizard, painted my face and polished my nails.

Mr. Al summoned me as soon as the polish had dried.

"This is so exciting. I just finished Rita's mom Vi an hour ago, and she looks fantastic," he exclaimed, kneading my scalp in the shampoo bowl.

"Now I'll do the same for you, dear girl. Where is it?" he asked, carefully toweling my wet hair. He paused a moment to admire his own reflection in the mirror as he seated me and pumped the chair up a foot.

"Where's what?" I asked.

"The veil."

No. I couldn't have.

"Mr. Al, I am so sorry. I forgot to bring it. I'm an emotional mess," I blinked fast as tears welled in the eyes that Amber had just decorated.

Yet another deception by father and son. And I am most likely a romantic rebound. Shut up, mind.

"God, don't cry," he pleaded. "You'll ruin your eye makeup. What does it look like?"

"It's a pearl tiara with white lacy stuff puffed around it."

"I know exactly what to do. Amber, we have a Burger King emergency."

Amber, who was entertaining herself by embedding rhinestones in the center of each of her ruby-red nails, left her station, hustled down the block, and scurried back carrying a gold cardboard crown.

"Thank you, my precious," Mr. Al said to Amber as he finished blow-drying my hair. He took the royal headdress from her and carefully positioned it on top of my head.

"Now a little tissue here and there. Voila!" Mr. Al exclaimed in pleasure. "A perfect functional model. My creative genius astounds me."

After a final spray, he handed me a bottle of Radiant Tress Gloss as a gift and gave me an air-kiss.

"Mustn't disturb the make-up. You look fabulous, dear girl. Go break a leg," he said and sent me off.

*   *   *

The drive home to Mom's was fraught with my see-sawing emotions, and that damnable elephant reappeared, filling the back seat of the VW.

Face it, I told myself.

If you don't tell Matt how upset you are, the marriage will be a sham—over before it's begun. He's distorted and withheld information, and his father's dominance has made you feel overlooked and second rate—not good enough to be an equal. And you really don't know where you stand.

You are *not* going to spend the rest of your life as a spineless doormat. Spit it out and if he walks, at least you'll have your self-respect. No more wishy-washy deference. To anyone.

The elephant snorted.

My watch read 2:30 p.m., and the bridesmaids were due at Mom's house at 4:00 p.m. to claim the dresses she'd taken hostage.

I made an illegal U-turn on Snake Road and drove straight to the chalet, not knowing if Matt was there or what I would say to him.

His Impala was in the carport. My hands were shaking too much to locate the house key in my bag, and I didn't want to barge in, anyway. The doorbell wasn't working, so I knocked on the door.

The expression on Matt's face when he opened the door was pure astonishment.

I guess I didn't look so good.

"Amy. What's wrong? We shouldn't see each other before the ceremony. Is everything all right?" He paled and alarm spread over his face.

"Everything but me." I willed my voice not to quiver. Matt moved to hold me, but I brushed passed him to sit on his dreadful brown sofa. I might never see it—or him—again. I took a deep breath and launched.

"Matt, I love you—and expect I will forever. But I needed to know about your previous marriage long before our engagement. Now, you tell me that your divorce wasn't final except for a bit of luck this morning. You led me to believe it all happened years ago. This is the second time I've been blindsided. Deception or dishonesty, even by omission, is not okay, and I'm numb."

The dam had burst. I couldn't hold it in and plunged on.

"And you and your father make decisions that may turn out great, but I feel overlooked and left out. It's my fault for not speaking up before, but I won't enter this marriage feeling disregarded."

Do not cry even if you have to bite off your tongue.

Matt settled on the edge of the sofa and listened—stricken into silence. Then he cleared his throat.

"Amy, the entire business of my marriage was a nightmare, and I wanted to make it disappear. Stepping out of the baby's life hurt, but it was the best outcome for the kid. My ex refused to let me even see the baby. I'm still reacting emotionally and can't talk about it."

He reached out, took my hand, and sighed.

"Guess I've blown it again, and I'm sorry. I thought the paperwork would be finished in plenty of time, but there were glitches every step of the way. I didn't want to lie to you, or not tell you, but I was afraid you'd slip away." He cleared his throat.

"I fell in love with you the first day we met. There you were, an hour late, standing on the sidewalk in the cold without a coat, and obviously freezing. Your stockings were torn up and looked like miniature ladders, and when we went inside that restaurant, you smelled like a stale bar—booze and cigarettes.

"Geez, I thought, what's Lynn got me into? At first, you seemed fragile, but when we talked about your job, I saw strength and compassion and sincerity.

"That's what I see now. You've risked everything to tell me this. I was an idiot not to tell you up front about the marriage and stalled divorce. I swear, no more secrets, ever. And you're right-on about my dad. He's aggressive, and sometimes it's easier to go with the tide. Maybe I've relied on him too much, but I've never had a real partner—and you're it. We'll work through whatever we need to, together."

Our eyes locked, and my heart knew—Matt was not placating me. He might not be perfect, but he was committed and sincere. He loved me. And who was I to fault him for deferring to Big Matt? I'd spent most of my life afraid to face down Mom.

I also realized, for the first time, that the pressure to

marry was as great for him as it was for me, signifying for each of us an acceptance within society. A coming-of-age passage declaring, "I'm mature, responsible, and ready to take my place in an adult world."

His rush to marry me was not so much a romantic rebound as it was a need to sluff off the failure of his collapsed marriage. The dynamic was crystal clear—as obvious as the raw pain in his mesmerizing blue eyes, and I understood his vulnerability.

The weight of that enormous elephant lifted, and it lumbered off, making room for the wave of relief that engulfed me.

He is my man, for better or for worse.

"I've got to get to Mom's before she sends out a search party. She can't find out I've been here." I squeezed his hand and jumped up before I choked up.

"You're not leaving without a kiss and a waltz." He took me into his arms and whirled me around to the front door.

"Just one question," he said as I exited, breathless and as besotted as ever.

"Why are you wearing that Burger King crown?"

CHAPTER FORTY-FIVE

"Your mother is making us crazy. Where the hell were you?"

Maisie jumped up from the bench in Mom's garden and startled me with her question. She was wearing cropped orange stretch pants and wreathed in a cloud of Parliament smoke.

"I had unfinished business, and Mom makes everybody crazy. Why aren't you changed?" I asked, picking my way carefully to the bottom of the brick stairs.

"She won't give out the dresses—insists they stay wrapped in cellophane until the last minute, so we won't mess them up. Everyone is hiding from her in your bedroom."

"Let's go in, and I'll corner her in the kitchen so you can escape to my room.

Maisie nodded yes, buried her cigarette stub in a geranium pot, and the two of us walked into the house.

I blocked the door to the kitchen as Maisie skittered by, and Mom looked up from the pile of lists, notes, and file boxes littering the kitchen table.

"What in God's name is on your head? Where's your veil?" She bellowed and her eyes reflected extreme frenzy. A hairpin cascaded from the taut roll of hair winding up the back of her head to a rounded bun on top.

No more cowering—confront her.

I ignored the question, stared her straight in the eye, and said, "If you don't hand over the dresses right now, Matt and I will skip the church ceremony and go over to the courthouse."

The building wasn't open on Saturdays, but Mom was too flummoxed by my threat of mutiny to think it through. She looked startled. Then she puffed up and turned on her heel, but the drama of her exit was spoiled because she had on satin pumps, dyed to match her Emily-blue dress, that were two inches higher than her usual Keds. She lost her balance and was forced into ignominious retreat as she groped her way out of the kitchen clutching the edges of the hutch.

I turned to go in the opposite direction to my room, which was packed with perfectly coifed and made-up maids. They were still dressed in casual Saturday shift dresses or stirrup pants and wore tight, too-polite expressions.

Embarrassed beyond words, I apologized as best I could.

"I'm sorry you all had to put up with this. First Mom heists your dresses, then she holds you captive here. It's almost over, and I hope you know how much I appreciate your support and friendship."

Taut faces softened amid murmurs of, "It's okay, Amy."

Then I handed each maid her gift and smiles and squeals took over as the packages were opened.

The little china treasure boxes were a definite hit, and when livid Mom exploded through the door carrying the gowns, she cast an envious eye.

Always take the high road, Mrs. Dickson had hammered through-out four years of Latin. I swallowed my aggravation, took Mom's package out of the drawer, and handed it to her.

"Just a token, Mom. But thanks for everything. I know how hard you've worked."

Her eyes glimmered for a moment with what might have been a tear or two, and she gave me a quick hug. I couldn't remember the last hug we had exchanged—probably years ago. Mom was not the hugging type. Nor was she one to wallow in sentiment. She pulled away and reverted to her true self.

"Get a move on, girls. We can't be late."

Clothes flew, and I tackled my headpiece. Mr. Al deserved every accolade he gave himself, because the Burger King crown slipped off and the veil slid on like magic. Almost a vision, I told myself.

Lynn, burbling over her matchmaking coup, slipped out of her roomy shift dress, took her sheath off its hanger, and carefully slithered into it. She pulled—and squiggled and tugged and squirmed. Then she caught sight of herself in the mirror.

"Oh, my God. I can't be seen in public. I look like a bag of marshmallows!"

Right on, Lynn. We all gasped.

"What happened?"

"Pizza. I should have knocked off the pepperoni after the fitting. What should I do?"

Mom verged on outright hysteria. Her eyes were not teary. They were glazed. First, I had challenged her, and now, this chubby hussy, who'd aced out Bob and produced the wrong groom, was about to ruin her entire production.

She called out to the kitchen where Dad was futilely searching for his bottle of bourbon. Mom had hidden it well.

"Henry, you'll have to run over to Capwells and buy Lynn a girdle."

Dad's answer was swift and firm.

"No way, Harriet."

Lynn intervened.

"Don't worry, Mrs. Archer. I'll just call Pete. He can stop in the store on his way to the church." She picked up the extension in my bedroom and dialed him.

"You want me to pick up what?" Pete squawked so loudly over the phone that we all heard him.

"Not a problem," Lynn assured him. "I'll call the lingerie department, tell them what I need, and have them hold it at the cash register under my name. Just ask the salesclerk for it."

So, we eased into vehicles in various stages of dress. I slid into the back seat of Dad's Ford with my train draped halfway around me and over the back of the seat. Dad put the garment bag containing my going-away clothes, my suitcase, and his duffel bag stuffed with my cosmetics into the trunk.

Mom, as always, insisted on the last word before we all sped off to the church.

"Girls, no creases and lots of happy faces."

*   *   *

The suspense in the church's bridal quarters was intense. Could spandex contain Lynn's Rubenesque lumps enough for her dress to fit?

Best-man Jack trotted over from the groom's territory to deliver the smart-looking cosmetic case Matt had bought, and we diverted ourselves by re-packing my face goo while waiting for Pete.

When Pete arrived, he was in a frazzle worse than Mom's. He sailed the shopping bag through the door to Lynn with his beefy hand and galloped for the male stronghold on the opposite side of the church.

Why is Pete so upset? I wondered.

The spandex had a lot to squish, and Lynn struggled. She grappled and strained and squeezed.

"God, this damn thing is so tight, I'll throw up if I bend over,' she wheezed.

The disclosure escalated Mom's tizzy, but the garment worked. Lynn looked as sleek and smooth as the other maids. Maisie grimaced when Mom fussed over and centered her detested tiara, and she retaliated by jamming additional hairpins into the knob on Mom's head. A collaborative success, and we were ready .

"Line up, girls," Mom ordered in a hushed tone as we entered the small vestibule. "Don't walk behind Amy. Her train needs to fall in elegant folds. No footprints on it."

Mom moved to the front of the line, impatient to make her imperial entrance. Once again, we waited. And waited. A crisis was occurring, but what?

Dad, dapper in his wedding finery, slipped out of the guy's quarters and came to my side.

"What's happening in there?" I asked in a whisper. Had Matt got cold feet? My hands trembled, making my bouquet shake.

"Bit of a glitch," Dad murmured. "That kid Pete is having a meltdown. The girdle freaked him out. 'Lynn wants to get married on my eighteenth birthday and now she's fat and has to wear old-lady underwear. My life is over, and I'm toast at seventeen,' he says.

"But Big Matt got right on it. 'Son, diets and divorces are easy to come by,' he told him. 'Pull yourself together, and if there's a problem down the road, I'll handle it. Life holds lots worse. Get out there and march Harriet Archer down the aisle.'"

Mom was up front and out of earshot, but Lynn was in close range and heard Dad. She made a peculiar sound, but spandex compressed her diaphragm and no words came out.

The organist and the singer launched into a third song to cover for the delay. Pete finally opened the creaky door from the men's territory. He shuffled reluctantly to Mom's side.

"You ready to roll, ma'am?" he politely asked her as Pastor Tom's wife flung open the arched doors to the chapel.

Mom gripped Pete's arm, but before she could respond, he took off like a rocket. He roared down the white carpet with her on his arm, obliterating her expectation of a regal entrance.

The maids and Maisie followed, teetering carefully to the measured cadence of the processional music wafting through the chapel.

Matt, tall and resplendent in his tuxedo, stood in the sanctuary, framed by the brilliant shades of the stained-glass windows behind him. His colossal smile filled the room— and my heart.

I took Dad's arm, held it lightly, and we stepped onto the white carpet.

All eyes were on me, and I didn't falter. I wasn't afraid to be the center of attention. My stride was steady and sure, despite my ankle, and I knew exactly where I was going. To join Matt, the man I loved, come what may.

*   *   *

The walk up the aisle on Dad's arm was the longest and shortest of my life. Mom scowled in her seat of honor in the first pew, and Vi beamed from a few rows back.

Pastor Tom welcomed the congregates, confirming they were about to witness the marriage of Amy Archer and Matt Willis. He had just begun the service when Mom rose to her feet and her voice rang out.

"I, Harriet Archer, mother of the bride, hereby give her away. So does her father."

Dad jerked her back into her seat, but the damage had been done.

My mind, already a jumble of emotions, was as fried as my nerves. I looked up at the beatific angel residing in the stained-glass pane high above us. I imagined her zooming down headfirst, her white robe flowing, to slap a strip of duct tape over Mom's mouth.

Dear God, what's Mom going to do when the pastor asks if anyone has objections? I asked myself.

Pastor Tom must have intercepted my prayer and solved the problem by skipping that part of the service. Relieved, I tried to focus on his words, but I felt disoriented—possibly because the angel's face had morphed mid-flight into that of a gargoyle's.

Somehow, I pulled myself together enough to speak my vows, and Matt recited his. But even though we stood facing each other, only two feet apart, I didn't hear what he said. It was as if I were looking on from afar, and I forgot to listen. My thoughts drifted.

Maybe the demonic angel might spirit Mom home and lock her in her potting shed.

Best-man Jack had tucked the rings into the breast pocket of his rented tuxedo jacket. When Pastor Tom requested them, Jack fished the rings out of his pocket, along with an errant green Jujube gum drop, and handed them over.

When Matt slipped the slim, white-gold band on my finger, my heart raced, and my eyes filled with tears, but I wasn't sure why. A scrambled mix—anxiety, relief, happiness—that I couldn't sort through.

Pastor Tom gave Matt permission to kiss the bride. I sensed that Matt was also in a strange space and felt relieved when he settled for a self-conscious, modest meeting of our lips.

Then it was over, just like that. Not quite believing it, I grasped Matt's arm as he led us back up the aisle to the vestibule. A brief wave of happiness swept over me when I realized I was leaving on the arm of my *husband.*

I am Mrs. Matt Willis, I told myself.

But deep down, I still felt disconnected, as if I were watching myself in a play or movie. Playing the part to perfection, but strangely removed.

The sea of faces filling the pews were a blur until Vi caught my eye by waving the tail of her 40s fox fur. She winked and blew a kiss.

"You done damn good, kid," she announced in her stage whisper.

I hope you're right, Vi.

CHAPTER FORTY-SIX

"Yikes. What *is* this stuff?" Matt gasped, cringed, and ducked.

"Birdseed," I said through the blizzard of tiny pellets assailing us as we left the church. "Pastor Tom told me that tossing rice isn't allowed in Berkeley. He gave out little pouches filled with the seeds local birds and wildlife eat."

We ran the traditional gauntlet to everyone else's amusement, shook ourselves off, and turned around to go back inside the church to complete official paperwork. Mom and Dad sped off across town to the reception venue, so Big Matt and Rose volunteered to stay behind as witnesses.

Guess they know the ropes. A snarky thought, but I was still reeling because no one in the Willis threesome of conspirators seemed concerned that if Big Matt had not found that judge on the golf course, this would not have been legal.

Stop thinking. Let it go.

The four of us scribbled our names on the papers where the pastor told us to, and he gathered up the documents.

"We're through. I'll have this marriage certificate recorded at the courthouse, and you folks can be on your way," Pastor Tom said.

At last—I'd be alone with Matt on the ride over to the country club. I was desperate to shake off this feeling of remoteness, to hold his hand, to connect. I needed his touch.

That demon angel whooshed down again and landed on Rose, who as a result threw an uncharacteristic mean curve ball.

With all good intentions, she said, "Amy, your dress is gorgeous, but that train's going to wrinkle, and the effect will be ruined if you scrunch up in Jack's Impala. Why don't you ride with us? The back seat of Big Matt's Cadillac is huge, and we can fluff out the train."

"Great idea, Mom," said my clueless husband of thirty-five minutes. I heard the angel snicker.

*   *   *

So Big Matt and Rose transported me in isolated splendor in the Cadillac's back seat, while Matt followed in his lesser vehicle. And when we arrived at the venue, Big Matt pulled into the parking space reserved for the groom, who then had to park on the steep hillside a block away because the parking lot was full.

Matt huffed his way up the hill as I exited Big Matt's car and Rose rearranged my train.

Sounds of merriment drifted toward us, indicating Mom's party was underway.

When Matt panted to my side, winded and tense, he gave me a distracted kiss on the cheek and nodded toward a back entrance leading to the patio.

Then his irresistible grin transformed his handsome face.

"Are you ready for your debut, Mrs. Willis?" he asked me.

That kicked off another attack of *my* nerves.

I wanted to be worthy of this man—and for him to be

ecstatic that he had chosen *me* as his wife. Vi's long-ago words of wisdom tumbled through my mind. "Make him proud you're on his arm.

Am I good enough?

I answered my own question.

"Let's go ace this." I flashed my most adoring smile. It never occurred to me to reverse the question—was he good enough for me?

*   *   *

A perfect warm July evening, and most of the guests gathered on the spacious patio, mesmerized as San Francisco's lights twinkled on across the Bay. Matt and I entered the patio through a fanciful wrought-iron gate and to my surprise, everyone greeted us with a round of applause.

A quick glance confirmed that all of Mom's minions had come through. The florist's efforts were spectacular. Garlands of hibiscus, cradling flickering candles, floated in the aqua pool. He'd scattered flaming tiki torches to light the patio dramatically, and he'd sectioned off cozy areas using enormous palm fronds.

At the bar, a distinguished-looking, middle-aged guy was pouring rapid fire and handled the knee-deep crowd with ease. He looked more like a college professor than a bartender. Rose's cousin Irma had stationed herself on a barstool, apparently settled in for the duration.

Waiters weaved through fire and fronds, passing Mom's selections of stuffed mushrooms and little meatballs bathed in grape jelly mixed with ketchup. Other catering staff prepared for the buffet. Mom had chosen chicken a la king for the entrée after verifying that its origins were British, not French.

Mom spotted us immediately and descended with an order.

"You two come over here right now," she said, gesturing to a spot by one of the tiki torches.

"Why?" Matt asked.

"So I can form the receiving line."

I felt Matt tense up, but I squeezed his hand to hush him. From now on, I would fight my own battles.

"Mom, you've put together a beautiful party. Thank you. But no one wants to stand in line for the next two hours. We'll just circulate and talk to everyone."

Her attack face emerged, but Matt had a momentary inspiration.

Staring over her shoulder, he frowned and whispered to her, "I think something's wrong in the kitchen. I see smoke."

Mom whirled around and charged to the kitchen, almost knocking over Aunt Jane, splendidly stylish in a pearl-gray sheath, who was threading her way to the bar.

"Brilliant strategy," I said to Matt.

"And you took her head on. Impressive. But we'd better mingle before she comes back." His stunning blue eyes scanned the scene.

"Let's start with the guys from work," I suggested. "I want to thank Anders for covering for me." I took Matt's hand and led him around two tiki torches to where Webber, Anders, and Moroni were hanging out.

Webber, wearing the same necktie he'd worn to work every day for as long as I could remember, was struggling with a meatball dripping purple-red jelly. One more spot would not make a difference.

"Hi, guys. Anders, thanks for looking out for Mrs. Parsons while I'm away," I said, surprised at his almost neat appearance. He'd even gotten a haircut.

"No sweat, Amy. I welcome any opportunity to screw the Housing Authority," he said, obviously revving up for one of his rants. Moroni interrupted.

"Congrats, you two. I'm desperate for a drink," he declared. He looked single and slick in a hand-tailored midnight-blue suit as he headed for the bar.

I watched as Irma, in her too-short, too-young cocktail mini dress, gave him the once-over. She perked up, eased off her barstool, and cut Moroni off as he approached. Batted her heavily mascaraed eyelashes, she gushed like an animated teenager.

Moroni listened to her chit-chat for several minutes and then said something that appeared to infuriate Irma. She gave him a drop-dead look, whirled around, and reclaimed her barstool.

"Don't know what set *her* off," he said, sauntering back with a drink in his hand. "I noticed a family resemblance. Thought she looked like you, Matt, so I asked her if she was your mother. And I asked if she would introduce me to that hot brunette over by the pool."

"Better lie low, man," Matt responded. "The brunette is my boss's secretary. I'm not too sure of the relationship, and he's a big guy."

We moved on, trying to out-mingle Mom, and I noticed that Irma had resumed tossing them down with Mom's second cousins. Described by Mom as distant relatives, the three rowdy louts were not distant enough for me. But Mom was adamant that kin are kin.

Vi looked spectacular. Mr. Al had tamed her frizz into flattering gray-blond waves, and her makeup was flawless. Swirling in a silvery chiffon caftan and sporting enough diamonds to rival sparkling San Francisco, she tottered over to give Matt and me hugs.

When she realized her portly husband Roy had wandered off to check out the bar and buffet, she excused herself.

"Damn that dud. Can't take him anywhere. He's gonna figure out the best place to sit to grab off the food when it comes outta the kitchen."

Champagne flowed and people made toasts, none of which I can remember. Mom was relentless as she ran the show page by page from Emily's book.

"Time for the wedding waltz," she ordered, and the quaking pianist could scarcely control his hands. Matt took me in his arms for our first dance as husband and wife. My eyes misted—this time clearly from happiness.

That's when I realized the pianist was playing "The Anniversary Waltz," Mom's favorite, and not Etta James's "At Last," which Matt and I had chosen.

Before I could protest, Dad cut in for the traditional father-daughter dance. I saw a flash of irritation cross Matt's face as he realized the switch in the song, but he carried on with his prescribed role, extending his hand to Mom. He steered her onto the dance floor and retaliated for the song by rising and falling to the beat like a rowboat caught in an ocean squall. I think he intended to make her seasick.

It won't work. She's indestructible.

Mom escaped to trot on the heels of the professional

photographer to assure that he captured every magic moment. Maisie's husband Hubert also followed the photographer. In true engineer fashion, he was absorbed with the workings of the new Kodak Automatic 35 camera he'd just bought and hoped to pick up a few pro tips.

Hubert took many more photos than the official guy and graciously offered to send copies to Matt and me. Then he made the near fatal mistake of telling Maisie he's snapped her a dozen or more times because she looked lovely in the tiara that she detested.

"That dorky sesame-seed husband of mine will sleep on the futon in the spare bedroom until he's carried out feet first." She hissed, and the tierra tilted sideways.

Mom popped up at my side. "We've got to keep on schedule. Time for you to gather the girls and toss your bouquet," she said.

"I'm not tossing it," I told her. "I've been humiliated too many times by having to brand myself publicly as single and be pummeled in a stampede trying to catch a bunch of flowers. As far as I can tell, only Lynn, Irma, and Aunt Jane are in the running. And possibly the brunette from Matt's office. I don't know her, Lynn has her bridesmaid bouquet, and Irma is sloshed. I'm going to hand it to Aunt Jane just before we leave."

"*My sister?* What has gotten into you, missy?"

"It might be called pluck, Mom."

*   *   *

Vi, primed with two boilermakers after the wedding waltz, parked Roy at a table with a mountain of food while she beguiled the timorous pianist into playing a few of her favorite love songs from the 30s and 40s. Squeezing on to the piano bench next to him, she snuggled up and sang.

"*Night and day, you are the one,*" she purred, and hearts melted. Vi enchanted everyone with the beautiful, romantic lyrics from softer times. Even Mom simmered down from the bouquet discussion.

Vi signed off with a wink and a grin. But she had introduced the pianist to boilermakers. His tremors ceased, and he cut loose on his own. Shake, rattle, and roll—and don't forget the Twist.

"This party *rocks*. Harriet, you outdid yourself. Thank you," Matt said and slapped his new mother-in-law on the back. We had sheltered behind the cake table where we had just carved the first piece of the lemon-chiffon confection. I had to avoid the cousins, and especially gross Buster, whose idea of a good time was smashing cake in someone's face.

"You're welcome, Matt," Mom responded stiffly. "I need the keys to your house, and then you have to leave."

"What?" Matt and I asked in unison.

"Did you even go into the side-room to see the gift display?" She was peeved.

"I thought that room was for coats, and nobody wore one. You hauled all that stuff over here?" I asked, incredulous.

"Yes, and now I'll take everything over to your place and get it all arranged while you're at Tahoe," Mom said. Her smile was smug.

Matt steamed.

"Harriet, no way and no key. You take the gifts back to

your house, and we'll pick them up when we get back. Now tell me why I'm being kicked out."

"Not just you, both of you. Emily Post says that no guests may leave before the bride and groom."

Matt and I processed that information while watching in fascination as Mom darted off to grab a plate and fork away from Lynn, who was still wrapped tight as a mummy in spandex. No upchucks allowed at this party.

Next, Mom charged to the bar where Aunt Jane was frolicking with Irma and the cousins. When Mom tried to evict her from her stool, Aunt Jane refused to budge. Matt and I moved in to hear what was going on, and Aunt Jane stood her ground.

"Look who's here—my dear baby sister," she said to Irma. "Harriet, get lost. You stole my man, but you will not ruin any more of my relationships. Irma is my new best friend."

"I am?" Irma asked, befuddled by bourbon and circumstance. "Do I know you?"

Aunt Jane pulled her silver-plated flask, etched with the art déco peacock, from her handbag, and Irma's face lit in recognition.

"Darling Jane with the big bird. Of course, I remember you from the shower. My dear buddy." Irma raised her glass. "Cheers. Let me buy us a round."

"Irma, the tab is on my sister Harriet, so order the good stuff." Aunt Jane smirked in defiance as Mom shot her an evil eye capable of felling Spartacus.

*　　　　　*　　　　　*

"*Wow*. Your Aunt Jane's a winner, but what's with your Mom? Why is she tossing us out?" Matt asked me, still disgruntled.

"Her blue book explains that the custom stems from ancient times when the groom couldn't wait to carry off his love."

"Oh." He wasn't budging any more than Aunt Jane was, and my frayed feelings were hurt that he didn't want to whisk me away.

Mom sneaked up from behind.

"If you two don't change clothes and go now, I'll have my beloved kin stuff all those gifts in your car, and you'll have to take them with you."

Outmaneuvered, we retreated, and Matt bolted toward the men's locker room. I made my way to the bar and handed my flowers to Aunt Jane. She was thrilled to tears with them.

"Amy, I'm deeply touched. But your mother will throw a colossal hissy-fit when she sees me with your beautiful bouquet."

"I already told her that I was giving it to you, Aunt Jane,"

"My God, that's brave as hell, Amy. I thought I was the only one with enough spunk to stand up to her."

"I'm developing the knack. Time for me to change now."

"Wait a minute." She leaned over to whisper, her back to Irma. "This bouquet is an omen, Amy. The bartender is a widower—a history teacher at Oakland High School. He moonlights to help out his sister, who owns the catering business."

She took a deep breath, and her eyes sparkled more than mine.

"He just invited me to have brunch tomorrow."

"That's wonderful, Aunt Jane. I'll keep my fingers crossed, and if you need any advice, go straight to Vi." I gave her a hug and then left to duck into the ladies' lounge to put on my lace outfit.

* * *

When I emerged, Matt was waiting for me outside in the hall, looking incredible in a blue linen blazer that brought out the crystal blue of his eyes. My heart leapt when I saw him.

I am married to this intoxicating man, I thought, still not quite believing it.

"Amy, you were a vision before, and now look at you—impossibly pretty. Come with me," he said, taking my hand.

Dazzled by his lavish words, I started toward the patio, but Matt tugged me in the opposite direction.

"I got turned around looking for the locker room. Come see what I found," he said.

Matt clicked the bolt-lock on a door labeled as service only, and it opened onto a small park-like outdoor area. He led me out to a narrow path that edged the lawn and wound behind a tall hedge of oleander.

A small white pergola, tucked out of sight behind the hedge, perched on a ledge overlooking the entire bay. A familiar scent was in the air. Even in the darkness, I knew the vines covering the arch of the pergola were wisteria— almost finished with their bloom, but still fragrant.

"Oh," I exclaimed, speechless as I realized my fantasy had become a reality. Then I turned to gaze at the four gleaming bridges spanning the dark bay water. Thousands of headlights flickered across them like chains of diamonds, and both shores glittered.

Matt moved to stand behind me and folded me into his arms. I leaned back against him as we gazed at the spectacular sight.

"I wanted to be alone with you, Amy. All this hoopla is making everyone else happy, but I don't want it."

He tightened his arms around me in a cozy hug and then said, "I only want you. He began to speak softly.

"I, Matt Willis, take you, precious Amy, to be my wife…"

He repeated his vows, and this time I heard him—every heartfelt word.

My heart flooded with love. This was the missing piece that was plaguing me. A deep need for emotional intimacy that had taken a backseat to all the pomp. And Matt had longed for it too.

I turned to look at him, the man I adored, standing under the wisteria-covered arbor that I dreamed about my entire life. This was real—an undeniable kismet.

We kissed—a fiery kiss promising a passionate future. I broke away, unable to stifle my joy, and saw that his grin was as huge as my smile.

"For keeps?" he asked.

I answered from my heart.

"For keeps."

EPILOGUE

Big Matt's lodge at Lake Tahoe, anchored on sturdy stilts, overlooked the rippling lake. A wide deck faced the enormous body of water, and stairs led from the weathered deck down to a compact pier spanning the rocky beach.

Convenient for launching small water-craft, Matt explained. But he'd shunned the family's cute little Sunfish sailboat to rent a toy at a local shop servicing tourists.

I huddled on the deck in a faux Adirondack chair and watched Matt astride the ear-splitting, grit-your-teeth-noisy Wet Jet. Zooming by, he bounced with abandon over the white-capped surface of the treacherous, deep blue lake.

He'll break his neck, sink into the depths of the icy water, and I'll be a widow three days after I've become a bride. And he doesn't even have life-insurance. Grim thoughts, born of hypothermia.

Matt neglected to warn me the lake was so large it created its own microclimate. I wrapped myself in a spare blanket, freezing in summer shorts and a pink gingham sleeveless blouse. Alternatives were limited—more shorts, cotton tops, and light-weight skinny pants. My white-lace going-away outfit was useless, as expected.

Vroom. Hour after hour, Matt roared through rolling whitecaps whipped up by the chill wind. Occasionally he zoomed near the shoreline to wave at me, and I waved back, feigning admiration through my chattering teeth.

Tahoe was no island paradise, but I'd overcome that disappointment by imagining that the vast lake was an ocean, the pine trees were palms, and the stuffy lodge was a frond-thatched hut. I wasn't sure why the place was called a lodge—it looked like an over-sized cedar-wood cabin to me.

A wood-burning Franklin stove dominated the lodge's main room and was its only source of warmth. Fortunately, the volatile heat Matt and I generated in the bedroom kept the rest of the premises toasty.

Matt basted himself with Sea and Ski before every outing on the lake, and the scent of the sunscreen was imbedded in my senses as an irresistible aphrodisiac.

His face browned with sun and windburn, transforming his eyes to an even more brilliant blue, and the bliss of my besotted state grew tenfold every day. His electrifying touch, melting kisses, wrap-around cuddles—how had I existed without him?

Awash in the passions of the heart and flesh, I resolved to be the best wife ever, and Matt was hell-bent on being the perfect husband after he reluctantly returned the rented Wet Jet. We shared an unspoken determination—to claim our place in adult society as a perfect couple.

Our return home to the chalet was marred only by Mom's hissy-fit when we called her to claim our wedding gifts.

"Missy, you only phoned me once. I'm outraged by your disrespect."

Matt and I had prepared and lied like politicians.

"Mom, there's no phone service at Big Matt's place, and

we had to drive miles to find a telephone booth to make that call. We missed you." *Ha.*

*   *   *

When I floated into work the following week, even grousing Webber couldn't dampen my honeymoon glow.

Two of our wedding gifts were on the back seat of the VW, tucked in nondescript brown bags. One of the three slow-cookers we had received, and one of two electric frying pans which I planned to deliver to Mrs. Parsons in Harbor Homes.

Anders had staved off her eviction with an injunction from Legal Aid, but the carcass of her stove remained. I hoped she could figure out how to use the cooking devises because I sure didn't know how.

When I sat down at my office desk, Maisie handed me a manila envelope with the photos her husband Hubert had taken at the reception.

"How thoughtful of him," I exclaimed. "Have you looked at them?" I asked her.

"Sure did. Tore up the ones of me wearing that damned gizmo on my head. And my hunch might have been right," she replied with a righteous air.

"What hunch?"

"See for yourself. Also, you need to go up to Human Resources to put in your name change."

I was dying to see the photos but decided it would be more fun to look at them with Matt. I tucked the envelope in my purse and brushed by Webber, sulking with his sour Monday morning face, on my way to the elevator. When I stepped off on the fifth floor and crossed the corridor, Mabel was comatose at her counter. I stopped, unexpectedly freaked out.

I need to think about this name business.

Disconcerted, I couldn't bring myself to jolt Mabel awake and ask for the form. Turning around, I got back on the elevator.

When I returned to my desk, I pretended to muddle through a multitude of messages, when I was actually muddling through the conflicts spiraling through my mind.

Something didn't feel right. I'd spent months dreaming about becoming Mrs. Matt Willis, and I was well-aware and grateful for the perks that accompanied the title—social acceptance, a bank account, even a credit card someday.

But I'd worked hard at becoming whole. Struggling to shed the deceptive comfort of diffidence, squirming in the unfamiliar cloak of assertiveness. Proud as I was to be Matt's wife, I realized that my evolving identity was about to be dissolved into his. Whoosh—and Amy Archer would cease to be.

After returning a few calls, I decided to finish out the day with the delivery to Mrs. Parsons and took off for Harbor Homes in the VW.

Because it was late afternoon, I parked the car on the safe side of the decaying barracks and took the back route to her door.

Mrs. Parsons greeted me with a broad smile and was overjoyed when she saw the pot and pan.

"Girl, you save the day. Got no way a cookin' nothin'. Gonna make pinto beans in the big pot," she said.

"I was lucky and found them at the Good Will store. But

be careful not to tell anybody," I cautioned her. "The rules say a social worker can't give a gift to anyone, and if someone thought I had given you something, I could be fired."

"Sure didn't come from no Good Will, but don't worry none. Not no way I squeal on you. Thank you kindly, Miss Archery."

As I guided the VW back over the rutted ramp and away from Harbor Homes, I wished I had magical powers to whisk the inhabitants of the rotting project over that road and into better lives.

And Mrs. Parson's parting words crystalized my decision. No more candy-ass wavering. I hoped Matt would understand.

Mrs. Matt Willis may define me socially, but *Amy Archer* will remain as my professional identity. I've fought for the recognition, and I'm not giving up the name. That's who I am in my working world.

And that was that.

*   *   *

Matt wasn't home yet when I arrived at the chalet a little after six o'clock, so I cautiously sat down on the miserable sofa that grew browner and uglier each time I looked at it. Too impatient to wait any longer, I opened the envelope from Maisie's husband and flipped through the pictures.

Hubert had captured every wonderful moment of the reception. The entire cast was included. Mom bossing everyone right and left. Lynn suffering in ridged Spandex. Big Matt and Dad shaking hands in a triumphant pose.

Smiling Rose, graciously coping with a stuffed mushroom.

A fabulous shot of Vi at the piano singing her heart out. The emboldened piano player giving his all to *Love Potion No.9*. Flirty Irma ogling slicked-up Moroni. Moroni gawking at the sultry brunette by the pool. Our first dance. Cutting the cake. Aunt Jane beaming with my bouquet. The hot brunette behind a palm frond and draped all over Matt— *what?*

This must be what Maisie was hinting about. I studied the photo. To my eyes, the brunette was clearly the aggressor. She lounged against him, one arm cuddling his shoulder. Matt had a champagne glass in one hand, a meatball on a toothpick in the other hand, and a look of desperation on his face.

Did I have pangs of anger, or jealousy, or anxiety? No. Just curiosity.

His boss's secretary, or whatever she was, had come on to Matt at his wedding reception. Soap-opera silly. I wondered, with my social-worker mentality, how Matt was going to maneuver the awkward situation at work.

All at once, the house shuddered and creaked, protesting the weight of the heavy Impala as Matt pulled into the carport. I heard him tromp across the deck. The door flew open.

"Where's my bride?" he called out.

My heart leapt and fluttered, as it always did, with the thrill of seeing him. My words tumbled from my heart.

"Right where she intends to be. By her husband's side. For keeps."

The End

ACKNOWLEDGEMENTS

I thank dear friends and talented writers who've contributed so much to bring this novel about.

The Mount Diablo Sages—Phyllis Houseman, Bill Yarborough, Corrienne Heinmann, and Kathleen Casey—have devoted years of Wednesday afternoons and countless hours to kindly critique with sharp eyes and astute suggestions.

And the smiling framed faces of the Friday Zoom group—Ceci Pugh, Robin Gigoux, June Gatewood, Sue Hummel, Gary Carr, Phyllis Houseman, and Corrienne Heinmann—who've soldiered through the pandemic offering much appreciated support and encouragement.

Professional expertise has come from the imaginative vision of editor Cherri Randall, the patient nurturing of editor Lyn Roberts, and the book would not exist without the wizardry of publisher Andrew Benzie. Thanks also to the California Writers Club, Mount Diablo Branch, for providing so many opportunities to connect and grow.

And of course, profound thanks to treasured friends for their invaluable encouragement.

I'm grateful to all.

ABOUT THE AUTHOR

California's East Bay has always been home to Chloe. Born in Oakland and educated at U.C. Berkeley, she spent many years working in public social services before retiring and moving a few miles east to quaint, quiet Clayton. When not writing, duplicate bridge and ballroom dance capture her fancy.

Literary achievements include publication of her novella, *Dream On, Dancing Queen,* which won the NABE Pinnacle Book Achievement Award for Best Romance, Summer 2016, Best Indie Book Competition Shelf Unbound Award Winner, 2016, and multiple five-star accolades on Amazon.

Two of her short stories, Something in the Wind, and Tango, appear in *Foresight, Hindsight, and Flights of Fancy,* an anthology published by the Shadow of the Mountain Literary Guild.

Currently, Chloe has again taken to the high seas, frolicking with dancing queen Cara and sidekick Josie for a return trip aboard the Star Sapphire—watch for *Lifeboat,* hopefully sailing soon.

9 781950 562312